WHEN THE SEA IS RISING RED

CAT HELLISEN

FARRAR STRAUS GIROUX
NEW YORK

macteenbooks.com

Library of Congress Cataloging-in-Publication Data
Hellisen, Cat.
    When the sea is rising red / Cat Hellisen. — 1st ed.
        p.   cm.
    Summary: Felicita fakes her own suicide to escape from the strict
confines of her aristocratic family and an arranged marriage, only to be
confronted with the harsh realities of living in the slums and the
ultimate discovery that the boy she has fallen in love with is plotting a
rebellion to destroy her family.
    ISBN: 978-0-374-36475-5
    [1. Fantasy.   2. Social classes—Fiction.   3. Magic—Fiction.
4. Vampires—Fiction.]   I. Title.

PZ7.H37444Wh 2012
[Fic]—dc23

                                                            2011012645

For my dad, who gave me all the dinosaurs I needed

1

SHE'S NOT HERE.

I hunch deeper into the protection of a small copse of stunted blackbarks. Condensed mist drips down the dark leaves and soaks my shawl.

Come on, Ilven. As if I could force her to appear by the power of thought.

Across the close-cropped lawn, House Malker's gray stone face waits, a patient prison. In just a few days Ilven's family will ship her off upriver to some Samar wine farmer, and today is the last chance we have to be alone together.

Mother won't miss me for ages yet—I can risk waiting a few minutes more for Ilven to show. My stomach churns. I hope that no servants saw me leave and that my mother is still at her writing desk, engaged in scribbling long missives to her beloved son, Owen. So beloved, in fact, that he never bothers to leave his town house to see her.

Mother's schedule is narrow and predictable. Like all the women in the High Houses, her life is ruled by a list of acceptable and appropriate behaviors, all of them dictated to her by men. First her father, then her husband, and now her son. One day that will be my lot, I suppose, and it's this thought that made me convince Ilven to run off with me into town to be nothing more than free Lammers for a brief afternoon. Excitement swirls in me and my breathing goes tight.

The minutes stretch, and my hands are slick from the cold and the dampness of my clothes.

Ilven's not going to make it. Her mother, for all that she's tiny and delicate as a glass doll, is a frightful drake. If that cold witch caught even the slightest wind of Ilven's jaunt, then my friend is probably locked in her room.

The memory of our last meeting returns to me. It seems a lifetime ago, and yet only a bare few days have passed. Lady Malker's words are still fresh as I remember the hate I felt when she stared me down, my friend cowering behind her.

ILVEN REFUSES TO LOOK AT ME. She twists the new silver band on her smallest finger around and around until the skin is red. I cannot draw my gaze away from this tiny detail that has changed everything between us.

"We have many preparations to make," says Lady Malker. There is something frosty about her, and when she talks I expect to feel her breath against my face like a winter sea-gale. Instead, her voice is calm and quiet, but hidden under it are snake-hisses and sneers. "Ilven will not be available for your games today, Felicita, dear." There is a subtle emphasis on *games* and *dear*. Nothing overt—I am, after all, from House Pelim—but enough for me to know that Malker are determined to claw their way up to their old level on the social scale. It's a warning of sorts.

I look past Lady Malker, ignoring her.

Ilven's shoulders are hunched. Her pale face is marked with tears, the shadows under her eyes bruised black and purple. Seeing her like this strikes at my very heart. If Lady Malker were not here I would fold Ilven in my arms and kiss her white-gold hair, tell her that everything will work out somehow. Instead, I clench my fists tighter and raise my head high. I cannot show weakness in this House. Rumors would spread, and my family would lose face.

"I thought you were going to come to university with me next year?" It's a stupid thing to say, but I have nothing else. I can hardly ask her about this marriage in front of her mother. I already know all they're going to tell me.

"Samar will have tutors," Ilven mumbles, staring at the polished white floor. Her pale hair is held back with a little metal pin decorated with the four-pointed emerald leaves of her family's crest. Those tiny green leaves are a lie—promising growth where there is none.

I want to scream. My friend doesn't mumble. She doesn't walk with her head down. She doesn't quietly accept that her education will be left in the hands of boys fresh from university.

"Ilven?" I want to remind her that she is a person who kicks off her shoes and stockings to run across the green fields behind our estates, that she once helped me play pranks on my idiot of a brother, that we are sister-friends, that we have kissed and sworn eternal friendship.

She looks up, and her eyes are pleading. She wants me to stay. She wants me to go.

"Perhaps we could arrange a little going-away party," Lady Malker says. "Something for the ladies." Her laugh is like the colored glass baubles the lower War-Singers make as frivolities.

A *going-away party*. We dress things up with pretty words. My friend is not going on a pleasure jaunt, or a holiday up-river to see the ruling city of MallenIve. They are selling her off to some nameless man with arable land. They are selling her for caskets of wine.

"It will be fun," she says. "I'll write you letters."

I hide a tight smile. Ilven's been locked up before, not allowed to see anyone for weeks on end, but we have a system. There are servants we can trust. I have Firell, and she, some poor sallow Hob girl, with one eye gone milky from a childhood illness. These two pass our letters between them, keeping our secrets. "And I'll write back," I say.

I bow my head to Lady Malker and take my leave.

There may be nothing I can do to stop Ilven's marriage, but I can try to make her last days here in Pelimburg ones she will remember.

THOSE LAST DAYS have crept by all too quickly, and instead of running with Ilven through the town as we planned, I am crouched in a spinney, getting progressively more rain-damp, while Ilven is trapped in her rooms, imprisoned by her mother. I shift position to ease cramps in my legs and stare across the misted lawns. Nothing.

There is a scrawled note in my pocket, and I take it out for the thousandth time. The oils of my fingers and the humid air have turned the ink blurry, the paper grubby and thin, covered with Ilven's small neat hand that, like her, tries not to draw attention to itself.

I read it again. No, this is the date she set—the only time when she would have the chance to leave the house un-noticed. My heart sinks. I feel like I've failed her, that some-how I should have just had the courage to walk out of my house and into hers, take her hand, and, without asking, with-out showing fear, lead her down to the town. There I would have bought her a gift, held her close, and kissed her goodbye.

However, I'm not willing to tuck tail and go back home yet. If Ilven can't be with me, she would be happy just to hear whatever stories I can bring back to her. The city is calling, full of promises. Ilven would want me to go.

A rational voice is telling me to forget about it—I'll have plenty of time to see Pelimburg properly soon enough, when I go to further my magic studies at Pelimburg's university. Then again, I've never been overly fond of rational thoughts.

Perhaps I could still buy Ilven a gift in town—something for her to look at and remember me by. So with my heart giddy-thumping like a lost uni-foal, I race through the gray drizzle and down the hillside to New Town. My mother's claustrophobic fears slip from me as I hurtle downhill. The cold leaves me exhilarated, shivering.

Pelimburg is a city of rain and mist and spray. It's supposed to be my home, but a lifetime lived in my mother's cage of a mansion means that I barely know it. I've only ever seen the city from the confines of a carriage; now I breathe deep, tasting how different the air is, how sweet the drops feel on my tongue. Up on the hillside, the rain seems bitter and darker.

The umbrella twirls in my hands, dancing. *Goodbye, Ilven.* I close my eyes for a moment, pushing away my sadness and letting my face go blank as the chalk cliff, before setting off again.

"Watch it," someone grumbles as I pass by, and water spins from my silk umbrella. Not a person here knows or cares that I am from the highest House in the whole city or that my family once owned every cobblestone of every street that webs Pelimburg, as my mother is wont to point out. Of course, that was before the scriven here ran out and half the Houses packed up to follow Mallen Gris to found the city-state of MallenIve. Now our House is a relic, a thing of former glory.

I take in the strangeness of a city that knows my name but not my face. There's a portrait of me in the University Gallery, as there is of every Pelim since my ancestor decided to raise the building, and I suppose were I to go to the center of New Town, where the oligarchy of the three remaining Great Houses—Pelim, Malker, and Eline—meet and make their plans, perhaps someone would recognize me. And if none of them did, there are a host of lower High Houses like Skellig and Evanist scrabbling for a place in the gaping holes of the Great House ranks; one of their members would sell me out, blacken my honor in order to play their power games. After all, we are the pinnacle and the very city is named for us.

Dogs, I think. All of them. Showing their bellies when they want something, snarling in packs when that doesn't work.

I want to be far away from that, from people who hate me because I was born into the Pelim name. And what is a Great House? As Ilven points out, we're merely the kings of the midden. The ranks of Houses below us do not understand that there is safety in powerlessness. No one is waiting for them to fall.

Instead of heading toward New Town, I take Spindle Way and cross the Levelling Bridge, plunging between its high dark houses, under the laundry lines that drip overhead, and over to that strange forbidden quarter where the aboriginal Hobs and the low-Lammers without magic mingle: Old Town.

Just past the end of the bridge, Spindle Way feeds into a broad road that runs along the curve of the Claw. Next to it is a slick promenade. The houses here are old-fashioned, and it is strange to think that once my family may have lived in one of these crow-stepped pastel buildings, back when Pelimburg was little more than a main street and a tiny harbor, when our magic was as strong as our fishing fleets, when of all the Great Houses, only Mallen stood higher than us. I run my fingers along the old walls, committing the gritty feel of the crumbling plaster to memory. Perhaps next time I'll try to find out which one was ours.

The houses overlook the wide mouth of the Casabi, where the river and the ocean meet and tangle, and I imagine some ancestor of mine looking down at the view from her white wooden window frame.

I close my umbrella and lean against the salt-bitten wall, paint flaking on my back. The chips fall to the ground, faded and pink. Hazy figures run along the promenade, through the veil of sea-rain, their hands over their heads or their whalebone-ribbed umbrellas snapped open against the deluge.

Beyond them the sea roars, gray and green. The white cliffs are invisible, shrouded by the rain and the raging ocean. My family house hides in the mist. And in that house, right now, my mother will be fretting, wringing her hands as she stalks the corridors, calling my name.

"Pelim Felicita?"

The man's voice makes me start. I turn so that my furled umbrella stands between us.

"You're far from home," he says, nodding to where the cliffs should be. "What brings you down here?"

He's black haired, skinny, with a nose too big and pointed to suit his thin face. Not Lammer, for certain—not with that pasty white skin. And the only bats in Pelimburg who would dare talk to me as an equal are limited to the families of the three freed-vampire Houses. He's no errand boy, then, for all their peculiar laws.

I have never spoken to one of the males before—the wray, they're called—and my understanding is that their House hierarchy puts them on the level of indentured servants. What do I say? I have no idea what the protocol is when speaking to a wray.

"You've met my sister," he says at my continued silence. His faint smile drops away, and he watches me with clouded eyes. Uncertainty has made him flick his opaque third eyelids into place.

"Roisin?" She's the only bat I know even the slightest bit. A Sandwalker—her House's star rises even as my own falls. A good acquaintance to encourage, I suppose, although the girl herself is a bore. House Sandwalker specializes in the rare art of perfumery, and Roisin is lucky to have nose and skill, for she possesses little in the way of brains. If it hadn't been for how our House suffered after the last Red Death wiped out so much of our fishing profit, I wouldn't even have bothered to know her name.

The bat leans against the wall next to me, and there is a shimmery displacement of air that feels almost like being tickled by a goose feather. "Jannik," he says, and holds out one hand, as if I were a House son.

He wants me to touch him. We do not touch them—we have pretended some status to the few in Pelimburg, but only because of money. In MallenIve, my brother says, the bats know their place. I know little of MallenIve except what Owen has told me. They still have the pass laws there. Owen approves, and I suppose I should too.

I make it a point to never be like my brother.

With this in mind, I gingerly brush my fingers against Jannik's. His hand is warm and dry from being in his pocket. A shiver of magic dances between us, then disappears as I let go. It leaves my skin numb and cold like at the start of the flu and I turn my head from him, uncertain of what to say. It's like no magic I've ever felt before and the hairs on my arms rise, tingling. I should say something. The silence between us is strained and awkward, and for a moment I'm certain he's laughing at me on the inside. A mocking glint is in his indigo eyes.

Normally I'm the first person to bristle at any insult, implied or otherwise. I take my pride too seriously, my mother says. But this time I feel lost, like a ketch in a storm. Something about Jannik has thrown me. It must be because I've never had any man talk to me as if I were his equal. Always the men treat us like we're simpletons to be herded through life, to be humored for our fancies, to be disciplined when we stray. And it's something I never really thought about till this moment.

For a dizzying instant, my whole world turns about, and an infinite set of new windows opens. I am looking out through someone else's eyes, and I hear myself gasp. Then the faintness falls away and the ground is once again solid.

I stare at Jannik. His mouth twitches. "I'm beginning to feel like I should be skinned and put on display," he says.

His words break through my disorientation and I shake my head. "I'm sorry. I never—" Something catches my eye.

In the distance, a familiar silver-gray carriage rounds the street corner. Four surf-white unicorns pull it forward. There is no hiding my family's ostentatiousness.

It's my brother's coach, and if he sees me out here in the dirty streets filled with magicless low-Lammers and Hobs, he'll find some way to punish me. Were he to see the bat standing this close to me, his fury would be painful at best. I open my umbrella with a snap, spraying Jannik with silver droplets and startling him into jerking away from the wall. "Here," I say as I thrust the umbrella into Jannik's hand. "Hide me."

Amusement flickers across his face as he props the black umbrella over one shoulder and pulls me close. From the road, we will look like nothing so much as two lovers on the street. "Someone you don't want to see?" he says against my ear. His breath is warm, stirring the tight curls at the nape of my neck. Again, that strange magic flutters against me, in time with his breathing. I have never been this close to a man. He is close enough to kiss. I push the thought away, concentrate on my brother instead.

"Someone I don't want to see *me*."

Jannik smells clean, without a hint of the telltale sweet-and-spice of scriven dust, so I've no idea where that prickle of magic comes from. I'd expect him to smell meaty, like fresh blood, and not of soap and musk, of amber and perfumes. Perhaps the vampires scrub their skin after they feed. The thought makes me ill.

"My brother," I explain, trying not to shiver as magic

crab-walks down my spine. From the corner of my eye, I can see the rough skin of his cheeks, freshly scraped with a razor. His heart is beating against mine. Despite the tales told, I know that bats are living, are far from immortal, but this is the first time I have been close to one, and it is this patter of his heart that makes it real. He is too warm when I expected coldness.

With every agonized breath I taste sweetness strange and heady. I need to get away from him and away from the lure of this unexpected magic. "Roisin never mentioned any brothers," I say, trying to change the subject as the clatter of wheels and hooves draws closer.

Wrapped together, we pretend that we are making small talk at a dinner table. "Not completely unexpected," he says. "I think our mother has made it quite plain to her that we are inconsequentials." He laughs, a humorless snort. "Yes, Roisin has brothers. Three, in fact."

Ah, the strange social system that the bats have—so different from ours—that puts the women in power. No one I know has ever seen the matriarch of House Sandwalker, although she's rumored to be an imposing sort. For a bat.

The sound of hooves on stones is fading now. "Move the umbrella a little," I tell him.

Jannik complies, and there goes the rear of the carriage, the gray bodywork fading into the mist and drizzle. With a touch of my hand, I motion for the bat to drop the umbrella and close it.

I've only so much free time left before my mother sends

someone to find me, and I still want to get Ilven a gift. "I should leave—go back to the house."

"What, after all that subterfuge?" Jannik steps back and looks at me from under his rain-damp hair. "Far be it from me to stop you, but all that hiding behind umbrellas and engaging in nefarious clinches is going to seem wasted." He grins. He is not afraid to show me his teeth.

Heat rises, flushing my cheeks. Bats do not show their fangs, they pretend they are like us.

Jannik's face goes closed, and he steps even farther away. He dips a brief bow in my direction. "My apologies." He turns to leave.

Oh Gris. He's mistaken my silence for contempt. Certainly, I've never had a bat attempt flirtation with me before, but there's a first time for everything. And oh, how it would drive my brother insane. "Wait." I catch his sleeve, the black MallenIve lace of his cuff falling over my hand. Again the magic needles my skin. Wait till I tell Ilven about this—she'll be so annoyed that she couldn't meet me.

The third eyelids are back, and he looks at me with white blank eyes, his face carefully schooled.

"Give my regards to your sister," I say, fumbling for some reason to keep him near me.

"I will." One corner of Jannik's mouth quirks up. "May I have my arm back?"

"Oh." I'm never going to live this down. I release my grip on his sleeve and bunch the offending hand into a fist. His magic slips away from me as he walks down the promenade.

I stare at his back, at the perfectly tailored flourish of his coat, the rain covering the charcoal material with a tracery of stars.

Jannik pauses to stare back at me, as if he's felt my eyes on him. A gust of wind blows strands of his black hair across his face, and he looks like an ink sketch partly obliterated by the gray rain. With his chalk skin and the milkiness of his covered eyes, he is utterly alien. Compelling.

My throat goes tight, and I can barely suck the damp air into my chest. This feeling, I'll call it *revulsion*. That's what it must be, this churning inside me, this ache in my lungs.

He raises one hand and flashes those needle-fangs at me once again. The third eyelids flick up, and I catch a glimpse of fathomless dark before he turns away.

I WANDER DOWN THE BEACH ROAD, my stomach somersaulting, my head giddy as I take the long route past the old part of the Claw's promenade, a place I have only ever seen on the hand-drawn maps that cover my father's study. Here in this quarter, the abandoned houses are crumbling together and littering the sidewalks with small stones and rounded clumps of brick. The rain is coming in hard from the ocean now, and I can just make out the dark sails of the returning fishing fleets as they scud across the frothing gray harbor toward the shelter of the docks. Usually the ships go out at night, but the look-fars' storm horn has been blaring all morning, its mournful wail a counterpoint to the wind and gulls. Up on the hillsides the look-fars are in their towers, watching for returning ships, portents of bad tides, and storms.

This part of Pelimburg is slowly returning to the sea. The people who once lived here have long since moved inland, away from the decay, up the hillsides, or farther upriver. You'd have to be mad to stay here now. Most of the houses look as if a particularly powerful gust will blow them right down. Some of them are rotting into the gray mud, sliding inexorably seaward.

"'Ere!"

I step back just in time to miss being clobbered by a piece of rotted windowsill.

"Clear off!" A small dark head stares down at me from the uppermost window of a house with faded green paint mostly chipped down to bare stone and decaying plaster. The girl is as brown as a selkie, and I wonder if she's a half-breed, if her mother was one of the beautiful seal women who sometimes marry Hobs. "Don't bring none of your bad luck this way," the girl says.

Bad luck? While it's true that I stand out here in my blue silk dress, the storm will have turned my auburn hair into a mess of mud-brown tangles. Fortunately. The reddish tint would have been a giveaway that I'm from one of the High Houses.

My heart patters into a panicked beat. There's no love lost between Hob and high-Lammer. The Hobs work our factories, sail our ships, wash our clothes. They are the beetle-back on which our city is built. And they do not have a gentle love for us.

I take a backward step.

If the half-breed finds out that I'm of House Pelim, things could go exceedingly badly. Idiots—don't they understand that without our ships, our scriv-magic, the Hobs would still be living in hunting packs, just barely surviving on what little they could glean from the rock pools? The Hobs seem oblivious to the reality that were it not for our whalers and fishing boats there would be no city, no jobs, no trade.

A little chill of fear crystallizes in my veins. Best to leave before I'm caught and stripped and trussed—and more than likely covered in fish guts—and left as a message to my family and our closed warehouses. How are we to help it that the catches have been small, the fish tainted by magic, inedible? Of course, it suits the Hobs to blame us for such bad luck. It's blame us or blame a sea-witch, and we make for a much closer and safer target.

"Go on then!" Another piece of rotted wood just misses me. I shrug and turn up the street.

"Keep your trash!" I yell. "I'm leaving." If I had just a few grains of scriv on me, I could teach the Hob a lesson. Like my mother and brother, I am a War-Singer, highest of the three magic castes, higher than Saints and Readers, and able to make the very air do as I will. Unfortunately, I have no scriv. That makes me terrifyingly weak in the face of Hob violence, and I step farther back, my fear building.

"Keep walking," says the dark little half-caste. "Or I'll track you down and burn your house to the ground."

It's not the brightest thing to engage them. I really should just ignore her. Besides, what is there to fight over? She lives in a falling-down building that even the sharif couldn't be bothered to condemn, and I live in a cliff-top mansion. Let her think she owns this little strip of land. There's no one else who'd want it anyway. I turn my back on her.

It's far to go before I'm home—I still have to walk past all of Old Town and cross the Levelling Bridge. Darkness is coming in fast as the sea-storm gathers. My sigh is swallowed by the wind.

It won't be long before I get a chance to speak to Ilven again. There'll be much to tell her, although I doubt she'll believe the bat story. She'll probably think I'm making it up just to entertain her—the way I used to make up hordes of imaginary brothers and sisters to people our childhood games.

I'll stop at one of the vendors on the way back and buy her a gift. With this thought I skip up toward the center of Old Town to where the market square is in full rumble.

I twist and weave through a crush of people who stink of work and cheap perfumes. It's so bad that I have to draw a kerchief from my pocket and walk with my nose and mouth covered, in case I breathe in some illness of theirs.

There are wooden tea wagons and wide tables set with fish of all kinds and vegetables and strings of sausages. Some people squat on the ground with their wares laid out on a cloth before them: herbs, seaweeds, carved ivory trinkets.

Not far from me, a gaggle of little Hoblings play skip rope with a piece of frayed and filthy cord. They chant fast and vicious, clapping and shrieking when someone gets caught out.

> *The sea is rising, one two three,*
> *What will that get for Ivy and me?*
> *Pelim House gave us bones.*
> *Pelim House gave us stones.*
> *When the sea is rising red,*
> *All of Pelim will drop dead.*

I rush past them, shaking my head. Little brats. Deeper into the market I go, exchanging the childish game for the clamor of the sellers. And what a racket they make. One shouts out his wares in a high breathless chant, and another calls to me, "Lammer, Lammer, Lammer," waving at her collection of sea-vomited trash. Bands of ragged children run wild, pickpocketing or worse. Sharif dot the crowd, obvious as diamonds in their starched uniforms. They rake the milling people with narrowed eyes, always keeping watch, policing the city.

I find myself oddly wary around them, even though, strictly speaking, I have done nothing wrong and the idea that my mother has alerted them to my absence is laughable. I dart past one distracted by a mob of street children and leave the pale uniform behind.

Finally, I am drawn to a small painted trolley festooned with garlands of shells. The vendor has draped a fine silk cloth of Ives blue over the top, and on it are set out the delicate shells of the paper nautiluses that I love so. It's these that first catch my eye, but then I spot the necklace.

It's made from the inner coils of the big sea-snails: little polished chips of mother-of-pearl strung on twists of silk with a larger piece edged in silver wire to make a pendant. Certainly it's the sort of cheap thing the Hobs would find charming, and I imagine Ilven's face when I present her with such a worthless treasure. Something to remind her of the sea, of Pelimburg, of me. The thought makes me smile, and for a moment I forget that my mother will probably lock me in my room until next year when I'm allowed to enter Pelim University and there embrace my few years of sequestered freedom.

"How much?"

The man takes in my gloves and my fashionable dress and champs his mustache. "Two brass bits."

I laugh in response, but I don't care that he's bluffing. What are two brass bits to me? While my brother, Owen, would probably have haggled him down until the poor man practically gave the necklace away, I dig through my purse for some change and toss the coins down on his silk.

The necklace shimmers, the colors changing as he hands it to me, and I think of Ilven—so pretty, so polished and changeable. It is the perfect gift.

With my dress plastered to my back by the rain and the

wind whipping my hair loose and free so that it blows constantly into my face, I set off back home, away from the stench of congealed fish and seaweed.

IT IS NOT my mother's worried face that greets me when I return. A servant ushers me through to the formal lounge, acting as if I am an inconvenient guest in my own home. Only when I see who is waiting for me among the polished furniture and glass statues do I understand why.

Owen scowls, his pale cheeks mottled. His eyes are storm black. Not the best of signs. My dearest brother is ten years older than me, and he has always regarded me as an unfortunate accident. I shiver and tuck my hand into my pocket, curling my fingers around the necklace. It seems to me that if I can keep clinging to it, I'll somehow weather this. I look to my mother for reassurance, but she is pointedly watching the floor, as if she will find some message or hieroglyph in the carpet.

"Where have you been?" Owen's tone is soft and calm, almost cajoling. It's the way he talks to the dragon-dogs when he wants to coax them from their kennels. He might as well be waving a cut of nilly-flesh at me.

"Out," I say. "Walking."

When he says nothing, I find myself trying to fill in the emptiness, even though I know this is what he wants me to do. I can't seem to stop myself, and inside I'm cringing at my own stupidity. "Up in the fields toward the woods." Under his cold stare, I'm babbling, pulling lies out of nowhere, compounding them. "I was supposed to meet Ilven, we were going to see if the sea-drakes were back—they're supposed to be heading into the bay, but she didn't meet me so I headed toward the woods." Short of clamping my hand over my own mouth, I don't seem to be able to stop. He didn't see me with the bat, I'm certain of it. If he had, he would have stopped the coach there and then and hauled me back home like a runaway dog.

"Are there many bats up in the woods these days?" he interjects, and I stutter into silence.

"I-I—"

The magic hits me before I can think of a response. It sucks me forward, pulling all the air from my lungs. The citrus tang of scriv is in the air, and I realize with a vague unfocused horror that my brother is truly angry.

Angrier than I've seen him in a long time.

Like me, my brother is a War-Singer, able to control the air. Unlike me, he's been to university for the full seven years, has trained to control his talent, to augment it with scriv. All my control comes from the little bit of tutoring I've been allowed. Perhaps if we were threatened with war, like in the past, I would have been better armed.

More than that, Owen has control of our household scriv. He hoards it, hands out thimblefuls as rewards, withholds it as punishment. And even though my natural talent for magic is greater than his, right now I can barely do more than raise the smallest breeze. Without scriv, I have no way of accessing my full power.

It's better not to fight, I know, so I let my body slump. The magical wind is cold, sharp as glass splinters, and it pricks into my skin, tearing at my clothes and hair. My eyes burn as I fight to shut them against the needles of air.

No good. He's keeping my eyelids pried open. The air forces me to face him, but my vision is blurring red and my chest is slowly being crushed.

I want so badly to kick, to lash out, but I know from a bitter childhood full of my brother's games that doing so will only make him play longer.

He's not entirely cruel. He gives me back my air before I pass out.

"I dislike leaving my wife," he says, and flicks at his fingernails before buffing them against his sleeve. He's not even looking at me anymore, but I know that this too is merely part of his act. I know this because he's let his magic lift me up so that my head is level with his, and he's made sure that I can do nothing but stare at his face. "I especially do not like it when the reason I have to come back up here"—and now he looks up from his manicure and around at the dark interior of the family home—"is because yapping Houses run to tell me they have spotted my sister in the city dallying with a bat."

My mother, who until now has been keeping white and quiet behind her precious son, finally takes the time to look up at me. "Felicita," she says, "there's been a terrible accident—"

"That can wait, Mother." Owen cuts her off.

She frowns and changes tack as easily as the little fishing

boats that litter the bay. "It's not true, is it?" she says to me. "I told him it couldn't have been you, that it's just someone trying to make our House look bad."

It's all she cares about. I feel defeated and irritated at the same time. "Of course it was me," I snap.

Cold threads of my brother's power tighten around my throat. Finally, I think, I've pushed him too far. This time he'll do more than lock me up in a cupboard for a day or leave me merely with bruises that will fade.

He drops me. I collapse against the black slate floor, my ankle twisting painfully under the sudden weight of my body. I gasp, trying to make up for the lack of air, or to somehow store it up in my body for another attack.

"Malker Ilven is dead," my brother says.

For a moment I think he's attacked me again. My throat is filled with grains of glass.

Then Owen walks past me, his boot heels thudding against the slate floor, and he is gone.

I can breathe. I just don't want to.

2

"Oh Gris!" My mother grabs me in her arms and pulls me so tightly against her that it feels like my spine will crack. Finally, I manage to work one hand free and I raise it to wipe her clinging hair out of my face. My mother never wears her hair loose.

"He's lying," I say. "Isn't he?" I push at her stiff arms until she lets me go. Her face is blotched, the powder in damp patches on her skin, gathering in the fine wrinkles by her eyes and mouth.

Her fear vanishes, and she presses her lips into a thin angry line. "You're never to leave the estate, you know that."

I'm House Pelim's little bird, the only daughter. After Father died, Mother kept me closed up, fearful that somehow I would go down like him—victim of a prole illness caught off a river-Hob or a hacking low-Lammer. "I wanted some fresh air." I cough the words out, then rub my neck gingerly, trying to massage away the pain.

She's regained her composure, and she scrapes one thin

hand through her silvered hair. "Never," she says again. "We've talked about this."

No. *You've talked about it.* I just had to sit and listen. The only person I can talk to is Ilven. We grew up together, shared the same flight space. And now, if my brother is to be believed, she's gone.

I pull away from my mother and race up to my room.

The turret room is probably my mother's sole concession to my state as perpetual prisoner. Technically, I should be in the family wing and not in this drafty little tower. But I like it up here, and as I'm the only daughter, my mother has allowed me this indulgence. Or maybe she just understood that I needed what little artificial freedom I could get to keep me sane. So I have this room that overlooks the chalk cliffs and fills and echoes with the sound of the sea mews squabbling over fish. The white gulls look like scraps of paper buffeted about the cliffs.

The rain has swollen the wooden frame, but a few hard shoves soon have the window open and salt-spray air and drizzle sweep in. The sea mews are louder, circling in great wheeling flocks, and below me is the rumbling crash of the surf.

"Felicita." My mother is standing outside my closed door. She's keeping an even tone.

I ignore her and pull up a footstool so that I can lean right out the window and stare down at the dizzying waves. They flash white around the humpback brown rocks, seething.

"Felicita!" she snaps. "We need to talk."

Across the bay, I can just see the gaslights dotted along the

Claw, blinking faint as night-worms. And there, like a stain on the horizon, a little ink blot, is Lambs' Island. Maybe next time I run, I'll get farther than the promenade. I'll steal a boat and make it all the way to the island and hide there with the Mekekana ghosts.

"Felicita."

If she says my name one more time I'm going to scream. They'll hear it all the way out in Old Town. It's not true, my brother just knows what lies will hurt me the most, that's all it is.

"You must forgive your brother," she says. "He was worried about you, and when he's worried he doesn't think." I can hear her breathing, a trembling, liquid sound. I think she's crying. "He shouldn't have told you the way he did."

It's not true. I clench my fists and force myself to stare out the window, to block out my mother's voice, but there's no need. She's fallen silent, waiting.

Ilven is almost my age, but blond and delicate in the way of House Malker. Glass fragile and dangerous. She's one of the few playmates I was ever allowed. I've known her my whole life. I crawl down from the window ledge and thrust one hand into my pocket and take hold of Ilven's gift before I open the door.

My mother twists her hands. "I'm sorry," she says. And I realize suddenly that she truly is.

My syrupy anger cools, and inside I feel breakable.

"How?" I say. My tongue is thick and heavy; I'm trying to talk with a mouth that isn't really mine.

"Oh, Felicita." She wrings her hands, over and over. "I didn't want you to find out like this."

"Tell me what happened." I let go of the necklace.

"She jumped."

That's all Mother needs to say. Our estate and House Malker's are built on the high cliffs along Pelim's Tooth. The Tooth, like its mirror the Claw, is a pincer of land that juts around the mouth of the Casabi river, making a protected bay.

But the cliff isn't called the Tooth all the time. In fact, most people call it Pelim's Leap.

Not to our faces, of course.

They don't like to remind us that our House has brought the Red Death to Pelimburg's shores before, that we have a history of suicides and ill luck.

I bite down, grinding my teeth, trying to stop the shaking from spreading through my limbs. None of the superstitions are true, but even now there will be talk through the Houses that Ilven has caused House Malker to lose face, that her death brings ill luck to our shores. If there are bad catches in the bay, if the whaling ships are lost in storms, or if another merciless red tide sweeps down the coastline, Hob and low-Lammer alike will whisper Ilven's name, and they will know at which House's door to lay their blame.

So Ilven took the Leap. My hands tremble and I bury them in the soft folds of my dress. "Are you certain?"

My mother nods. "They found her . . . body."

I hate to think what she means by *body*. It's a long drop to the bottom, to the rocks and the crushing waves. In my mind, Ilven's delicate face turns to a slab of hammered meat. I try to swallow down my nausea.

There will be *whys*—people gossiping and speculating as to what Meke-damned trial drove her to it. Whatever thoughts spurred her on, Ilven's not going to spill them now. And any ill luck that comes to Pelimburg now will be blamed on Ilven's dive, on the alchemy of falling girls and broken-glass sea. If her death wakes something in the deep, then she will bring more shame down on her House with that one act than she could have accomplished in a lifetime of disobedi-ence. They will hate her for it. I wonder if Lady Malker has already struck her daughter's name from the family tree.

"I think I want to sleep," I say. And I do, really, I do. The last thing I want is to be awake and to think about how Ilven escaped from the life she didn't want. And why she never spoke to me, told me, warned me. Perhaps I could have changed her mind. It occurs to me that she never meant to meet me under the trees—that she knew me well enough to predict that I would wait only so long before I left—because then she could take the Leap without any chance of me wit-nessing her from my tower. My heart goes small, and every limb feels too heavy to lift.

Perhaps my mother even understands a little about how I feel. She leaves, and a few minutes later Firell brings me honeybush tea.

"Firell," I say, and she curtseys in greeting.

She sets the ornate copper tray down and begins fiddling

with the pots and bowls. The thin liquid trill of tea poured into porcelain is soothing, and the faint sweet scent of the honeybush lingers in the air.

"Can I bring you anything else, miss?"

I shake my head. It's too heavy for my neck. I'm going to snap, break in two. If I could cry, perhaps my head would be lighter. I am a rain cloud, heavy before the storm.

She curtseys again, ready to leave, but I stop her before she can go.

"Here," I say, and fumble in my pocket for the little necklace that is weighing me down. She takes the gift, her eyes wide, nervous.

"Miss?"

"For you," I say. And it might as well be. Firell has served me as a lady's maid since she could carry a tray. I look at her again and really see her: her face olive complected, her dark hair drawn back into a neat pad low on her neck. Her starched uniform, marred by faint stains at the armpits, the burn on her arm, faded now, where she once caught at a falling teapot so that it wouldn't scald me. I realize now that I know nothing about Firell—she could be a magicless unwanted baby from a High House, or some serving girl's bastard. The latter's more likely; along with the tan skin, she has the short stature that points at Hob parentage. The High Houses try to keep their bloodlines pure, clinging to their magic. Ilven used to say that soon we high-Lammers would be nothing more than inbred monstrosities, lording it over one another as we play king of the midden.

It could be a true future that Ilven saw—she's a Saint after all. *Was*. Was a Saint.

"It's a gift," I say to Firell.

She takes the package with fluttering fingers and tucks it deep in her apron pocket without unwrapping it. "Thank you, miss. Thank you."

When she's gone, I feel empty. After a while, I take my teacup and blow, making tiny ripples across the reddish water.

There's a distinct bitter aftertaste of Lady's Gown in the tea, and I welcome it. Anything to sleep without dreaming.

I AM STILL GROGGY from a week spent in mourning, and my thoughts chase one another in ever-tightening spirals. This is not a good way to face my mother's neat and quiet revenge. The early sunlight hurts my puffy eyes and I squint, wishing the ache away. The low tea table is a bridge between us, or perhaps a wall. Carefully, I arrange the teapot, the little white cup, and the sugar bowl before me like an army. Defense? Or attack?

My mother sits crisply, folding and unfolding the letter she holds. Her weapon. It bears my brother's jagged script. How like him, to talk to us in a way that gives us no chance to argue or interrupt. My mother still deludes herself that the letters are written out of more than a desire to spend as little time in our company as possible. She likes to think he is still hers.

It seems we're pretending that nothing happened. My brother is with his wife and her expanding belly. It will not be long now before her lying-in, and we shall see even less of him than usual. I hope. He will stay in his town house in New Town, near enough to the docks that he can keep his eye over our wealth. His wealth.

As for Ilven, there is only the kind of silence that comes heavily weighted with the whispers of servants. They stop talking when they hear me coming. They do not look at my face.

My hand darts up to brush the high collar of my dress. Glass beads and thick embroidery press against the bruises they are meant to hide.

My mother fires the first volley. "Your brother has had some interest from House Canroth." She sets the letter down between us, then draws her cup closer to her but doesn't drink.

"Interest about what?"

"It's time you looked to a suitable match—"

"With House Canroth?" Anger makes my skin tight. "They're—they're not even a Great House." As if that matters; all the eligible bachelors from the Great Houses are practically decrepit. Even the next highest ranked, like the Skellig twins, are still in swaddling clothes. I try to dredge up what little knowledge I have of Canroth, but my mind is blank. Something about glass, I think. Ah, that's it, they make fine crystal, so they're mostly War-Singers. At the very least I suppose I should be glad Owen is not trying to tie me to a House overrun with Readers and Saints, all lost in auras and Visions. I do not want to spend the rest of my life trying not to feel too much, in case some Reader turns my inner-most desires against me. And if I think my life is measured and controlled now, how much worse would it be in a House ruled by Saints, constantly tracking futures and possibilities, their lives ruled by scriv-visions and the auguries of decks of cards? Perhaps Ilven not only foresaw her own death but also knew to an instant how long I would wait in the grove of trees before I left her to her chosen path.

I try to calm myself by sipping my tea, but it is too hot, and I burn the back of my throat, my tongue. Good. I focus on the pain, the tip of my tongue touching the shreds of burned skin on my palate. An image of a reedy little man drifts up through my memories. We met at my mother's last garden party—he's a nothing, a pale little nothing in his thirties. I don't even remember his name.

My knees bump the table as I stand, and tea spills over its polished surface. "I will not marry a Canroth," I tell her.

"You sit down," my mother hisses. "See, this is exactly the sort of nonsense that drove Ilven to—" She stops, just on the knife edge of tact. "Your brother will make the arrangements with Canroth Piers."

Piers. His face coalesces in my mind. His drab mustache is the only detail that made any impact on me. My innards knot and twist like live snakes. I understand why Ilven jumped. Even that damned bat on the promenade, even he—a hated vampire in a city that barely tolerates their existence—has more choice than I.

And there's nothing I can do. Owen is a decade older than

me, and with Father dead, I answer to him, to his whims and decisions. The Pelim line ends with Owen, and were he to die, I suppose I would then be in the charge of Mother's family in MallenIve. A ghastly thought in itself.

The letter on the table flutters in a sudden gust that brings with it the distant reek of seaweed. I grab the letter, sweep it up to my chest.

"Where are you going with that?" my mother asks as I stomp up to the large bay window that overlooks the short expanse of front lawn before the garden drops off to the sea.

There's no point in answering her, she'll know soon enough. I throw the right window wider, then fling the letter out. The thin leaves dance across the lawn before another sea-gust takes them, sending them flickering through the air. The sea mews crowd about the papers, calling to each other in excitement, wings flapping as they fight. Another gust sends the papers over the cliff, fluttering in looping spirals. A last sheet twirls on the lawn in a giddy solo, then tips over and is gone.

Like Ilven, it's taken Pelim's Leap.

"I'm so glad you've managed to get that out of your system. Now, if we could go back to our tea. You know better than to go against your brother's wishes."

I don't turn around. The wind pulls my hair loose and auburn curls slap at my face. "I hate you," I say.

A sigh comes from behind me. "Hate me all you want," she says. "It won't change matters." Her footsteps fade away, a measured *click* across the polished black slate. The sound is suddenly dampened, and I know that she's in the carpeted passageway.

"I hate you," I say again, softly, to the sea, to the cliff, to the fat-bellied clouds. To my brother's cruelty. To Pelim's Leap.

3

THIS TIME, I think as I fill my bag, this time, I won't come back. I've been hiding in my room since Owen's command that I marry into House Canroth, wondering what to do. My mother has given up knocking on my door.

Outside, the night is heavy and wet. There are no stars and the only sound is the sea breathing, the constant measured rasp of the surf. Dawn is not far off, and it won't be long before the starlings and servants awake. I've only a handful of brass left after buying Ilven's gift. I've never had to worry about money; if ever I needed something, the servants bought it for me, and transactions were handled discreetly, from accounts that I have never seen. Now I wish I'd asked for a coin here or there. A few brass bits won't buy me more than a worker's tea, but I take them anyway. Them and the contents of my jewelry box.

On second thought, I put most of the jewelry back. It will be too obvious. Instead, I take only a few of the older pieces—a necklace, a set of hideous earrings, and three old but still valuable hair clips. Small ones, ones that I last wore when I was five or six. No one will notice that these are missing. I shove them into my bag.

I pause at the tiny enameled scriv-box. It opens at the slightest pressure of my finger, revealing the meager amount of scriv inside. The dust is made of fine gray grains, like ashen sand, and smells like citrus and musk. The smell of magic. I should take this—without it I am nothing, powerless as a Hob.

Without it I have almost no magic. Like all high-Lammers, I am a lucky accident of birth, gifted with a talent that can be expanded by something as simple as a mineral. A mineral unfortunately rare and extremely addictive. This—this dust—rules our lives. Sometimes I wonder if it would be better had there been no magic at all.

There are tales of Hobs who had natural magic unfettered by a dependency on scriven, who were created after House Mallen opened the Well—the source of all the wild, un-controlled magic in our land—but the sharif-councils and the Great Houses have killed any of those Hobs that might once have existed.

The only ones who are allowed to use magic are the high-Lammers. We're bound to the scriv, so our magic is tem-pered. We can't accidentally flatten cities or bring down a plague. And of the Lammic practitioners of magic, there are only three accepted types: War-Singers like myself, who can manipulate air; Saints, who can see the future; and Readers, who can tell people's emotions from the flare of their auras.

The Well is sealed.

All the Hobs with magic have been destroyed. The animals twisted by the opening of the Well have been harnessed or hunted. The unicorns that were once goats are again our beasts of burden, the lions-turned-sphynxes are killed for their coats, even the little wyrms, tiny legless dragons, are no more than an occasional lucky find in a gardener's compost heap. Now there is only us—the Houses. Scriv.

I snort softly. Am I ready to give this up—to become like the mundane Hobs? The grains are cool against my fingertips, stirring up the sharp smell, the musty illusion of power. I have never been allotted more than the barest amount at a time; my brother controls exactly how much scriv my mother and I are allowed.

It is the same in all Houses. My status as War-Singer is little more than a hollow title. I will never be allowed to be truly powerful. I accepted that I would see only two years of real training at university, nothing like my brother's seven. Not unless there's another war with the Mekekana and we need every Lammer to fight them off. Not that there's any chance of that happening after their thorough trouncing.

I rub the scriv between my fingers and let it fall back. Of what use to me are illusions?

The scriv-box closes with a clean snap. The leaping silver dolphins on the lid, picked out against the blue enamel sea, grin up at me in gentle mockery. No one will believe my little fabrication if I take my scriven with me.

I ache to take it, to not leave it here to waste.

Instead, I force myself to turn away.

The shawl I've chosen for tonight is my favorite—golden-brown sea silk in a delicate scallop pattern, beaded with the smallest of amber glass seeds. I wrap it around a pair of embroidered shoes and tuck the bundle under my arm. I'm wearing my oldest, shabbiest dress, thick woolen stockings against the chill, a rough coat, and a pair of sturdy boots. They were meant for walking, but I've never had much chance to use them and the leather is stiff and uncomfortable.

They also squeak. I curse the Gris-damned boots under my breath. I'll never get out of the house without using magic.

I turn back to the little box sitting expectantly on the mantelpiece and exhale a long breath I didn't even know I was holding. Just one pinch, that's all it'll take. And this will be the last I have.

No one will notice if a few grains are missing. I step forward to press the catch.

The last time. You should make the most of it, I tell myself, as I take the smallest pinch of scriv possible. The dust fills my nose with the sharp smell of magic, and then, all around me, the air is real, solid. Carefully, I use my scriv-enhanced abilities to hold sound in place as I step over the collection of cold tea things outside my doorway and creep down the winding turret stairs, past the second-floor wing where my mother sleeps, past the ranks of servants' rooms, farther and farther down, till I am in the long open tearoom.

The house is held still and silent with my magic, but

already I can feel the edges of sound filtering back in. I barely took enough to last five minutes. There's no going back.

The last of the scriv-high fades just as I turn the bone key in the front door. Outside, the night waits, clammy-handed.

The door shuts softly.

In the kennels, one of my brother's dragon-dogs whines, perhaps hearing the faint click of the lock. My breath held, I wait, the seconds slipping past. The dog shuffles. The steady *thump thump thump* of its heavy tail against the wood is like a fist beating on a door. It makes me pant faster, just trying to suck some air down a too-tight throat. The throbbing bruises on my neck feel like they go all the way to the inside. The sound fades, and the air tastes like burning copper when I am finally able to breathe normally again. Damning myself for not taking more scriv, I inch along the path.

The darkness is a blanket. I stumble over the shadows of things that are not there, falling and scraping my knees and palms on the seashell grit that edges each paving stone. This time the dog must hear me, for it yaps once into the starless night. Another dog joins it, and soon all my brother's damned dragon-dogs are baying and barking in a frenzy. Their howls echo against the distant forested hills.

Not bothering to be silent now, I run for the long shadows of the box firs that grow alongside our house. Protected from the worst of the sea-winds, they grow tall. I huddle in between them, the fresh piney scent filling my nostrils. Under it is the heady loam of the soil, grounding me.

"There anyone out?" calls a woman's voice. Firell.

I shut my eyes and press myself against the wall, dampening the back of my coat. *Go away.*

Instead of magically hearing my thoughts and disappearing back into the house, Firell walks down the pathway. Her boots thud on the stone. She pauses, and I want to scream. Then the footsteps fade away.

Oh Gris. Thank all the Old Saints that Hobs aren't any more magical than a handful of dried beans. I'm about to leave my little piney sanctuary when I hear her voice again, soft and coaxing, and the rattle of the wooden latch to the dogs' enclosure. The hounds have stopped barking, and while there's nothing for me to fear from the dogs, I suddenly wish that I had spent less time with them.

The first comes haring up the pathway, claws clicking on stone. I close my eyes again and tip my head back against the wall in resignation. A few seconds later a cold nose is touching my hand. The bitch whines and licks at my fingers.

"Go away, Mar," I whisper. "Shoo!"

Mar sits down on her haunches and gazes up at me with brown-eyed devotion, her long red tail sweeping the paving.

"No treats," I hiss. "Go on! Shoo!" I flap at her with my hands, but the dog is used to getting little tidbits or scraps of meat from me, not being shoved away. She just sits there and whines low.

"What's there, girl?" Firell's voice is nervous. She must have a lantern because a warm orange spill of light is bouncing along the ground, lapping at my hiding place.

It's no use. I push my hands against the wall in anger and then step out into the light.

Firell almost drops the fatcandle lamp. "Miss!" She presses one hand to her mouth and then lets it fall again. Her eyes narrow. "What are you doing out here? You'll catch your death."

"Firell."

She stops her solicitations over my health and takes in the clothes I'm wearing. A frown gathers across her face. "I don't understand," she whispers.

"Can you keep a secret?"

"I-I—"

"Look," I snap. "It's simple. You're not to say you've seen me here tonight, no matter who asks." I smile at her. "Come now, Firell, sweet. I brought you a gift. Are we not friends?"

The Hob stares at me, her free hand going automatically to the little bulge in her apron pocket.

"Please," I say, resorting to begging. "I just can't stay here." I look wildly about me, expecting that any minute now, alerted by the noise, my mother will come trundling down from the house with her clothes in disarray and servants following her like the tide.

"Miss," she says again. "Miss, I can't lie to your mother." Her face is almost pale in the darkness, ashy with fright. "You know I can't."

"You're a Hob," I say. "You lie to her all the time—about how much sugar you put in your tea or how many slices of bread you've taken."

"That I don't," Firell says. "Here." She pulls the necklace from her pocket and throws it at my feet. "I don't want none of your gifts."

"Firell, please." I'm desperate now. "I'm sorry, sorry. I didn't mean it, truly. Keep the necklace, but please just do me this one thing, and I'll never ask anything more of you." I hug myself, shivering at the thought of being forced into a future I don't want. Or of the punishment that waits for me if I don't do as I'm told. Owen is not a man prone to forgiveness.

She looks at me with sudden understanding. "When I was just a Hobling," she says, "my mam told me I'd be coming here to help look after a little girl—a little high-Lammer girl. And I didn't have no say in the matter."

I stay quiet, watching her, my fingers tightening on my coat lapels.

"I thought you were lucky—no scrubbing nothing, clothes laid out for you every morning, tea in bed. And all I wanted was to go back to being a Hobling in Stilt City, at play. I hated you so much, every day for years." She kneels and takes Mar by the collar, holding her still. "Go on then," she says. "I didn't never see you here tonight."

"Thank you." But the Hob woman has already turned away, dragging the dog with her. On the ground, the little gift still lies. I drop to one knee, scoop it up, and jam it deep into my coat pocket.

I wait a few heartbeats, letting the silence of the night drift around me in a thick mist before I set off again. This time I keep to the long shadows where the darkness gathers

42

thickest, picking my way across the silvery damp grass until I reach the edge of the world. Below, the rocks and waves are grinding against each other, and the wind sucks at me, begging me to take one more step, to throw myself down. *Sacrifice*, the water says in its sea-witch voice, full of whispers and promises. Sometimes I have to wonder if the Hob belief that the sea is animate, alive and full of magic, is more than just primitive nonsense.

Instead, I kneel and pull a rock free from the cliff edge. The wind tugs at the golden-brown silk as I unwind and rewrap the shawl around the shoes and the lump of pale chalk. Then I stand, take a careful step away from the edge, and hurl the shawl out into the ocean.

That's all the sharif will find of me.

4

BY THE TIME I see the Levelling Bridge, the sun is streaking the horizon pink. Gold edges the last of the smeared clouds, and the sails of the returning fish boats are cheerily white. My feet, however, are far from cheery. The whole of my right heel feels like one huge blister—the boots are certainly a size too small. My toes are pinched and sore. With my teeth gritted, I hoist my little holdall higher and walk down Spindle Way, drawing closer and closer to the bridge. Around me the first of the early-morning delivery carts are *clip-clopping* past. The large goatlike nillies with yellow eyes—unicorns who have had their horns sawed off to feed our need for a cut-rate replacement for scriv—shove at one another, and the stone road is already covered with the little black pellets of their dung. Straw and mud have been tracked here, and they mingle with the fine white sand that blows in from the harbor.

I stand with one foot on the bridge. The bridge-houses loom on either side of me, packed close as cards in a Saint's deck.

Once I cross and lose myself in Old Town, it'll be done. *That's what you want, Felicita.*

Or I could be a little bird again and fly back to my tower. And then what? A lifetime of dull and careful parties, a marriage engineered for Pelim's fortune, and then a long stretch into eternity. Gray and featureless.

Old Town might stink of fish and feces, but it still has to be better than *that*.

Even the thought of my mother's face creased in anguish can't slow me. She will soon forget any heartache, I'm sure. After all, she has Owen. If I return before my mother has time to panic, all that will happen is that I'll be watched more closely, have less privilege. A few months and then I'll be trapped in House Canroth, watching Piers blow baubles of glass. Perhaps, dutifully, I'll even make my own.

I imagine his white fingers touching me, slug-like in the dark, and I shudder. A show of weakness that I can't allow myself. If there's one thing my mother taught me, it is how to wear the perfect mask. Never show them what you're really feeling because that's how they hurt you. I picture my mother's face when she must go out in public with Owen, the cold arrogant look she wears, as if the whole world is filth before her. It is an expression I've learned to copy well, and like all roles, if you can believe it, you can be it. I press my hands to my face and push, smoothing the worry and fear away. I'm better than them. Better than Owen, than Canroth Piers. They can never really control me because they cannot bridle my thoughts.

It works. I'm calm again. Let Piers and Owen make the wedding arrangements, just don't expect the bride to be there like a dog called to heel. I'll choose my own Gris-damned husband, thank you. If I even want one, and I'm not exactly certain of that. I want life on my own terms, not on the dictates of tradition and of haggling over power and land.

I will never let myself be caught like that—any marriage I make will be my own. A choice. A free one.

Idiot girl. Owen always called me that. And perhaps now it is truer than ever, but I don't care.

The thought of my future husband isn't easily forgotten, so I try to replace it. In my head I turn Piers's pasty fingers to long white ones, the overpowering smell of scriv to that strange subtle magic I got off the bat on the promenade . . . I shake my head, breathe deeply.

The stench of Pelimburg thickens as I go farther across the bridge. A few hardy souls have already set up open-air tea stalls, and fat Hob women with dark faces and screeching voices call out as I pass. "Tea's champ," they say. "Hot for the girls and cold for the boys." Another one fries elvers in oil and wraps them in flat-bread cones. The air smells of shellfish, sweat, rotting seaweed, and strong tea. I wrinkle my nose and wonder if pressing a kerchief to my mouth will give me away as a House Lammer. If people remember seeing me, and talk to the sharif, then my game will be up.

A sudden chill stops me. Someone did spot me before and told my brother where I was. How long before word reaches him and I am hauled back, on a tightened chain? I need to do something. I look this way and that, suddenly terrified that everyone is staring at me and wondering why it is I'm here in Old Town, dressed in tat.

Then I see them.

Two bats are standing outside one of the bridge tailor shops, waiting for it to open. Most businesses will only serve them at prearranged times or unlikely hours so that more respectable Houses will not have to endure the bats' presence. They're watching me. One walks away from his kin, toward me, frowning. While bats all look similar, there is something about him that tugs at me, about the way he stands, as if he is not really a part of this world, as if he is merely someone looking on. I lower my head and walk faster, pretending that I don't notice, that he is not the Sandwalker bat I met the last time I ran. The memory of his scent and magic makes my breathing tight.

"Felicita?" he says. It is him. *Please, please,* I whisper under my breath. *Please go away. Please don't remember seeing me.* I do not look up. If I make eye contact, then he will know that it's me.

He doesn't call my name again, and after a few moments, I risk a backward glance. The bats are gone. The tailor has ushered them into the shop. Curiosity, or something like it, makes me backtrack. I peer through the dusty windows into the warm glow. The spry little tailor is talking to them. The bats have their backs to me. I linger, my palms pressed to the glass, just watching the shorter one as he stands with an easy, casual grace, his hands in his trouser pockets.

Then, as if a string has tightened between us, he turns around and sees me.

I jerk away from the window and lurch down the pavement, blindly knocking pedestrians out of my path.

A cleaning-Hob flicks her street-broom at me. I step out into the street, trying to avoid the press of bodies.

"What about this," says one Hob, her hand reaching out for me. "Lost, are you, little Lam?"

I rush past her and pull my ugly brown shawl from my holdall and cover my head. I'm too recognizable as a Great House Lammer—the auburn is a dead giveaway. It won't be long before I'm caught out for what I am. Gris-damn the Pelim red in my hair.

I pause in my tracks.

Some of the low-Lammers dye their hair red. It's a cheap dark color, with no subtlety or life.

Perfect. And for the first time since I left my prison, I find myself smiling.

"Here! Out of the way, frail-bit," yells a man, and a cart clatters past me with a full load, a tangle of tarred ropes and netting. I twist out of his way and hurry on down the sidewalk. All I need to do is keep my nose high and wait till I smell the distinctive pungent aroma of hair paste.

It doesn't take long. The hairdresser's is a dark little shop squeezed between a fish stall and a nilly-runner's. Already a line is streaming from the runner's door, as the men place bets on the racing.

The hairdresser's glass-and-wood door is grimy, and I push

it open gingerly, wondering if my mother is not completely insane in her belief that all the Hobs and low-Lammers carry filthy diseases. A little ivory bell clacks, and a girl with her hair in many long thin braids looks up. She's leaning on the counter, and next to her elbow is a fatcandle, its oily smoke drifting about her head. Her hands are stained a deep red as if she's wearing bloody gloves, and she stares at me over her interlaced fingers. Her wide eyes are slanted, the deep gray green of true Hobs. Her skin is warmed gold by the candle-lamps, and she looks otherworldly, beautiful.

"Clear off," she says, giving me a dismissive glance. "You're in the wrong shop."

She can make it so that no high-Lam or bat with a passing acquaintance could possibly recognize me. Carefully, I straighten my shoulders and pull the shawl from my head.

"Oh." She taps at her teeth with a brown fingernail. "Definitely in the wrong shop."

"I want you to dye my hair," I say. I try to stare her down but she just looks at me, her forehead puckered. She's still tapping at her teeth.

Tap tap tap.

Tap.

"All right, then," she says, just as I'm about to pull the shawl back up and look for another shop. "But it's no money back if you don't like it none."

"How much?"

She peers sidelong at me. "Three bits."

"I'll give you one."

"Cheap little whore," she says with a shrug. "Fine. One bit it is."

A few minutes later, she's got me sitting on a three-legged stool, my knees up awkwardly high and a stained piece of waxed silk over my shoulders. She slaps paste onto my coiled-up hair with an even precision, then works the muck into my scalp.

"'S a shame to dye this lot," she says. "But you won't be the first little bastard to go on the game an not want your da seeing you." Her fingers knead and pull, spreading the paste over every strand.

"I'm not—" I grit my teeth.

"Oho! Really." I don't have to see her face to know that she's smirking at me. Her voice just has that quality. Sharp fingernails scrape my scalp. "Next you're going to tell me that it ain't your da you're running from. There's no other reason for a high-Lammer to run—you're in trouble. You've lost your House face, and now you're running." She pauses. "Mind you, I'd run too." Her fingers tremble against my scalp, pulling the hair. "Whatcha do? You in trouble with a boy, is it?"

"That's not it," I whisper. "There are other reasons—" I stop. The less I say, the better.

Her hands have begun their rhythmic massaging again, and with each long slow stroke the silence gathers. "Are you one of ours?" she finally asks, in a voice unlike her earlier one. No longer jocular and mocking. Her tone is heavy.

I do not know what she means or how to respond. "Ours?"

She snorts. "Never mind. It was a stupid thought. We got no use for your kind an you ain't got no pity for ours."

Anger bristles through me and then fizzles out in confusion. I've no idea what she's talking about, but there is one thing she has right: high-Lammers have no pity for Hobs. At best, we think of them as children we need to discipline. I remember my parting words to Firell, and a vague guilt chews through me, making me ache.

Water sluices over my head, washing away the excess dye, washing away the picture of myself as a pampered little House daughter.

"Take this," I say after the girl is done, and hand her the necklace Firell threw back at me. Nervous, I try my best at the city patois. "Don't tell no one that you saw me." It sounds strange on my tongue, stilted, the vowels not flat enough. The look the Hob gives me makes me flush, but she grins again and snatches the gift from my hand.

The mother-of-pearl necklace clatters onto her table. She examines it in the dim light, then waggles her head, as if she can't decide between a no and a yes. "Fine." She sweeps it off the table and undoes the clasp. As she pushes her hair up away from her neck, I see bruises and wounds on her flesh. It looks like someone's stabbed her repeatedly with an awl. Then her hair drops back down, and the marks are hidden by her beads and braids.

The largest piece of mother-of-pearl sits between her breasts. She looks down at it, her fingers twisting it this way and that. "It'll do. I ain't seen nothin'." Then she stills, her red-dyed hands at her new bauble. "You made a good choice."

I pause at the threshold.

"To run," she says. "Bad things are coming to the Houses, and you're best out of there."

"Bad things?"

Instead of answering, she squints. Then with a final dismissive wave she says, "Head down Whelk Street way."

"Why?"

"You go down that way and ask out for Dash. Tell him Anja sent you. He'll see you straight," she says, and then the door closes behind me with a sharp *snick*.

My hair feels rough and strange. I've little idea how bad it looks, but no one on the street even gives me a second look. With my clothing already spattered with dung and roadside dirt, and my hair a tangled mess of fake red, I'm just another low-Lammer on her way to work. Whether I'm working a street corner or a market stall, well, that's none of their business unless they're buying. The anonymity is comfortable, like going around draped in magic, hidden from view. The thought of never having scriv again pulls at me, but only a little. We're so rationed here in Pelimburg anyway, what with those MallenIve prats charging an arm and a leg for even the tiniest thimbleful.

Still, I never had to worry about that before. And now . . .

And now, my mother will have discovered that I'm gone. How long before the golden-brown shawl or an embroidered slipper washes up against the rocks? Will they lower sharif on long silk-thin ropes to inspect? Till they find anything I'm just missing once again, and I'm relying on my mother's sense of House honor to keep quiet about it for as long as possible.

ON EITHER SIDE OF ME, the bridge buildings drop away, and Spindle Way diverges and dips toward the mudflats. If I keep along the raised stone promenade, I will reach the tip of the Claw. There are only squatters and Hobs living in that area, and no one will think to look for me there.

Or I could go straight on through Old Town and lose myself in the Hob-infested marshes of Stilt City. *Ugh*. I'm safer on the Claw, among the fish-gangs. At least the houses there are built on solid land. Solid mud, anyway.

A wind rises in the east, winding around the jut of the cliffs and blowing across the harbor. The masts wail eerily and the smells of kelp and tarred wood compete with the stench of dye whelks rotting in barrels. It's strong enough to make me gag.

Certainly, I won't be getting a job on the wharf.

A job.

I'll think about that later. For now, all I want is a place where I can hole up and wait for the sharif to find my "remains." I ask a Hob leaning against a wall for directions to Whelk Street. He stares at me strangely, then tells me. His directions lead me to a place that seems horribly familiar.

It's only mid-morning and the weather is already changing. The easterly brings clouds scudding in from the ocean, gathering thick and low. Soon it will be raining again, and with the promise of rain comes the smothering kiss of the fog. I need to find some kind of shelter. The end of the promenade with its rows of dilapidated buildings—that's where I need to go. Back to where the selkie-girl threw a piece of windowsill at me. The place is a tangle of squats.

My feet won't move.

No one will recognize me, I tell myself as I pat my hair reassuringly. There's no chance that I look like a House Lammer now. And I stink. The rough cotton of my housedress and coat smells of sweat and dirt and dye. Still, I'm nervous as I trudge forward.

The sun slips behind the cloud blanket, and the day goes dark, the shadows lengthen. It feels like late afternoon even though I know full well that it isn't.

Pelimburg has always been a city confused by time, running on rhythms set not by clocks and minute hands but by the internal lollop of its sea-heart. Tidal beat. I match pace with the waves that crash into the promenade wall and keep my eyes open for a likely shelter.

I'm so busy peering through the shuttered, glassless windows, and dubiously eyeing the damp-rotted walls, that I don't notice the gang until they have already circled me.

The leader of the pack grins, doglike. They're Hobs. Dirty and ragged, with a feral look, like the marsh-jackals that hunt rats in the long salt grass and steal food from the rubbish dumps on the edges of the city. They close in tight.

I'm frozen.

"Lost are you, kitty-girl?" says the leader, drifting close

enough to me that I can see the dirt in the pores of his brown face. "You won't find paying customers down the Claw."

The next person to assume that I'm a streetwalker is going to get punched. I ball my fist and try to keep my breathing calm. It's hard—my heartbeat is skipping and stammering, and I'm cold. My breaths are beginning to sound more like gasps than anything else. I wonder if the Hobs can smell fear the way dogs can.

Perhaps I should ask them if they know who Dash is, but the air has become claustrophobic and tight.

The pack crowds closer and I hug my bag to my chest. I want to cry, there is a prickling at the corners of my eyes. I should have stayed at home and accepted my planned-out future. I wonder if it's safe to go back, if by some turn of luck no one will have noticed that I'm gone and there will be no punishment waiting for me. The longer I'm gone, the harder it will be to go back, the greater the dishonor.

I think of what Owen will do to me.

"Sphynx got your tongue?"

I try not to let my lip tremble, but it's useless. "I'm not looking for customers." The words sound like brass bits falling one by one onto a glass table. Precise, clipped, and too loud in the otherwise empty street.

"That's good," he says. "'Cause I weren't looking to pay."

I close my eyes and hug my bag tighter. I can't run, there's too many of them, and my boots are too tight and my legs ache from walking and right now all I want is to be back home.

His breath smells of fish and vinegary cockles. It's on my face—hot and sweet-sour and overwhelming.

They're so close now that the heat radiates from them. One touches my hair, and I snap.

I go from frozen statue to spitting fury. Even if what's going to happen is inevitable, I'm going to do my best to scratch their Gris-damned eyes out or deprive a few of them of any future Hoblings. I grab the leader's genitals and twist, just as one of his lackeys throws a punch at my cheek.

He yelps and I screech. My terror is still there, let loose on them. What I wouldn't do for a pinch of scriv now.

The noise erupts as the Hobs lay into me. Someone knocks me to the ground and I curl up on my side, trying to protect my belly and breasts and also to get in a few well-aimed kicks. At least these ugly boots are good for slamming into soft flesh. Tears are streaming down my face because even though I keep fighting, I know it's futile. I'm outnumbered. I'm soft and I know nothing about fisticuffs. Owen used to taunt me when our mother wasn't looking, and I feel the same defeated fear now that I felt then.

"Oi. What the fuck are you lot doing down our way?" a girl asks over the noise of the scuffling, her voice a fish-market drawl.

The Hobs still. The leader stands, pats nonchalantly at his trousers, and grins. "Weren't doing nothing," he says, and aims a sly kick at my back. Pain bruises down my spine.

I can't see the girl who's talking, just a forest of bare feet, hobnailed boots, and dirty patched trousers. Already my right eye is swelling up. It feels hot and watery and sticky all at the same time.

"If you've touched one of ours, boyo, and Dash hears about it, then I wouldn't want to be in your skin."

Dash. A flicker of relief. I don't even know why—I've nothing more to go on than the word of a Hob hairdresser and a feeling that, somehow, this Dash will help me. The girl is one of his, a friend or partner, I suppose, and she's stepped up to protect me. It's something to cling to.

My attacker speaks again. "We were just leaving, Lilya, darling. No need to get all stormed up," he says. He walks past, grins, and cocks his hat at me. The pack follows him, and I'm left in the middle of the street. A faint drizzle is misting around me, covering my hair with a veil of tiny droplets.

"And who the fuck might you be?" the girl says as she drops to a crouch to get a better look. "Not one of ours, Gris knows. You're a long way from Kitty Lane."

"I am not," I say through my split lip, "a Gris-damned prostitute."

"Says you." Lilya is short and dark, with sizable hips that soften her otherwise hard figure. Her waxed hair is pulled back in a tight bun, pinned close to her scalp with an assortment of glinting pins, revealing wide cheeks and slanted eyes. She has a fish-worker's blood-and-scale-spattered apron slung over her shoulder. She holds out one calloused hand. "Come on then, up ya get, kitty-girl." She smirks as she says this, and there is the faintest trace of bitter humor.

Lilya's hand is warm and rough, and she hauls me up with

ease. Her arms might be skinny under rolled-up sleeves, but it's all wiry muscle.

"They really did you over," she says, after peering at my bruised face. "This way, we'll get you sorted out." She's not friendly, just abrupt and sharp, like she's dealing with another problem in her long day.

"Thank you," I say, but it's becoming increasingly hard to talk. My lip is swelling up and going oddly numb, and my right eye is tingling, hot from the bruising. I can barely see through the puffed-up lids, and the whole side of my face aches. Not to mention the sharp pains shooting along my ribs. I keep one arm clutched across my side, like that's going to help. I'm about to ask her about Dash when she sighs loudly.

"*Gris.*" She sweeps up my bag, casually flinging it over her shoulder. "Dash is gonna love this like a punch to the face. Like we need another mucking stray hanging around."

Best to keep my mouth shut until I know exactly where I stand. Silently, I hobble after her, barely keeping up as she strides down the street toward a house that I recognize. It's green and faded. Lilya pushes open a door that just barely qualifies and leads me into a musty narrow entrance. Someone has tied an old sheet over the next doorway, and Lilya holds it aside and beckons me through.

The whole place smells of rotting wood—a curiously loamy and pleasant smell—and of smoked fish. The latter is decidedly less pleasant. A layer of sucking gray mud coats the floor.

"We don't use the downstairs much," Lilya says, and nods at a flight of rickety stairs. "Head on up." She shoos me with her hands, and, clutching the rail for safety, I edge up the staircase. The boards creak ominously underfoot, but as I reach the second and then the third floor, I realize why the squatters prefer to use the upstairs part of the house.

The gloom falls away. Faint streaks of sunlight poke through the cloud cover and stream in the windows and dapple the walls and floors, and the wind blows through the empty windows, bringing the clean sharp ocean scent with it.

I stop. The upper floor is wide open, with only fragments of the dividing walls remaining. A few sheets and blankets here and there cordon off private areas, but most of the space seems to be taken up by a common area demarcated by a filthy piece of wool carpet.

There's another girl of perhaps fifteen or sixteen lounging against a collection of stuffed sacks, her hands busy with needle and thread. Like me, her hair is red, but hers isn't dyed. It's a carroty mass of flyaway tangles, and she has the pale porcelain skin of a Mata. No House child ever looked so pinched and underfed though. My immediate guess is that she's one of the bastards that House Mata seems to set out like spores, though we're a long sight from MallenIve and the Mata High Lord.

She lowers her embroidery and tucks her bare feet under her thin skirt. "Lils," she says, "I thought *I* was supposed to bring home strays, not you."

Lilya drops my bag. "Jaxon's lads had got a hold of her

down near the bend. What was I supposed to do—leave her there for their sport?" She thumps down next to the redhead, then looks at me. "Sit. Nala's good with fixing people up."

"Am I now?" Nala laughs and gets to her feet. She's tall and thin. A strong breeze could probably send her sailing off over the sea. "You best do what my Lils says."

So I sit. I'm relieved. My head is swimming with pain, and the dizziness keeps threatening to send me careening to the floor. I have to keep my movements slow so as not to make the pain in my ribs flare. With my free hand, I wipe at the itchy dried-up tears on my face.

Nala winces. "Lils, put some water on for us, dear." She walks over to me with an armful of the burlap cushions and plumps them under my back. "Oh," she says. "That's a nasty cut." With careful fingers, she brushes the loose dirt from my face. "Jaxon's a little rat turd, coming all the way down to our side. Wonder who he damn well thinks he is."

She's not really talking to me, I don't think, just nattering on in a way that is rather soothing. I relax a little into the rough cushions.

"Here." Lilya is back with a bowl of warm water. Nala grins at her friend's scowl and wets a small scrap of cleanish cloth in the steaming bowl.

The water stings my cuts, but I keep quiet as she dabs at the open wounds. "Bit of meat on that eye would work wonders," she tells me, "but there's no chance of that. You just keep this wet cloth on it and hope for the best." Nala wrings out the rag, wads it up, and puts it over my swollen eye. The warmth helps a little. I close my other eye and let the grayness swirl around me. All I want to do is sleep, but the pain keeps me lingering on the edge of consciousness. Voices drift over me, distant and meaningless.

"Soon as it wakes, you're gonna have to walk it back up to New Town," says Lilya. "It can't stay here. Dash doesn't need another charity case."

Nala laughs. "Me? I didn't drag it in here. And why take it back anyway? Are you scared of Dash?"

"Isn't everyone?"

Nala laughs again. It's a carefree sound, full of fluttering leaves and white wisps of cloud. I decide that I like it—it's a laugh that makes fires grow brighter. "You've known him for years, he'll say nothing if you make like it was your idea. Besides, she has well-kept hands, soft like a House Lammer's. Dash won't mind a kitty-girl of his very own. He'll let her stay."

Lilya snorts. "Little frail-bit says she's not one."

"Only kitty-girls dye their hair." Nala shifts, and I realize she's stretched out alongside me, warm as a blanket. "Anyway, he let Kirren stay."

"Kirren's a dog. At least he's useful."

"So?" Nala touches my matted hair. "Maybe he'll find a kitty-girl useful too. Especially a kitty-girl with a manner so *polished.*"

Gris. Out of the frying pan and into the fire.

5

METAL CLANGS AGAINST METAL, and when that sound fades, the shrieks of the seabirds rise. The melancholy cry of a look-far's horn drifts in with the faint breeze: a storm warning. The day will bring wind-lashed misery down on Pelimburg.

I'm awake.

My right eye is sealed tight, gummed together with hard-ened pus. The left is fine, and I open it to stare at a ceiling dusty with cobwebs and the carcasses of brittle-winged sand-dragons. The thought of those bugs flying in and out of the room makes my skin crawl. Carefully, I tease the gunk from my eyelashes, crumbling it between my fingers until I can force my eyelids apart. The skin still feels tight and tender, and a touch assures me that my right eye is swollen and the whole side of my face disfigured. It feels bruised. Huge.

There are people talking in low voices, just murmured conversation. Someone says *kitty-girl* and I focus.

"I'm not wasting good tea and water on her," says Lilya.

"We've barely enough for us, and Esta will be back from the docks soon."

"She's awake."

I turn my head and take a good look at Nala, sitting on the carpet with her legs stretched out, wiggling her long pale toes at me. "Would you like a spot of tea?" A wide urn of tea sits on a crate next to her, steam rising and making the air seem clean and comforting.

"Oh go on. Next you'll be offering her cake and berries and real cream and calling her miss."

Nala answers by stretching her foot over to poke Lilya in the thigh. The Hob girl scowls and pushes Nala's foot away. The scowl doesn't last long though—Lilya is fighting to not smile. The smile changes her face, makes her look younger.

A creak whispers up from the stairs, the old wood sighing.

"Esta!" Nala yells. "Come see what strange manner of fish Lils brought us yesterday."

Yesterday. Can I really have slept all through the afternoon and night? The light falling through the window is pale, and a pink-lined mass of cloud hangs low in the sky. It's early morning.

I struggle into a sitting position, and my bones scream at me. I'm bruised all over.

As I rise, a young girl of perhaps eleven or twelve, with silvery-black hair sheared close to her skull, ascends the staircase. She's darker than most Hobs, her skin like heartwood. Gray eyes and her strange, sleek hair give her away as a half-breed. It's amazing that she doesn't stink like a selkie too. She looks at me flatly, says nothing, then turns her attention to the tea urn.

"Storm warning," she says, glaring at me.

Oh damn, it's the girl who threw the wood. *Please, please, don't recognize me.* I look down at my hands, hoping that the hair falling across my face is a good enough disguise.

"Wonderful," Lilya says. "I thought I heard the bloody thing. Another day with no wages. And Verrel says the whalers have seen witch-sign."

"Pelim ship didn't come in last night." The selkie-cross helps herself to a small bowl of tea and slumps down on a pile of burlap bags.

It's as if a cold wind has blown through the room, darkening and chilling the squat. Everyone is silent for a moment, then Nala rises and pours a bowl of tea for me. I take it gratefully—my stomach is tight with hunger and even a little tea would go a long way toward easing that.

Esta finishes her tea in three swallows, then balances the bowl on her knees. "Be the third ship Pelim's lost this year, counting them two little ketches last month," she says to the teabowl. She looks up. "Not all they lost last night neither, rumor says."

The black tea is bitter and strong.

"What d'ya mean?" Lilya pours more tea for Esta.

"Jaxon's runner heard from the sharif that the Pelim wretch took the Leap."

I swallow hard, bow my head lower so as not to look at their faces.

"Second girl this month. What are those nilly-mucking Houses doing to them?" Lilya snorts in derision. "Besides clapping the daft things in iron and wasting their talents. What Dash could do with one of them in his palm, I don't know . . ."

"It's bad luck, these girls," Nala says. "They'll bring things out of the deep. And Pelim's the worst of the lot for bringing bad fortune down on the city. It won't be the first time they've brought a sea-witch to the shores."

Witch-sign, they said. Little eddies, like miniature storms breaking the surface of the ocean. Witch-signs rise up in great numbers, last a few minutes, and then disappear. When the whirlpools are gone, all that's left is floating petals. Black sea roses.

Anomalies.

I'm not afraid. A queer chill settles into my bones, and I huddle, pulling my knees closer to my chest. What if Ilven's death really did raise something up out of the waters? But those stories Nala is talking about—they're just . . . fancies. There's no real truth to them, they're Hob tales. That's what our House crake taught me. Of course, Ilven always did find the old stories fascinating and told me how she secretly wished that they were still real, that there was more to magic than just the scriv-forced power of the Houses.

Oh Ilven. Bound now below the sea, caught in the kelp

forests, nibbled at, her hair full of crabs and little ghost shrimp, a ghost herself. I choke on a sadness so sharp that it has sliced me in two.

"Hush." Lilya waves her hand. "There'll be no talk of bad-luck girls and boggerts and sacrifices and all that rubbish. That's the sort of shite only idiots gab about. And it's all just rumor. Till there's a body washed up, we don't know nothing about the Pelim wretch." She narrows her eyes and turns her attention back to Esta. "Have House Pelim gone and made an official announcement about the ship?"

Esta shakes her head. "They're still hoping the ship comes in. And that's all they damn well care about—their precious *Silver Dancer.*"

The name makes me shiver. There are paintings of our ships all over the house, and my brother would often point to this one with pride. To me the ships meant nothing, merely a means to an end, but Owen loved those monstrosities. The *Silver Dancer,* bright with harpoons, the huge lamp-whales cresting the sea around her.

Nala cocks her head. "But Rin's on board . . ."

"I bloody know he is!" Esta stands, throwing the bowl to the ground. She disappears behind a curtained partition and the drape flaps, then drops still behind her.

"Shite," says Lilya. She picks up the bowl. "I best go have a word before we all go up in flames."

Nala turns her own empty bowl around in her hands as if she has never seen it before. Then she looks up, smiling at me. Her voice gives her away though, all falsely brittle bright.

"Rise and shine, kitty-girl. I'll walk you back up to New Town, make sure you get to your lane nice and safe."

"No!" My hands claw at the thin blanket, pulling it up to my face. The thought of being set out on the streets again, with no idea of where I'm going or what I'm doing—that Hob boy from yesterday, he will just be the first. And in New Town there's still the chance that someone will see past the mess of my hair and somehow recognize me. And if they do, Owen will hunt me down.

Fear lances through me. He will make me suffer. I remember the last time I saw him, the black in his eyes. I don't think I would fare well in another such meeting.

Heat flares in the corners of my eyes, sharp as needles, but I won't let myself cry. "I—can't I stay here?" Even as the words slip out I realize how feeble and desperate I sound.

Nala sighs and sets down her empty teabowl. "And bring your clients here?" She shakes her head. "Come on, sweet. You'll be better off with your own, anyway."

"Please. You don't understand. I'm not a kitty-girl. I r—" I can still tell the truth, in my own way. "I ran away from home, dyed my hair so that my mo—mam wouldn't find me. If I go back to New Town, she'll spot me. Or someone will."

The red-haired girl is frowning. "I won't ask you what your business is, 'cause it's none of mine," she says. "And I know what it's like to run, for sure." She leans her head back and stares at the ceiling, like she's looking for answers trapped there in the webs with the insect husks. Finally, she faces me.

"I'm not in charge of Whelk Street though, and I've no say in the matter."

"Who is?" I crawl out from under the thin blankets and stand, careful and slow. "Is there someone I can speak to?" Beg, in other words. Or bribe, if I still have my trinkets and the Hobs haven't robbed me while I slept. I keep my knowledge of Dash to myself. I want to see him before I decide to trust him. And I certainly don't know if I trust Anja.

"Well, it's Dash who has the say-so here." Her face brightens. "And he comes and goes as he pleases, so I've no idea when he'll be back."

"Can't I stay until he gets in? I can ask him then. There must be something I can do?" Panic makes my words rush. I can't go back home, not now—in disgrace. If the sharif are already saying that I must have jumped, then there is no future for me in the Houses.

The wind picks up, threading through the glassless windows and ruffling Nala's hair. She doesn't answer me, but she's deep in thought again, her brow furrowed with the effort. I wrap my arms around my bruised ribs and wait. In the silence, the faint sound of sobbing and the soft slow soothing of Lilya's voice come from the curtained-off area.

Someone here died, I realize. Someone these people loved and cared for. I'm not the only person in the world tangled up in grief.

Maybe the *Silver Dancer* will limp into harbor later today, and no one will be dead. There's still a chance.

I snap out of my morbid thoughts when Nala stands and holds out her hand. "C'mon then," she says, and winks at me. "We'd best go find you a job if you're to have any chance of Dash letting you stay."

Every bone and muscle in my body might ache, but I want to be out of this death-house. At the back of my tongue is a strange bitter taste that I can't swallow away. It feels like metal in my mouth.

Scriv-withdrawal.

Not possible. I've never taken much at a time.

On the other hand, the stuff has poisoned me for sixteen years, and hardly a day goes by when I don't take at least a tiny pinch. My face goes cold and numb, and I fumble at my cheeks with fingers that feel wrapped in layers of wool. Then the panic passes, and I make myself still. It will be fine. I can get through this.

Nala shows me where they catch the rainwater on a rickety balcony and brings me a small pail so I can wash myself as best I can and tidy my hair and dress. In the broken shard of an age-spotted mirror, I look like a whore after a bad night. My hair is a tangle of knots that I can barely comb out with my fingers, and my eye remains a sticky mess.

The cold water is soothing, washing some of the heated ache away from my skin.

Passable, with my hair braided back and the gunk washed from my face, I try my best to shake the creases from my dress. No one is ever going to give me a job, I think, as I stare at the mess in the mirror. The new red of my hair is cheap and ugly, and against it, my skin is sallow, leaving me looking ill. The bruises don't help. I wouldn't hire me.

"Come along, kitty," Nala says. "We can't sit here all day waiting for the weather to change and good fortune to fly in through the windows."

I cover the worst of the skirt's wrinkles with my coat. It will have to do.

Already the wind has turned, and the ships will have to tack against strong westerlies to be able to make it in to port safely. And there's no guarantee that they will. The Tooth and Claw have claimed many a ship in Pelimburg's eight-hundred-year history.

Even so, I hold out hope that the *Silver Dancer* will limp home.

6

NALA, STILL BAREFOOT, walks ahead of me, her feet slapping against the paving stones. The storm clouds are here now, black and heavy with lightning.

The wind whips her carrot tangles about her face, but she seems to barely notice. She's skipped a few lengths ahead while I try my best to keep up, cursing my toe-pinching boots and my stubbornness and Jaxon all the way.

"So what's your name, little kitty-kitty?" she calls back at me, hollering through her funneled hands.

I wait till I've caught up before I answer. "Firell," I pant. It's a common name and close enough to my own that I hopefully won't stumble over it too often.

"So you say you don't work the street corners?"

I nod.

"Quiet type?"

Nod.

"There anything you good at?"

A shrug this time. I'm good with oil paints and I have an

excellent reading voice, but somehow, I don't think these are appropriate skills for a low-Lammer. I can also make the air do what I want, mostly. If I have scriv. Definitely *not* appropriate for a low-Lammer. Low-Lammers are weak points in our lineage. They are the non-magical masses, the families of all the mundane and useless progeny that we forced from the Houses. We can't have their blood tainting ours, thinning our magic.

"Well if you're able to stand ten hours and scrub teabowls, there's an opening at the Crake."

Whatever—I don't even know what or where she's talking about, so I nod.

"The Crake it is then." She twirls on her toes, hair spinning about her. The layers of thin skirts and thinner petticoats are a whirling flurry about her skinny thighs. I wonder if she's insane, boggert-touched. Boggerts are ghosts who don't know they're dead. They come into your house in the night, feed off the living, try to be part of our world again. Of course, it's just a story. Doesn't stop one from wondering though—especially when someone is flighty and fey and barely there—if the boggerts have been feeding off her. Boggerts are like the look-fars' horns: warnings of worse to come. Things follow them out of the deep.

That's what the Hobs say, that boggerts draw out the things that should stay lost in the ocean trenches. First comes the witch-sign, then the ghosts who want to live, and finally, awake and hungry, the sea-witch. It's the same thing Lilya was talking about back in the squat. I suppose out here in the city I'll be forced to hear more of the Hobs' superstitious prattle. I sigh and trot as fast as my aching feet will allow me, following Nala down the narrow lanes that serpentine through Old Town.

The Crake turns out to be a tea shop. It's a corner building full of awkward angles, mismatched windows, and little stone gargoyles. The unifying theme of architectural style appears to be Ugly. Someone, in an attempt to disguise this, has painted the walls yellow and put yellow-and-white-striped awnings over the wide pavement. It doesn't help.

A wooden sign bangs in the rising wind: THE TWICE-DROWNED CRAKE. Under the faded gold lettering is a picture of a little speckled bird paddling in a teabowl.

Funny thing, to name a tea shop after the poet whom the infamous Mallen Gris tried to have drowned on several occasions. Gris only finally managed to kill Esker Davyt when he forced him to drink a bowl of poisoned tea. The story goes that the poet wrote a scathing epic prose poem that exposed all the secret histories of House Mallen and that in revenge Mallen Gris had him silenced.

The truth is that Gris murdered him because he was a dreadfully bad poet and an embarrassment to all of Pelimburg. It's said that Mallen Gris had the unfortunate poet's body ground into patties and fed to a party of Davyt's fellow crakes. Gris apparently held up a forkful of meat before the stunned guests and called it "the finest contribution Esker Davyt made to the world of verse." Sounds like something the madman would do.

A motley collection of tables and chairs covers the side-walk outside the Crake's entrance, and every available space is filled with morose men: some young, some old, some hard to tell. They mutter into their tea or scribble furiously on parchments spread out and pinned down with elbows and upturned bowls.

All of them have the same disheveled look, hair awry and clothes wrinkled, skin pale and waxy, eyes fever bright. So familiar—every House in Pelimburg has one in its employ, to write their praises, or to double as history and language tutors.

Crakes.

Dear Gris, if there's one thing I can't abide it's a bad poet. And the crakes, the poets of Pelimburg, are seldom anything but. Our own House crake taught me to read and write, read to me the basics of magical control from an ancient textbook, and instilled in me a healthy dislike of anything remotely resembling verse.

Thank Gris the old goat wouldn't be caught dead in an Old Town teahouse like this. These must be the truly awful poets if they're gathering here. I take a moment to contemplate the enormousness of that thought.

Nala hears my little moan of distress. "I know," she says. "It's terrible, isn't it?" She pulls me up to the door. "Still, even the talentless must have tea, and where better to come for it than here. Besides," she says as she shoves me ahead of her into the shop, "we like to think it's the only place where you can have your crake and eat it too."

Mad. Obviously mad. I eye her for some sign that a

boggert has been feeding off her. She's pale . . . Do they drink blood like the bats do? I've never stopped to wonder what the stories meant by "draining the living."

Nala leads me through the cramped interior to where a woman is tending a huge copper urn above a fire. The woman twists the spout and measures loose-leaf tea into an assortment of mismatched pots, muttering under her breath as she fills the orders written on a chalkboard behind her.

She holds up one finger as Nala and I approach. "Not now," she says, and carries on muttering. "Redbush, a pinch of sweet aloe; blackbark nut, honeybush, plain; honeybush, pinch poisonink—oh Gris, as if that's going to help stir the imagination . . ." When she's caught up with the round of orders, and a quick-fingered low-Lammer youth has rushed off carrying the tray of pots and bowls above his head, she turns to us. "What's this, then, Nala, love?"

"Dash had word you needed a bowl-girl in the kitchens." Nala presses one hand gently against my spine, forcing me forward. "And so I've brought you one."

The woman stares at me for a moment and frowns. Before she can turn us away, Nala says, "She's not a kitty-girl, just has the bad taste to look like one."

"Bad taste, maybe. Don't think I'll take her just on your say-so, Nala. It's been a long time since you worked here," says the woman, and grabs my hands suddenly in hers. "You're a soft sort of thing under all those scratches. Think you can wash bowls till your hands turn raw?" Her own hands are thin, papery, the joints rounded with arthritis.

"I—yes." I nod. It's got to be a better option than working at the fish markets or, indeed, going on the game.

She lets go of my hands. "I'll start you off on a trial day. You work hard, no complaints, and you're hired."

The boy shouts an order across the counter to her, and she writes it down in a seamless scribble as he does. "Nala, you show her the scullery and get her started," she says, and with that, I am dismissed, and her attention is once again engulfed in tea making.

I wash dishes for seven hours. Never in my life have I even rinsed out a cup and here I am, elbow deep in sudsy lukewarm water, scrubbing out teabowl after teabowl.

My eyes sting. My hands smart. I wipe away burning tears with my sleeve. My gut wrenches, and I'm pale and shaky. Sweat films my body.

Would it have been so bad to stay home and marry whoever my brother told me to? There would be books to read, and tea and fresh-baked sugar biscuits, still warm from the oven. My clothes would be laundered and soft.

There would be scriv. A crashing dizziness threatens to send me to my knees, and I cling to the edge of the sink with both hands, waiting for it to pass.

My stomach is a burning hole, but after a few long gasping sobs, I manage to push the pain down.

Here I am in dirt-stiff tat, desperate to go pee in an outside latrine that seems to consist of nothing more than a wooden box-seat over a shallow drop and a handy bucket of ash. There is dirt worked into my skin, and my hands are wrinkled and white. My stomach growls at me all through the day. If I don't eat something soon, I'm going to drop down right here and most likely drown in filthy dishwater. That'll teach me to run away.

I grab another bowl and plunge it into the water and scrub the tea stains with salt. If I go back now, I will be a disgrace, bringing shame and dishonor down on the Pelim name. The best I could hope for is that my brother would take revenge by marrying me off to some disreputable House, a name with nothing more than shallow rowboats in their fleets, or weak magic-lines. He'd make sure I looked back on Canroth Piers as a lost prize. Owen would see me disgraced, thrown down.

When the old woman finally comes into the cramped little scullery and leans on the stone sink, I wonder if it would be better if she decided not to hire me. My hands are now red and stinging; deep cuts in my fingers bleed a pale watery red. I fold them over my stomach as if that will somehow settle it, stop the incessant twisting inside. My eyes feel peeled raw, and my cheeks burn.

"Mrs. Danningbread," she says, introducing herself. Obviously I've passed some secret test. "You're to be here tomorrow morning at six sharp to help set up. Wages is five bits a day and all the tea you can drink." She hands me a hunk of yellow cake. "It's a mite stale," Mrs. Danningbread says. "But I'm afraid the others got to the sweetbrown first. This is all that's left."

I don't care. I manage to thank her before I shove the wedge of gritty cake into my mouth. I don't think anything has ever tasted this good. It's sweet and dry, and it fills the hole in my belly.

Outside the tea shop, Nala is sitting on a low flower-bed wall. There are no flowers growing there, just weeds and a few dead sea roses, their red-black leaves shriveled and dusty. Nala's feet are splattered with mud, and the front of her dress has great muddy paw prints and streaks on it. She looks like she's been attacked by half-grown sphynxes, but she seems happy enough and grins when she sees me.

"Come," she says. "We'll have to run if we're to get back before the storm breaks."

I groan. All day the skies have been black faced, the winds buffeting Pelimburg, so much so that Mrs. Danningbread had all the outside chairs and tables brought in to the already cramped shop and rolled up her awnings. Finally, the much-awaited storm has roared in, hours after the warnings were first sounded. The last thing I want to do now is run across town in my hated boots, with the wind—and more than likely the rain—slamming me around the whole way. Not to mention that just the thought of running makes me turn green. My ribs and cheeks are still aching. And I ate that Gris-damned cake a bit too fast.

As it is, we don't make it back before the rain starts. I limp into the squat and up the stairs, dripping all the way. I'm cold, I'm aching, I'm still hungry despite the thin slice of cake, and all I want to do is curl up tight and cry until I am dried and empty, an old eggshell.

Nala doesn't stop dancing. She bounds up the stairs, feet flying, her white soles flashing to me like sailor's code. I think I hate her.

The only thing that saves me from complete collapse is the smell of cockles and mussels frying in lard. I recognize it from the House kitchens, although I've never tried it myself. Right now, I'd eat dried cuttlefish if someone gave it to me.

Lilya is sitting cross-legged in front of the little portable stove, stirring a blackened pan. A war-scarred brindled terrier with bowlegs and a wide, blunt face is lying spread out on a tattered scrap of blanket near the stove. There's no sign of Esta, or the mysterious Dash. Lilya has fastened heavy canvas bags over the windows in an attempt to stop the wind from tearing up the room, and they billow like sails.

"So we're keeping her then?" Lilya asks without turning to look at us. "Just as long as you're the one to break it to His Flashness."

Nala grins. "She's a good enough little worker. The Bread-loaf took her on, so there'll be coin in the bowl. Dash won't mind, if she brings in a steady wage."

The only answer Lilya has for her is a grumpy snort.

"Here, you lump," Nala says, and hauls a bone from her bag. The terrier perks up one jaunty ear and whines lazily. Nala tosses the bone with a laugh, and the terrier snaps it up before it hits the ground. "Still fast on your feet, Kirren, old boy." She scratches the dog's head.

A sudden clatter of boots on the stairs has us all on our

feet. I'm shaking inside, although I try to hold myself together. If this is Dash, then my reckoning has come. *Anja sent me.* I hold the name on my tongue and wait.

Instead of Dash, a sharp familiar face appears at the head of the stairs.

"Esta," says Lilya. "Any news?"

"Ship came in." She doesn't smile. Gripped tightly in one hand is a small paper box.

The *Silver Dancer* is safe, thank goodness. Loss of an entire ship eats in even to our fortunes, and we are one of the wealthiest Houses in Pelimburg.

"Half the men washed over," she continues, and the pit of my stomach draws tighter. I feel guilty, as if somehow I am responsible for these unknown men and their deaths. Owen will pay their families for the loss. It's more than some Houses do.

"And Rin?" asks Nala, although the answer is writ plain on the little girl's face. My stomach twists more, and now I can't tell if this is hunger or guilt or the lack of scriv or all of them tangled up in my insides like fishing line.

"Come now," Lilya says, stepping away from the food. "Hand those over, Esta, my love." She motions at the small rectangle in Esta's hand. "There'll be no setting this house on fire."

Esta throws the box down. It has a small print of a red sphynx on the front. Matches. "Going out," she says, and turns away from us.

"Where?"

Esta stares back at Lilya.

"We can go look for your brother." Nala draws a little closer to the half-selkie. "Kirren's got a good nose. We can give him one of Rin's shirts to sniff at, and then we can all go down to the shore and look—"

"For what?" Esta screams. "His body?"

An uncomfortable silence settles through the house. Esta turns and walks back down the stairs. No one makes any move to stop her.

"Would that Verrel were here," says Lilya. "He's the only one of us who can talk to her and—her and . . . Rin." She turns her attention back to the meal, stirring the pan. "Hope he comes home soon."

Nala takes a chipped ceramic bowl from a wooden crate that serves as a cupboard, and I follow her and do the same. "He's as bad as Dash for coming and going," Nala says softly.

"I'll go look for Verrel later," Lilya says. "Tell him that Esta's down walking the strand, looking for Rin's body."

Nala says nothing, and we three eat in silence. The food, a solid, salty, fatty lump, hits my empty stomach. I've never tasted anything better. I forget about the boy called Rin, a faceless person whom I have never met, who means nothing to me. With a precision I normally feel only when I use scriv, I push my tangled-up feelings into a little ball and seal them away.

Afterward, I scrub my one pair of stockings and my dress clean in a small pot of cold water and hang them to dry. I'm so tired I can barely stand, and I sway as I wring the water out of my stockings.

"Here," says Nala. "I've made you up a bed in the corner." She leads me to a curtained-off space near the stairs.

It's little more than a pile of burlap bags, loosely stuffed with sea grass. She hands over a neatly folded gray blanket. "It's all there is," she says. "Maybe tomorrow Lils can see what she can find. She's good at finding things."

The blanket is thin, and I have to add my slightly rain-damp coat over it to keep warm. I curl up like an alley cat on the pile of bags. The storm beats about the crumbling house.

I sleep in my shift, while my dress and stockings drip on a line that stretches across the remains of what was once a tiled washroom. This is the first time in my life that I have ever washed my own clothes or known that in the morning I would have to wear the same outfit again.

If Esta comes back during the night, I don't hear her over the screaming of the wind.

7

THREE DAYS LATER and I'm sick to the teeth of the smell of tea and cakes, the feel of soapy water, and the lamentations of crakes. I can hear them from the scullery. Every now and then one stands up and orates at length to the unfortunate crowd, after which he bows to their scattered applause. Personally, I think they'd be better served by plates broken over their heads than by hand-claps.

And if I'm correct, more than a few of their recent verses make mockery at my House's expense. Crakes—always biting the hand that feeds. Ilven used to tell me that my hatred of poetry and poets had more to do with being forced to study under our House crake than with the actual quality of the verse, and that one day I would see the beauty in what they did. Somehow I doubt that.

"Firell?" A head pops around the doorway. It's the day-shift waitress, a low-Lam girl everyone calls Perkins. She has a narrow nose in a moonish face, and her eyes are wide and dark as winter storms.

"Yes?"

"Can you pick up a table for me? Charl has all the outside tables so he's too busy."

Of course he's busy. It's market day, and the place is packed from floor to wall. I dry my hands on my apron and squint at her. "I've never served a table in my life. Why can't you do it?"

"I—just can't." Perkins huffs and blows a loose strand of dirty blond hair from her flushed cheeks. "Please, all you have to do is take his order and bring it to him, I swear. And he tips well, so you'll get a bit for your troubles."

It must be some regular that she can't face. And a bit is nothing to sniff at. "Fine. I'll do it." I take off the stained scullery apron and hang it on a peg. "Just point me to him."

"Thanks, Firell. I'll owe you one."

After checking my dress to make sure that it's serviceable, I follow Perkins into the chaos of the Crake's interior. Poets are clustered about high tables scribbling away or angrily gesticulating at each other as they argue some fine point of meter and rhyme. Perkins points to one of the low tables near the door and its single occupant. Unusual enough in this crowded place that he would have a table to himself.

His back is to us, and all I can see of him is that he's wearing a fine black coat and that his long dark hair is loose, falling over his shoulders in a sleek wave. One of the better-groomed crakes then. A wide-brimmed hat is on the table next to his elbow—an odd fashion choice on this windy day.

I squeeze my way between the tables and chairs, muttering *excuse me*s until I reach his table. He's bowed over a notebook, his quill flying over the cream pages. This close to him the air feels stretched and tight. Uncomfortable.

"Sir? Can I get you something to drink?"

He answers while he writes. "Water, please, and a redbush tea, no honey." He looks up then, and I recognize him.

He's the bat from the promenade. The one who held me to him so that Owen wouldn't see me, who sparked with magic and smelled of white soap and musk. A little shiver runs through my center.

I can't remember his name, but he's from House Sand-walker, that much I know.

The bat frowns. "Pelim Felicita?" he says. "I *thought* it was you I saw—"

I drop to a crouch so that I'm level with his face. "Shut up!" I hiss at him, then change my tone. "Please, don't say a word." I glance around to see if anyone heard him or noticed what happened, but the crakes are deep in their own worlds.

If he turns me over to the sharif, if he tells my family that I'm here— No. I will not go back. Desperate to guarantee his silence, I say the first thing that pops into my head. "I'll give you whatever you want if you'll pretend you never saw me." Then I put both hands over my mouth and damn myself for a fool.

He stares at me.

Slowly, I lower my hands and grip the edge of his table. Dizziness is rushing up inside me, making my head light. Then he drops one white hand over mine and draws my hand closer to him, pinning my palm to the table.

The subtle prickle of his magic wars with my building nausea, and shivers run up my arms.

He leans closer, and I can see the tips of his fangs when he speaks. "Whatever I want?" He sounds amused. The flicker of magic dances between our skin.

"I didn't mean it like that," I say, and try to pull my hand free, but he grabs my wrist and keeps me there.

He smiles. The fangs are more obvious than ever. "I know you didn't." He releases my hand and I almost land flat on my bottom. "Are you free five days from now, in the evening, I mean?"

"What—I—yes, I suppose so." I stand, jerking my dress straight. Fury is now replacing the terror and I glare at him.

"Don't be like that," he says. "I'm inviting you to a party."

A *party.* "Are you insane? I can't go to a party. What if someone sees me?"

"Trust me on this, no one will recognize you at this particular social event."

My mouth drops open in disbelief. "I'll just fetch your tea," I say.

He grins in response, and I can feel him watching me as I thread my way to the counter and give Mrs. Danningbread the order.

She peers at me. "Why are you up front here—"

I point at the bat.

"Oh," she says with a sniff. "Perkins needs to get over her little prejudice very, very quickly. I can't have that sort of nonsense. They're citizens, whether she likes it or not."

The bat is back to scribbling in his book. Perhaps he's hoping to become a crake in his own house. Stranger things have happened. I lean my elbow on the counter and wonder what I'm going to say to him. The wood is warm and satin smooth under my elbow and I fight the desire to just lay my head down on the counter and start screaming at the mess of my life.

If I agree to go to this party of his, then Gris alone knows what I'm letting myself in for. On the other hand, I really don't want him going to my mother, or worse yet, Owen, and informing them that I'm still alive, working in a tea and cake shop and looking like a cheap whore. *Argh.* I grit my teeth.

"Here you go, dear." Mrs. Danningbread puts a small tea urn and bowl on my tray, and a glass of fresh-pumped water. I set my shoulders and carry the drinks to him.

"If I go to this little . . . social event of yours," I say as I set down his bowl and pour the tea in a smooth arc, "can I be sure that this thing between us is clear, or will I have to spend the rest of my life running at your beck and call?"

He smiles thinly. "It wasn't meant to make a slave of you."

I arch an eyebrow in answer. He holds my future in his hands, and he knows it.

The bat sighs and rubs a hand over his face. When he looks at me again, I see that he's slid the third eyelids down, and his eyes are milky white and expressionless. "You have my word that it will be just this one time," he says softly.

"Fine. Five days' time."

The bat smiles again and he looks genuinely happy. I realize then that he can't be much older than me—he's maybe seventeen or eighteen and not yet well versed in schooling his face. The third eyelids recede a little and I can just make out the edge of his indigo pupils. "I'll see you then, Felicita."

"It's Firell."

He nods. "Can I meet you here?"

Well I certainly don't want him knowing where I live. "That will have to do. What time?"

"About eight?" He sounds so uncertain that I almost feel sorry for him. Then I want to start laughing because I have just agreed to accompany a bat to a party. I wonder if this counts as stepping out.

I will the damn bat to leave so that I can get back to the bowls piling up in the kitchen. Perhaps he's something like a Lammer Reader, able to see emotion, because he drinks quickly, scribbles a bit more, and then picks up his hat and his letters-bag and heads for the door. He's left coins on the table, and already I can see he's paid double—a fair tip indeed. He pauses at the counter and hands Danningbread a small envelope. Danning-bread nods and puts the note into her apron pocket.

It's only after he leaves that I remember his name: Jannik.

When I'm back in the safety of the scullery, I lean against the wall and bury my face in my hanging apron. I scrunch the damp material up against my cheeks. A choked noise es-capes me, something between a laugh and a sob. This day better not get any worse.

THE NEXT MORNING DRAGS, leaving my hands still and my mind too busy. After my first day of work, Nala left me to find my own way there and back, and mostly, I haven't managed to get myself too lost. I've seen Esta once, sat with Lilya and Nala while they talked and made supper, and spotted a gangling low-Lammer youth leaving the house, his coat over his shoulder. Of the infamous Dash, there has been no sign.

I'm not even sure if he exists. Perhaps he's just some bogeyman that the Whelk Streeters use to keep the other gangs of squatters at bay. Whatever, it seems to work. Dash's name is like a pass-letter, and people melt out of your way if they know you're one of his.

And I will be one of his, I tell myself. Lilya says that as long as I'm putting brass in the bowl, he'll be happy enough. I hope she's right.

Mrs. Danningbread comes into the back room. "It's quiet," she says. "You go on and take a seat outside with some tea." It's true, we seem to have hit a mid-morning slump and I haven't had to wash a teabowl for a good few minutes. Everything is clean, the dishes scrubbed down to creamy white, stacked up and drying. I wipe my hands on a mangy-looking tea towel and untie my apron.

Charl, the low-Lammer boy who works alternate days, is sitting down at one of the outside tables enjoying a bowl of steaming tea. There are two plates set out before him, both with a thick slice of dark cake. He nods at the other chair and pushes the second plate over for me. Flustered, I take a seat.

The cake is a heavy chocolate, soaked in brandy and covered in clotted cream and berries. It's so rich that I have to eat it slowly, savoring every cream-covered sweet sliver.

"You're one of Dash's," says Charl. He's never spoken to me before.

I nod, even though I'm not exactly certain that I am. Even if Dash accepts me, I still have to make myself indispensable in some way, prove myself to Lils. I've already worked out that stern, unsmiling Lilya is the paste that holds Whelk Street together. She seems to know everyone and everything: all the best places to steal bruised fruit and where to scrounge the last of the half-rotten vegetables off the barrows. She even knows how to climb the cliff for eggs, and without her, I think the Whelk Streeters would starve. She's hard and dry as ship's tack though. Luckily, she's tempered by Nala, who softens some of her brusqueness.

Charl swallows a huge forkful of cake, seemingly without chewing. "My mate says there's poisonink down at the dock, waiting to head upriver. You let Dash know to meet us at the usual." He sips his tea and stares at me.

"Um," I say. "I—I haven't seen him around, but I'll let Lils know."

He nods. "That'll do. Now eat your cake."

A black carriage rattles past us, drawn by a bevy of dark unicorns. Their cloven hooves clatter on the stone, and they swing their heavy horns back as they shake their heads.

"Bloody show-offs," says Charl. "Can't bloody use nillies like normal folk. Have to rub everyone's face in it. More money than they ought to have."

"Who is it?" I don't recognize the carriage, and there is no House insignia on the door.

"Gris-damned bats," he says, before spitting on the ground. "Think they own the bloody city nowadays. New money, new power. But still the same as the old lot. No better than mucking House Lams."

The coachman flicks his whip over the backs of the unis, and they pull away, forcing the other, smaller carriages out of their path. The back of the coach glints like black oil spilled on water. Bats. I shiver, remembering the feel of Jannik's magic ghosting over my skin. The smell of musk and soap, and the way his hair brushed against my neck as he hid me from my brother. He's ugly, I have to remind myself. He's pale and skinny and he lives on nilly-blood.

I wonder if it's his coach, if he's inside there now, watching me. My mouth goes dry, my palms sweaty. All day I've been trying not to think of this damned party I'm supposed to attend, but it's hanging over me. Anything could happen. All I know of Jannik is what I've gleaned from two chance meetings. For all I know, once he has me at his party I'll be caught and trotted back to my family's home. Why not—after all, the bats need to find ways to sweeten their relationships with the Great Houses. For all the talk of equality, everyone knows the bat Houses continue in Pelimburg on our sufferance only. A step in the wrong direction and the three vampire Houses could lose everything.

I'm being ridiculous. If he wanted to curry favor with my family, he could have merely tipped them off that I'm here at the Crake.

There's something else that he wants from me, and I'll be damned as a Saint who told a bad future if I know what it is.

A moment later, I spot a familiar bird's nest of red hair. Nala trots up the wide sidewalk, her hands full of leashes. She's walking a collection of dragon-dogs. They are tall and thin, with high, sloping shoulders and long jaws with wolfish teeth. People move quickly out of her way. She doesn't stop when she sees me, but she flashes a white smile and sort of waves her fist a little. The dogs strain on the leather and pull her onward.

Bemused, I wave back.

THE TOWNSPEOPLE ARE SHUTTING UP SHOP, and street children are picking through the garbage on the sidewalks. I try to avoid the gangs—I'm still nervous after my attack—so I take the wide central road, where the street theaters are busy packing up now that the last shows are done for the day. As I rush through the homeward-bound crowds, someone yells my name. Or at least, the name I've stolen.

My heart jumps, and I try to pretend I didn't hear the shout.

"Firell! Oi, you! The girl in blue. Kitty-girl!"

Gris-damn it all. I turn slowly. My heart is doing double-time. I can feel how the blood has drained from my face. My skin is cold.

A tall, skinny young man is waving at me. He's standing at a street-theater wagon. Is this the infamous Dash? I doubt it, I'm sure I've seen this one leaving the Whelk Street house, and he's a mild, gangling sort of person. With my breathing as steady as I can hold it, I smooth down my skirts and walk toward him.

He's got a friendly face and hair in a long ragged cut. Low-Lammer, for sure. "You're the new girl?" he says as I draw closer.

I nod.

"Verrel." He pulls a bag of tobacco from his paint-spattered jacket and begins to roll himself a 'grit. His fingers are deft and fast. "Smoke?"

"N-no thanks." Verrel is one of the Whelk Streeters, and relief warms my skin. Lilya said he keeps to his own time, out chasing skirts and keeping the pubs in business. When he's not playing at being a theater boy. Everything she's told me about him makes him sound like a reprobate, but instead, he comes across as affable and charming. Perhaps he is all three, and then he will have been well named after the infamous progenitor of House Ives. It's even possible that he's some bastard cousin to the current Ives' line, saddled with a name like that.

Verrel shakes his head and licks the paper closed, his tongue darting smoothly. After he's lit it and taken a long suck on the smoke, he cocks his head at me, as friendly as if he were one of my brother's dragon-dogs.

"Lils described you pretty good." He grins. "You're heading back?"

Before I can even answer, he's rummaging in his pockets again. "I'm going to be late, got a night show. We have candle-lanterns and everything."

"I see." I don't, not really. I've never paid Hob street theater much mind. He's so excited that he doesn't notice my lack of enthusiasm.

"Here then, there you are," he says to the small brown paper packet he's finally retrieved from his bulging pockets. "Give them to Esta for me, will ya?"

The packet smells sweet and minty, and inside it are hard roundish lumps.

"Humbugs," he says. "Tell her not to set any Lammers on fire, and I'll take her out for cakes when I get my day off."

"Oh, oh—yes. I'll do that." I shove the packet into my little tote.

He grins and takes another long drag. "Poor thing," he says. "Not much of a girlhood if there's no one giving you sweets and toys."

I try to picture sullen little Esta ever playing with dolls or wooden and ivory blocks. It seems unlikely.

"Nice meeting you," he says, just as a Hob, portly and covered in greasepaint and wearing a voluminous fake beard, yells at him to stop chatting up the lasses. "Say hey to the rest." He touches his hand to his ragged hair in a friendly salute and turns back to packing up the sets.

I stand there for a moment, thoughts swirling through my head, then trot on toward home.

BACK AT THE SQUAT, Lils is crouched in the washroom, wearing nothing but a graying shift, while Esta pours jugs of water over her head. Lils's hair is still tightly pinned up. It makes no sense. Wordlessly, I hand Esta the crumpled, sticky packet. She scowls.

"From Verrel," I tell her, but she doesn't say anything back, just fishes out one striped golden-brown sweet and pops it into her mouth.

Uncertain, I stand there, waiting for a chance to give Lils the message.

Lils wipes water from her face and glares at me. "What do you want?" Her shift is wet, clinging to her body and almost see-through. She looks vulnerable, like a hermit crab changing shells.

"Oh . . . uh . . . I have a message from Charl at the Crake—"

"I know who he is. What does the little chancer want?" She touches her damp hair, then looks to Esta. "Another bucket, need to be sure it's wet all the way through before I let it down."

Esta goes to fetch another bucket, leaving us alone.

"The message is for Dash," I mumble.

Lils snorts. "Give me it."

"Something about poisonink, and meet Charl at the usual." I spread my hands in apology. "He didn't say much."

Her brow wrinkles into a frown, then after a moment's thought, she nods. "I'll let Dash know, sure enough," she says. "Verrel spotted him down at Market Way earlier." Lils squints at me. "His Flashness'll be pleased to hear that bit of news, right enough."

"So he'll let me stay?"

"Can't right say." She turns away. "Depends on if you got what he wants." Lils turns her back to me and begins to pull hairpins loose, slowly, one by one, setting them out neatly before her.

For a moment I can smell the meadows behind my house, the must of nillies and leather. A childhood recollection of trying to follow Owen on a hunt, of a fall made nightmarish by the passing of years. The crack of bone, followed by almost unbelievable pain. I remember sweat sticking my dress to my skin, and how my arm throbbed, hardly feeling like it belonged to me. Walking home alone across the heath because Owen did not want to stop his chase.

Water splashes on the tiles, spattering my boots and dress as Lils dumps a bucket over her loosened curls.

I am back in the present, and I frown at the memory as it slips back to where it belongs, hidden and best forgotten.

If I've got what Dash wants?

My heart flutters, and I will it to slow. Just what exactly does she mean by that, I wonder.

8

THE NEXT AFTERNOON when I hang up my apron at the end of my shift, I get my first pay packet. I've worked six whole days, and the thirty brass bits clinking inside the envelope seems like both a fortune and a pittance. I pick my way nervously through Old Town, aware of the strange heaviness in my coat pocket. I wonder if I walk naturally, or if there's an extra swing to my arms, a giddiness to my walk that might make me a target for Jaxon, or someone like him.

Tomorrow is my day off, and I plan to head down to Old Town market early to trade in my pilfered trinkets from Pelim House and my boots, and get a pair that fits and a change of clothes. A whisper flutters through my head, about how if I worked harder, longer, perhaps I could save up enough for a smidgen of scriv. The thought makes me laugh aloud, choking on my own naïve hope.

I'll never be able to afford scriv now. Even uni-horn—a barely passable substitute—trades on the market at thirty-two copper bits an eighth. And trade in scriv is strictly controlled.

The few merchants will sell only to House Heads or their official representatives. *Never again, Felicita.* Shaken by this realization, I lurch around the curve of the promenade and up Whelk to where the shabby green house is waiting.

Upstairs, Lils is already home, although there's no sign of Nala or Esta. Verrel from the street theater is stretched out on the carpet smoking a roll-up and staring at the ceiling. Every now and again he hums a snatch of a tune from one of the popular low musicals that are all the rage in Old Town. Lils is deep in conversation with a skinny little Hob who is sitting cross-legged on a tea crate, stripping the husks off some withered green maize that must have fallen off one of the vegetable barrows. He looks my age, maybe a year or two older, and he has the leanness of poverty, the old eyes in a young face. All around him are white linen-wrapped bales, smelling sweet and dusty. They seem to have taken over the squat, covering every available surface. He's one of Charl's lackeys, I gather, come to drop off the 'ink.

"—and not," the Hob says, jabbering away so fast that the words melt into each other, "for any reason. No reason that they can give, of course. Typical fucking Houses, ya know?"

"I know." Lils prods at the stock she's boiling up out of end-of-day market pickings.

"Just where do they get off? I mean, the best they can do is tell Esta that they'll give'r compensation. What's that worth? What do you pay someone when their family is dead? I mean, Rin's 'er brother, he's all she fucking has—had—left, and they think a handful of brass is gonna heal all ills?" He keeps asking questions, but doesn't wait for anyone to answer. "Fucking Lammers," he says. "Present company excluded."

"Exclusion accepted," says Verrel, and he sings a line from *Merriweather's Fortune* before taking another protracted drag of his smoke.

The Hob is high. I've seen them a lot now around Old Town, strung out on the little silvery-gray leaves of poisonink. 'Ink can give you visions, make you think you can solve all the world's problems, but it also tends to make you talk a load of absolute nonsense. The crakes take it. For inspiration, they say.

"Is this lot ready?" the Hob asks, hands twitching as he waves at the pot.

Lils sighs, stabs at the contents with her wooden spoon, and says in a patient voice, "Not for hours yet. Why don't you go lie down and I'll give you a shout when I dish up."

But he's not listening. He's spotted me, and he hops down from the crate. The Hob is a little taller than he looked sitting down, but not by much, and he has a roguish grin that reminds me of Jaxon. I step back and brush a tangled lock of hair behind my ear.

"And this," he crows as he approaches me, "this must be the latest addition to our happy little family. You're the kitty-girl, right? Lils told me all about you."

"I—" I take a deep breath because I have really had enough of this now. "Am. Not. A. Gris-damned. Kitty-girl. Will you lot get that through your thick Hob skulls!"

Lils laughs and keeps stirring. Verrel coughs on his hand-rolled 'grit.

"Oh," says the Hob. "I like you." He holds out one hand. "I'm Dash, by the way, kitty dearest."

Right. I stare at the Hob. Even Jaxon was more impressive. He grins back at me as I scrutinize him. Like most Hobs, his olive skin is tanned a deep brown, and his hair is thick and black and unruly. It curls down to his collar and falls over his gray-green eyes. There are salt stains on his clothing, although, for a Hob, it's pretty fine clothing. His waistcoat is silk, emerald green, and the buttons are black ivory from a sphynx's tooth. He's wearing a black neckcloth, loosely knotted in a lopsided bow.

"Shake his hand," says Lils, "before he decides to throw himself from a window or something."

So I extend my hand and take his. His grip is firm, his palms dry, and he seems utterly at ease with handshakes. Most Hobs are not interested in the practice. "Wonderful," he says. "I'm off to bed." And with that, Dash disappears behind the longest curtain, to an area of the house I've not yet been in.

"High as a Hob-kite," says Verrel.

"Verrel, you go put a water-urn by him. Stupid bugger is going to need it when he wakes. Otherwise he'll be bitching about his bad head for the whole of tomorrer," says Lils.

Verrel sits up and stubs out the dog-end of his 'grit in a mermaid's-ear shell near his hip. "Lucky me," he says. "Lucky, lucky me." He fills a small urn from one of the water pails that are spread out along the balcony and lopes off to Dash's room, stepping carefully over the scattered bales.

"Here," I say, nervous now, worried that I've botched this meeting and that when Dash wakes he'll find a reason to throw me out onto the street. I fumble in my pocket and hand Lils the rough paper envelope. "For the bowl," I say, nodding at the communal bowl that takes pride of place on the highest crate.

"You don't have to give me all of it, you daft Lam," she says, and tips five bits back into my palm. "Now you go get some sleep. I'll introduce you to Dash when he's himself again."

"You mean . . . he's not always like that?"

"Sweet Gris, no." She makes a growly *huk huk* sound that for Lils is what passes for laughter. "We'd have strung him out on the rooftops long since if he was." Lils takes a sip of her stock and licks her lips. "He has his moments, and when he does, we just leave him be until he's worked through them. Then things get back to normal sharp-like."

I cast a glance at the closed curtain and wonder just what kind of person he can be to somehow have all these people at his heel.

9

THERE'S NO SIGN of Lils the following morning. With the fading of the spring storms, she's back at work in the fish markets before dawn.

Dash is there though, talking quietly with Esta. He looks up as I push my curtain open but continues speaking in a low whisper, so as not to wake the others. The selkie-girl is curled up tight with her arms wrapped around her knees and her head bowed. She nods as she listens but says nothing. She blinks when she sees me, her dark seal eyes fathomless as a wild animal's.

"I have to go," Esta says as I draw closer. She leaps up and is running down the stairs before I even get a chance to greet her.

Dash raises one eyebrow at me. "And that?"

I shrug. "I've no idea—she hasn't liked me from the first day we met." I neglect to mention that the first time we met she tried to brain me with a piece of windowsill.

"How interesting. Normally she reserves her hatred for old

men and House Lams." He pats the cushioned sacks next to him. "Sit. Believe it's time you and me had a little chat." Then he grins at me. "I'll make us tea." He's clean, dressed in unstained clothes, the stubble scraped from his chin. There's still a slight bitter herbal smell to him from the poisonink, but it's barely noticeable.

My heart is pattering as I sit uncomfortably cross-legged. The burlap is rough, and all I'm wearing is my long shift. I feel exposed.

"See now," Dash says as he flicks a match against his thumb and lights the bundle of driftwood in the stove, then sets the little copper urn to boil. "Isn't this cozy?" He half smiles at me.

Uncertain, I half smile back and wish I'd just stayed in bed.

"You're working down at the Crake?" He tosses the spent match into the fire.

"I've paid my share into the bowl," I say, already on the defensive.

"I daresay you have." The little fire flickers, catching on the dry wood. Soon he'll have the water at a rolling boil. "Do you like it there, working for old Breadloaf?"

"It's . . . fine." What does he expect me to say?

"Yeah, she's a good sort—makes you work like a dog but it's not like we're not used to that. Leastwise she pays on time and there's cake if you're lucky."

"Yeah," I murmur in agreement. "Every little bit helps." I relax. All he wants to do is make sure I'm bringing in my wages and helping to feed and look after the rest of the crew.

Dash grins. "Soon we'll be bonding over redbush, sharing secrets like old friends, and you'll feel all like you're ready to trust me, and then you'll tell me exactly why it is that a House Lammer is hiding out in Whelk Street with a bunch of half-breeds and Hobs." Dash glances at the urn, then back at me. "Won't you?"

"I—I'm not a House Lammer."

"'Course you're not. Firell, is it?"

I nod vigorously and will the water to boil faster so that I can have a cup to hide behind. Something—anything—to do with my hands to hide their shaking.

"You're no low-Lammer," he says. "Do you know how I know that?"

"How?" I swallow, and watch the steam rising so that I don't have to look him in the face.

"Your hands are too white." Dash takes the urn from the fire and adds a generous pinch from the tea box. "Your accent is wrong." He glances over at me, smiles thinly, and sets the redbush to steep.

Someone has shoved a lump of coal down my throat and I can't swallow properly. "My mother was a servant and for all that I'm a bastard, my father raised me in his House—gave me the best tutelage—" I cough, a small dry sound.

"A likely story. Pass us the teabowls, *Firell*."

The porcelain bowls are cheap, made of thick white clay, cracked and chipped. I take two from the crate and hand them to him. If I keep my mouth shut, I can leave him to his guesswork.

After a few slow sips of hot tea, Dash speaks again. "Sphynx got your tongue?"

"Why should I say anything if you won't even try to believe me?" I sit straighter and glare at him. I won't be cowed by a Hob.

Dash laughs. "What House?"

"Pardon?"

"What House did your mam work for?"

Thoughts race through my head, and I settle on the first and most likely story I can imagine. "Malker."

Dash swishes tea in his mouth, then twists his body so he can spit out the window. "The witch-cursed House. Go on."

And with that, he's given me my lie. Inwardly, I'm smiling, but I keep my voice shaky and nervous. "I left after Malker Ilven took the Leap." I even let myself shiver—just a slight tremble of the shoulders—before continuing my story. "I couldn't stay there, not after that. The bad luck would have killed me, driven me mad. You know what they say about suicides crawling back from the deep and bringing death with them." I put my half-empty bowl down on the floor and pull my knees to my chest. "Don't make me go back," I mumble. "Please."

Dash frowns, and I feel him staring hard at me. It's like spiders crawling over my skin, and I want to shake my head, scrub at my face with my fingernails.

"And so you came here," he says very softly, his eyes never leaving my face. "Why?"

"I—Anja said I should go to you." The hairdresser's words,

an instruction I never really questioned until now. I try to keep myself steady, to not blink or waver. "She said to tell you that."

He watches me for a moment more, his face smooth, expressionless, then he quirks one side of his mouth up in amusement. "Welcome to Whelk Street, Firell." He stands and straightens his rolled sleeves and his emerald-green waistcoat. "See that the teabowls are washed before Lils gets back," Dash says. "Girl can get right shirty if she thinks you're skiving." He grabs a dark blue scarf from one of the lines that crisscross the room, picks his way through the piles of material, and heads downstairs without another word to me.

After a few minutes I pick up the teabowls and go to fetch a pail of fresh water for rinsing them. Water, icy from the night, slops over my shift, and I curl my toes and mutter a few newly learned expletives. Working at the Crake has taught me more than merely the ins and outs of dish washing.

I hope the arrogant little gutter-dandy stays away for another week.

He's very . . .

. . . tiring.

ALAS, I HAVE NO SUCH LUCK.

Dash returns just after we've eaten breakfast. Nala's still here with Verrel, gathering her bag so she can buy bones from the butcher and treat her dogs. Verrel is sitting by the window, blowing smoke out into the morning air. The room smells like salt and tobacco.

"All right, crew," Dash says. "I need everyone here to buckle down."

Nala stares at him. "Dash," she says patiently, "I've dogs that need walking." Her bag is slung over one shoulder.

"Walk them later." He stoops over to grab a slice of flame-blackened toast and chews it hurriedly. "I need this lot shifted before the sharif get wind of it." He gestures at the covered bundles stacked on the floor.

Nala scowls and crosses her arms. "It's illegal?"

"Not really." He shrugs, then kneels down to untie the twine around the first of the white-shrouded bales. "It is stolen though."

"Oh sweet Gris, Dash! You said last time was the . . . last."

"Too good an offer to pass up, Nala. Now, run down apothecary way and get as many glass jars as you can carry. Money's in the bowl."

She scowls and turns away, but not before digging through the communal bowl for a handful of brass. The slap of her bare feet against the wood falls to silence, and then it is only Dash, Verrel, and me. We stare at one another. Verrel raises one eyebrow as Dash pulls the bale open to reveal a mess of stems with tiny furred gray leaves. Poisonink.

"And you want us to do what with it?" Verrel rolls a new 'grit with one hand and drinks tea with the other.

"Sort it, pack it. We've got a buyer for the finished product, and the sharif are only looking for the raw stuff."

"The sharif? Wonderful." Verrel takes a deep, thoughtful drag and eyes the poisonink. I look at it in horror. The damn stuff will get me caught—ruin me.

Dash looks across at me and grins. "You ever sorted 'ink before?"

He knows I haven't, the little shit. I scowl at him and shake my head. If he brings the sharif down on us and they realize who I am . . . Damn. I need to get this stuff away from me as soon as possible. "What do I have to do?" I say between gritted teeth.

"Here." He kneels down and lifts a single branch. "Go like this." Dash runs his hand loosely down the branch, and the twisted gray outer leaves fall onto the white sheet. "That's the stuff you want to get rid of. What's left"—he flicks the small tightly furled new leaves—"that's what you want to put in the jars."

"And this?" I point at the mess of dried leaves on the open sheet.

"Ah, save that for me," Verrel says. "I can compost it for the garden."

Garden? The whole house is slowly sinking into mud. Obviously, Verrel is as insane as the rest of the Whelk Streeters.

Dash just nods as if this is the most normal conversation in the world. He unwraps another bale and then opens up a second sheet. "Good stuff here." He points at the one sheet. "Compost there."

I stare at him.

"Get on it then, kitty," he says.

"Firell."

"*Firell.*" He smiles, then shakes his head.

Verrel stubs out his 'grit and drinks the last of his tea in one gulp before sitting cross-legged on the floor and taking a branch. With a sigh, I fold my skirt over my legs and sit down next to him.

It's mindless work and strangely soothing. The poisonink leaves a sticky black residue all over my fingers and thumbs, but after a while I find myself feeling almost content. The sweet sharp scent of the 'ink cleans the air of the sour smell of bodies and poverty. Verrel sings and hums while he works, and occasionally Dash will join in. Verrel's voice is strong and sure, while Dash's is thin, although, thankfully, in tune.

Nala gets back after about an hour. We can hear her coming up the stairs, swearing and clinking glass. Dash puts down his branch and rises to go give her a hand.

"This is the last time, Dash." Her voice comes up from downstairs. "And I need to go to work, or I'm going to lose my job."

"You can get another."

"I *like* this job. I'm not the same as you, always running off to find something else to do." Dash and Nala appear at the top of the stairs holding a large burlap bag between them. "Besides, the dogs love me, and I'd miss them." She sets her end of the bag down. "I'm going now, all right?"

He stares at her, mouth twitching, then looks over at where Verrel and I are making considerable progress through the collection of bales. "Fine." He drags the bag the rest of the way to us and starts pulling out glass jars. He sets them out with a meticulousness I didn't expect from him, all the jars in order of size and shape.

"Dash . . ."

"What?" he snaps back at Nala. "Go on then, I said it was fine."

"You're going to hold this against me?"

He pauses with an opal jar in his hands, turning it over and over. Finally, Dash shakes his head. "No," he says. "Go before your dogs all die of broken hearts." But he says it with a smile, and his voice is easy.

"You're a changeable little monster, you do know that?" Nala says.

Next to me, Verrel laughs and begins to fill the first jar, packing the 'ink in tight. "Of course he does."

"It's part of my charm," Dash adds.

"*Charm*—is that what they're calling it now?" Nala's relief is clear in her voice. I do not think that Dash is always so easily mollified.

By mid-morning, we've done most of the bales. There are two left, and we've filled about fourteen of the glass containers. My hands are black and so sticky I can barely touch anything. I crick my neck from side to side, trying to ease the tense muscles.

Esta's come back from combing the beach with Kirren for signs of her brother and is sullenly making tea.

"Time for a break." Dash stands. He stretches his arms

high above his head, exposing a flash of stomach. He is the very opposite of Jannik, brown and wiry with workman's muscles. I copy him, pretending I haven't seen this arc of skin. Verrel also stretches; something in his back *clicks* loudly, and we laugh at each other.

"Shite," says Esta from her spot near the window. "Dash? Come here."

Dash picks his way over the debris and joins Esta by the little stove. They both stare out the window for a few seconds, then Dash hisses under his breath, swearing. He puts one sticky hand to his face and grimaces. "Verrel, start moving everything next door."

"Sharif?"

Dash nods. There's a black mark on his face left there by the gummy residue from his fingers.

I'm going to vomit. Verrel must see the panic on my face because he rests one hand on my shoulder. "Don't worry," he says. "Help me gather this." He points at the sheet where we've been throwing all the waste leaves. I nod hurriedly and knot it together into a bag, while Verrel grabs as many jars as he can carry. "This way."

He leads me to the cracked and tiled washroom and through a broken panel into a cramped, gloomy passage.

"Where are we going?"

"Up," he says, and jerks his head at the ceiling. There's a small square piece of board, and Verrel uses a length of broken timber to push it away to reveal a hole. "Up you go," he says, and cups his hands for a footrest.

"You're joking."

"Not at all. I'll boost you and then hand everything up."

The hole is pitch-dark, and I stare at it in dismay.

"Come on, time's wasting."

My fear of being found by the sharif and sent back to my House in disgrace overrides my fear of the dark. I scramble up into a narrow attic space with sloping walls. After a few blinks, the gloom takes on shape and shadow. I reach down and start hauling up all the contraband.

We work fast and quiet, and in a surprisingly short time, all the jars of 'ink have been transferred into the attic.

Dash gives Verrel a lift into the loft and then slides the board shut, enveloping us in utter darkness.

"Now what?" I whisper. "We just sit here until they leave?"

"Not a chance."

"What?" My eyes adjust again, and I can make out Verrel's face near me, calm and expressionless. "What then?"

"We're moving it across." He shuffles off on hands and knees, one jar clamped under his arm. "You need to be careful and stay on a beam or else you'll go right through the ceiling," he says. "Now follow me."

Obediently, I gather as much as I can and crawl after Verrel, my fingers gripping the wood so tightly that I'm probably going to be picking splinters out from under my nails for weeks.

What was I thinking? I should have bloody well run back home to Mother the day I left and hoped for the best.

At the end of the loft, Verrel shifts a segment of broken

wood out of the way, and we crawl into the sunlight-dappled attic of the adjoining house. The beams creak ominously as we settle our stolen 'ink here.

"It's not going to fall down, is it?" I look up at the straining wood beams of the ceiling, at the huge gaps between the slate tiles.

"Not today," says Verrel. "Hopefully."

After several excruciatingly slow trips, we've moved every-thing across. Verrel seals the join between the two houses and leans back with a sigh.

The house groans in the wind, creaking and snapping. "Oh sweet Gris," I say. "If this place collapses and I die, I'm going to come back and haunt that little bastard like a bog-gert." I shiver and pull my legs up to my chin. "What are we supposed to do?"

Verrel laughs softly. "Now we sit tight until Dash gives the all clear."

"What about the others?"

"Dash can talk his way out of just about anything, don't you worry about him. He knows half the bloody sharif by name and what they had for breakfast. Right now he's proba-bly giving them the grand tour and asking them about their mams' gout."

"I'm not worried about *him*," I snap, and hug my knees tighter.

The minutes barely scrape by. A sharp wind blows through the dilapidated roof, and I shiver. I hear dogs barking, the distant rumble of the sea, the rag-and-bone man's desultory handbell. But for all I strain my ears, I can hear no voices, no sharif calling out. No Dash. In the silence, I'm left to thinking, and all my thoughts are either about scriv or that damn bat Jannik. As much as I try to think about something else, my mind keeps wandering back to them. I miss magic.

I breathe out slowly, imagining that my lungs are full of power, that all around me the air is gathering, ready to do as I say. It does nothing to rid me of the dull itch in my mind. I need to taste scriv—citrus bright—in my throat or feel the teasing prickle of the bat's magic.

Below us come scritching noises, rustles and scratches.

"What's that?"

Verrel shifts. "Hmm? Rats, most likely."

Wonderful.

"Kirren's probably chasing them about down there. Having a whale of a time while we sit here with our arses going numb." He rubs gum off his fingers onto his coat, then pulls a packet of tobacco out of his pocket. "Want?"

I shake my head.

"You're like Esta then? Got a sweet tooth?"

"Not particularly." I sigh, scratching patterns in the dirty wood with my thumbnail. "I like MallenIve salt licorice." I think of the delicacies we sometimes got from the capital city. Things I am unlikely to ever taste again. *Scriv.* Stop it, I tell myself, and flex my fingers against my stomach as if that will still the hunger. "Ama seeds." Hot and bitter, and small as fingernail parings. I used to eat them while reading, popping the tiny burning seeds onto the tip of my tongue to see how long I could stand it before swallowing them.

That surprises a laugh. "Expensive and odd tastes you got there," he says.

"Reminds me of my father." There are other things that make me think of him, although I keep these to myself. The smell of tobacco and vai. Leather and hounds. I squeeze my eyes shut. "Tell me about Dash."

All I can hear is Verrel's slow exhale. Then: "There's not much to say. He keeps secrets, and that's all there is to it."

"Secrets?"

"Well they wouldn't be secrets if I was going about telling them, now would they?"

I laugh softly. "So how did you end up here?"

"I knew Esta and Rin, and they needed a safe place to hide, so I brought them here. Didn't want to leave them alone, so I asked Dash if I could stay on."

"And he just said yes?"

"Not hardly. Then he found out I work the street theaters and he became a bit chummier." He coughs. "Now I'm his glorified message boy, but it's all right, 'cause, whatever else, Esta's safe. There's no one in Stilt City or Old Town that would even think of crossing Dash."

"Why's that?"

Verrel shrugs and flicks ash down between the beams. "Long story."

"I think we have time."

"Ah, was long before I met him, right. Back when he was

just a Hobling, him and Lils, well, they were neighbors, and Lils—well, there's something about her, and—" He suddenly looks uncomfortable. "I shouldn't say nothing."

I keep quiet, and he apparently takes that as reason enough to trust me, at least a little. "So anyway, there's some stupid Hob, just gone old enough to want to be bringing in some money for his family but still young enough not to realize you don't sell out your own people. And he thinks he's going to turn our Lils over to the sharif."

I squirrel this information away, wondering what fish-market Lils, common as anything, can possibly be hiding that would warrant the interest of the sharif.

"Now, Lils and Dash—I mean, they're just barely turned nine—they don't know how to stop this when they hear him say he's gonna go turn her in. Lils thinks to go to her mam and hope that she can talk some sense into this Hobling lad. So she goes home, and that's that, because the next day the Hobling is gone."

"To the sharif?"

"Well, that's what everyone thinks. And all the neighbors are talking in whispers, and Lils's mam is getting ready to take her into the deep marshes and go into hiding and live on raw fish and crabs, and Dash is just being all Dash, grinning like it's all some huge mucking joke. That's how I heard it told, anyway."

"He thought it was funny?" I can't keep the disgust out of my voice.

"He *knew* it was funny, because not two weeks later,

someone pulls this half-eaten body out of the marshes and the only way they could identify him was from his boots and shirt."

It takes a moment for this to sink in. "I'm sorry—are you saying Dash at age nine killed another person to keep Lils safe?" There's no disguising my disbelief.

Verrel laughs. "Nothing of the sort. Dash never gets his hands dirty. What he does do is put the right word in the right ear and do a favor for this one or that and the next thing you know . . . things happen."

"At age nine?" I repeat. Then I shake my head. "You must think I'm an imbecile, telling me that and expecting me to fall for it like a little fish with a fly."

"Believe what you want," Verrel says. "There's others who could tell you better tales. And maybe they're truer, and maybe they're not."

I think of the Hob downstairs, a gadabout, a skinny boy barely older than me, and all the things Verrel seems to think he's done or is capable of.

"Secrets, huh?" I say after a while. I have run to a house tangled with secrets and deceptions, bringing my own with me. The light falling through the holes in the slate roof is growing fainter, and the air has the smell of rain. I tuck my feet close to my body, wondering how much longer we'll be forced to stay up here.

Three 'grits later, a voice calls from the other attic. Verrel sighs in relief, pulls the board back, and shoves his head through. "We're all right, then?"

"Right as rain," says Dash cheerfully. "Sharif have sailed off for fishier waters."

I grit my teeth and wonder if it would matter if I strangled Dash in his sleep. Or poisoned his tea. I wonder what his neck would feel like under my fingers.

We crawl out across the roof beams and back into the squat. I'm just passing down the last of the glass jars to Verrel when I hear a familiar gruff voice from the main room.

"What bloody happened here?" Lils says. "Market's bloody crawling with sharif, all asking nosy questions."

"Tea?" says Dash.

Lils mutters something I don't catch.

"It'll all be gone by afternoon. Charl and his lads are coming to collect it."

I ease my legs and body through the hole and then let go to land lightly on the passage floor. Verrel grins and holds out two jars. "It doesn't happen that often," he says. "It's all part of Dash's grand plan, he needs the money."

"What grand plan?" I mutter as I brush dust and cobwebs and shreds of poisonink leaves off my dress, then grab the jars out of his hands.

"His plan to destroy Pelimburg, of course."

Of course.

10

AFTER MY UNFORTUNATE ENCOUNTER with Dash and the wrong side of the law, I've been wandering through the market on what's left of my day off, keeping an eye open for a vendor who will neither look twice nor ask questions about my old hair clips and jewelry. Even though it's rather quiet, there is a crowd under the vast tree that shades the center of the market, and the air is thick with nervous excitement.

I follow the people toward the center, to the old tumbled stone stage where they used to stake and burn bats, before the Houses gave them citizenship. Public punishments are still a spectacle, with people gathering to watch the condemned suffer for their crimes. Usually it's a thief, bound in place while the sharif use an iron ax to relieve him of a finger. There's a punishment to suit every crime, and the sharif seem to take no small pleasure in putting out an eye or slitting a tongue.

The crowd is made up mostly of gawkers, bystanders, and the kind of old women who revel in the suffering of others.

There's a girl on the stone stage, held in place with iron manacles. I can smell how they burn the skin at her wrists.

"What did she do?" I ask the man standing next to me, and he grunts, then shrugs. Another Hob overhears my question.

"Spoke out agin House Pelim—her lad was washed over. One of the *Silver Dancer*'s crew. Said it weren't right that all they get is a few brass bits. She's got little ones to care for—"

"Oh hush," says the older man. "'Less you feel like getting up there with her."

I stare at the girl. So she's spoken out against my House. She's not all that many years older than me, but her poverty and the children she's borne have sucked her dry, left her withered. Only her eyes are bright and fierce.

A sharif steps up to her, an iron blade in one gloved hand. In his other hand is a contraption for holding the jaw open.

She stands straighter. "Fuck you, an all," she says. "House dog."

One of the sharif holding her clouts her jaw, and she laughs. It's a manic sound. "I stand by it. Everyone knows it's true. What's a life to a House, handful of brass and thank you very much—" She doesn't get to finish what she's saying. They force the mouthpiece in and pull her tongue straight with iron pliers. She shrieks, a ululating sound, the howling of a struggling cat.

Angry mutters sweep through the crowd, and I force myself to watch while they split her tongue in two like a viper's.

Before they are done, I'm pushing through the crowd,

desperate to be away. I've only ever heard of these punishments, never before witnessed them. The way Owen spoke, he made it sound like they deserved it.

They don't.

Gris. No one does.

ONCE I'VE EXCHANGED MY FEW TRINKETS for a handful of brass, and bought new comfortable boots for working in and a dark blue summer dress that won't show tea spills and dirt, I decide to treat myself to an ice-cone.

The day has turned hot and muggy, and midges are swarming in clouds about the fruit stands, a sure sign that the last of spring will soon give way to summer and we'll have days of clear skies if we're lucky. My face is flushed from walking and haggling. There is still a feeling of sticky anger and resentment in the air even though the blood has been washed from the stones. With my cone in hand, I sit on a rough-hewn bench near the center stage and listen to the news criers read from the *Courant*. They call out the day's weather predictions, gossip, and news from the surrounding towns. Even news from as far upriver as MallenIve.

I find out that I'm dead while eating spoonfuls of shaved ice from a paper cone. My official death notice. Lemon flavored.

I hear my name and realize that the crier is talking about my suicide. About the slipper they found in a trawler's net. About the remnants of a golden-brown shawl that snagged on the rocks below Pelim's Leap.

My body is yet to be recovered.

Naturally.

I'm sure my mother tried to keep my supposed death as quiet as possible, but she can't control all of Pelimburg, and tongues will wag. The rumors have been building since I disappeared, and now we have the truth of it. Or at least the truth as far as Pelimburg knows.

The sour lemon ice melts and turns the paper cone soggy, runs down my hand in sticky drips. A bee, sensing opportunity, hovers near my face, and I wave it away and get up to throw my cone in a nearby gutter. It's time to head back home.

There's nothing more that I want to hear.

I leave the market with my new boots already laced on and my dress packed in my shoulder bag. One of the street theaters is in full swing, and a large crowd has gathered around the makeshift set. I'm not one for the tunes and over-acted dramas that the theaters put on, but this way is the shortest route back to the promenade.

The crowd is singing along jovially. I know the song now—Verrel practically sings it in his sleep. It's the lament from *Merriweather's Fortune*. From what I can tell, Merriweather, a rather rough-cut stand-in for Mata Blaise, newly crowned monarch of MallenIve, has lost everything in a fire that has burned MallenIve to the ground. I think at this point in the story he's standing over the crushed and lifeless form of his wife, one of the countless vapid blondes of House Eline, raging against the ill winds.

It's supposed to be full of pathos, but the Hob and low-Lam crowd bawl in off-key happiness at the House's misfortune.

Verrel is standing behind the hastily built stage. He sees me and beckons me over.

"You need to run down to the flats," he says as I approach.

"Why? What's happening?" I have a vision of the sharif climbing all over the hidden poisonink, of Dash caught, of Esta setting fire to my brother's ships. "They haven't—"

"Dash is calling all the Whelk Streeters who can make it to join him there." He pauses to drop a lever. A new backdrop unrolls with a solid thump, sending sand gusting across the floorboards. He tugs on a rope and slowly winds up the old drop. "Seems someone found Rin's body washed up while they were out clam digging."

So the faceless boy will have a face. I don't really want to go, but nor do I want to give Dash a reason to turn his attention back to me.

"Right," I say. A burst of applause drowns me out. "I better get going then." The last thing I want to see is this dead boy, a reminder of Ilven.

Verrel wipes a dirty hand across his brow and leans back on his rope. "Tell Dash I'll come along as soon as the late show is done," he says.

I trudge down the main road toward the Levelling Bridge and then turn off to the promenade. The tide is out and the mudflats stretch slick and stinking away from the stone wall.

Sea mews pick at washed-up fish and long branches of rotting kelp, and sandpipers run along the mud, probing here and there for mollusks.

The promenade curves, and in the distance a crowd has gathered near the water's edge. The figures are dark and tiny as flies, but I catch a glimpse of the white uniforms of the sharif.

My stomach twists, and fear makes my insides cold. I pull my brown shawl out of my bag and knot it over my head. Why are the sharif there? Isn't Rin just another half-breed lost to a storm? I pick up my pace, running along the low wall, looking for a safe place to jump down to the gray sludge. If I keep my head lowered and stay near the back of the crowd, hopefully they won't pay me any attention.

The crowd is bunched together, and I slip behind the sharif. Lils isn't here, but Nala is, with her fists holding tight to the leashes of the huge hunchbacked dogs that the Houses once used to hunt river-drakes. She sees me and nods grimly. Esta is talking to a sharif, and Dash is at her side watching the proceedings. He keeps a hand low on her back, propping her up and offering silent comfort. Kirren presses his blunt face against Esta's legs, tail wagging low.

I edge closer. It's not that I want to see the body. But I am curious about what the sharif are asking Esta.

The sight of the corpse makes me gasp, and I clap my hand over my mouth to stifle the sound.

Rin is lying stomach-down on the mud, one arm pillowing his cheek. His body is intact, strange enough considering that he's been in the water for more than a few days. In fact, he's not bloated, or gnawed on, or disintegrating.

Instead, he is perfect, like he's asleep on the mud.

Except for one thing: he is as clear and gelatinous as the box jellyfish that sometimes wash up on the beaches. His bones are faint and silvery, the lines of his organs barely visible. It's as if the seawater has leached all the color from his naked body. I've never seen anything like it before. It is far worse than witch-sign.

Through him, I can see the indentation of his body in the soft ground. There are rag worms nosing from the mud, nudging at his flesh, and sea-beetles scuttling around his corpse. They leave feather-fine tracks around him.

"Boggert done this," someone whispers from behind me. "There'll be worse to come, you mark me. There's bad tides coming."

I look up in horror, and Dash catches my eye. He shakes his head, frowns, and with a quick jerk of his hand, signals me to head back to the house. He wanted me to see this, I realize, and now he wants me gone.

Heart pounding, I run all the way back to where the green house is standing stubborn-faced to the wind.

"THE SHARIF THINK IT'S ONE OF US," says Nala, "that there's Hob magic at work." Kirren is lying against her feet, tongue lolling. Every now and again he whacks the floorboards with his tail.

We're all of us gathered together—the first time I have

seen every one of the Whelk Streeters in the same place. Dash has filled the stove with driftwood, and the flames crackle in merry counterpoint to our somber mood.

"Don't you worry about that," says Dash. "I'll keep the damn sharif off our back." He pokes at the fire. An urn is warming on top, and Lils is carefully mixing dried tea in a bowl. Her fingers measure out equal amounts of redbush and sweet aloe as a base, and then she takes Lady's Gown for calm and the smallest pinch of poisonink, just enough to take the edge off reality.

"I don't like this none," says Nala. "It's magic. Not scriv, wild magic." She glances at Lils, her eyes wide. "They know."

"Don't matter," says Dash. "They've no idea how to stop it. And I—we can use this."

"Use my brother's death?" says Esta, rather too calmly.

Everyone pauses, uncertain, and Dash gives the smoking twigs another vicious jab. "You want someone to blame," he says, "you don't look to us. You look to those bastards in Malker and Pelim. You look to them."

Esta makes a hiccuping sound and hugs her knees close to her chest. Dash stops tormenting the fire and sits down next to her. "I'm sorry, my sweet," he says into her hair. "But we'll make it even, you'll see." He hugs her close, and she lets him. "We'll make them pay."

Lils presses her lips together in a thin line and shakes her head in warning.

I watch them, my hands folded in my lap. Everyone else seems to be trying to keep themselves occupied: Verrel rolling countless 'grits, pulling them apart and rolling them again, Lils with the tea, Nala stroking her hands down her thin bare ankles, over and over, and Esta, poor Esta, is holding Dash's coat with her fingers so clenched that the knuckle bones look like they are about to poke through her skin.

Dash has her half sitting on his lap, one arm around her, pulling her close. She turns her face against his lapel and sobs. He looks up helplessly and sees me doing nothing.

"Go through to my side of the house. Second crate to your immediate left you'll find a bottle or two. Bring me a vai."

Lils glances up from her tea making and squints at me. Her face is blank, but suspicion emanates from her. She looks back at Dash, one eyebrow raised.

"Come now, Lils," Dash says. "Can't have a proper wake without a drop of the blood."

"That's not what I mean, and you know it."

"It's time the girl got involved," he says. "She'll be useful."

A creeping flush of anger spreads up toward my face. I hate it when people discuss me as if I were too feebleminded to understand anything. Owen and my mother did it all the time.

Lils touches her tightly coiled hair and frowns at Dash. "It's on your own head, then," she says. "I don't like it. None of it—you're messing with what you can't control."

"You don't have to like it, Lils, but you keep your trap. I know exactly what I'm doing. Everyone has their place here, and we'll soon find kitty-girl her own spot in the war."

War. I stare at Dash. He's still stroking Esta's head.

"You're too trusting." The water is boiling and Lils turns her attention back to her tea making. "You'll tell anyone anything if you think it'll get them to help your cause."

"It's not my cause," he says. "This is for all of us. We'll level things. We'll purify the city and make it like it was before the first Lammer ships came."

"And you think you'll build a perfect world from the ashes."

"And you, Lils, dear, have no vision. You used to trust me, what happened to that?"

Lils narrows her eyes. "I still do. And you know I always will. Just sometimes I wonder about your methods."

"Well, don't. Pretend we're Hoblings again and things are still the same as they ever was."

"And you're the one getting us out of the same trouble you got us into in the first place?" Her voice is gently mocking, but I can tell that the argument is already over, that Dash has won.

"Just that exactly." Dash rocks Esta, patting her back like a mother will do with a hurt child: soft, soothing monotony. He looks over Esta's shoulder, straight at me. "Go on then," he says. "Go grab that vai."

In a way, I'm glad he's ordering me about. It gives me an opportunity to leave the close atmosphere. Listening to Esta sob over her lost brother reminds me that in my old home my mother is weeping over my death.

"And don't go touching nothing," Dash shouts at me as I pull the corner of his curtain aside and head into the previously forbidden territory of his room. Kirren has followed me, and his nails *click* against the wood. The dog's presence is reassuring. I forgot how much I missed the comfort of my brother's dogs, their unassuming friendship. I lean down and scratch Kirren's head.

It's dark here. The sun has slipped behind the bank of clouds on the horizon and all the windows on this side seem to be shuttered. It's a moment before I see the crates stacked up on my left.

The second one is filled with bottles. One or two, he said. I laugh drily. There's a veritable fortune in here. It's not hard to work out how Dash keeps the look-fars and sharif paid off. I grab a bottle of vai and then pause to look at the rest of the room. Kirren whines and edges backward as if aware we are overstaying our welcome. There's a narrow bed against one wall—clearly Dash doesn't bring his lady friends here for entertainment purposes. A small book sits next to his bed, but before I can have a look at what it is, Dash calls out to me from the common room.

"Have you bloody well managed to get lost in there?"

"Uh," I shout back. "No!" Quick as I can, I carry the vai to where they're waiting. Dash meets my eyes and does his weird half-grin thing at me. "You can do us the honors," he says, indicating the waiting teabowls. I pour a generous shot of vai into each one. This should be interesting: Hobs especially tend to feel the effects of the scriv in vai like a hallucinogenic. Add the high alcohol content and the poisonink in the tea and . . . I wonder exactly what Dash wants to achieve.

Esta drinks her bowl fast and immediately holds it out for another drink. Obviously, she's planning on obliterating tonight from her memory. Old before her time, she acts more like a seasoned drinker than a little girl. Not that I really blame her. There have been nights lately when I wished I could do the same—stop Ilven's frightened, desperate face from taking over my dreams and nightmares.

I've never seen anything like Rin's corpse before. Never heard of such a thing happening.

Boggert, someone said. If that's true . . .

If it's not laid to rest, then Pelimburg is in deep trouble. I stare at Dash, wondering if he had anything to do with Rin's death, using it to fuel whatever he's planning. If somehow he has control over sea-witches and boggerts and other strange creatures. Then I shake my head—sea-witch—please. I'm getting all caught up in Hob fancies. Next I'll be thinking that there really is Hob magic at work and that Dash knows how to manipulate it.

Dash stares back at me, his expression flat, as if he can read my mind.

The drinking actually seems to help. Esta's gone quietly catatonic, and Dash lifts her easily. "Time for bed, sweet," he tells her. She mumbles something in response and grips his coat harder. "Hush," he says. "Sleep."

He disappears behind Esta's curtain, and we can just hear the soft sound of his voice but not the words.

"Want a 'grit?" Verrel asks when Dash comes back.

"Only if our delightful Lils will add a little 'ink to the mix." He sits down. Right next to me.

Lils sighs and shakes her head but hands over some dried poisonink anyway. Verrel crumbles the leaves into one of the 'grits, rolls it one-handed, then passes it over.

"What are we going to do?" Lils says, and takes a hesitant sip of her vai-laced tea.

"About what?" says Dash.

"About Esta. She's barely here."

He shrugs and flicks ash into the mermaid's-ear ashtray. "Keep her away from matches?" He sighs out smoke. "I really don't know. We'll have to keep an eye on her, or maybe distract her. I'll think of something."

Verrel leans forward. "And someone needs to make sure she stays far away from the Pelim boatyard."

"Indeed."

Nala finally looks up. "I could do that, take her out with me when I walk the dogs."

"That's a start." Dash leans back, and his arm brushes mine. I pull away, but he pays no attention. "She's not to be left alone. I'll go deal with the sharif tomorrow. A couple of bribes should see them forget about Rin."

"And the boggert?"

He glances at me before looking back at Nala. "There's no such thing. No boggert, and no sea-witch coming after it."

She runs one hand through her wild frizz of hair and glares at him. "What if there is? You know of anything else that turns a body into a jellyfish? Boggert drained him, everyone knows the way of these things."

"There is. No. Boggert." He frowns at the 'grit smoldering between his fingers. "So stop talking about it." He looks up, his eyes bright. "Now would someone be so kind as to pour me another vai?"

I don't know how he can drink more vai on top of all the 'ink he's been doing. So far it doesn't seem to have had any effect on him, but I'm feeling the lazy buzz of the scriv tickling down my spine. The fine hairs on my arms are standing up, fuzzing my skin.

"Cold?" says Dash in my ear.

"No." I shift away from him and run my damp palms down my legs. "I—I think I'll have another vai too, please."

Lils and Nala exchange a look, and I try to ignore them. The vai might have only the tiniest bit of scriv in it, but it makes my mouth dry with anticipation. I can feel the air against my skin like a live thing, and I want to twist it, manipulate it, make it do my bidding.

Dash stands and holds out his hand to me.

"What?" I say.

"We're going to watch the sun set," he says. "I'm not sitting here any longer. Too much misery in this room. I need out."

Lils sneers. "And you want us to all traipse off to the garden and watch the sun set because you hate dealing with reality?"

"I can deal with reality perfectly well," he says back, grinning. "I just don't see why I should."

"He's right, though." Verrel lazily flicks ash. "Better to be out there than in here." He clambers to his feet.

"Fine." Lils grabs the vai, and at her nod, Nala goes to check that little Esta is sleeping soundly.

"Out as can be," she says after peeking around the curtain.

"And she won't wake for a while, neither," says Dash. "Not with that much vai in her." His hand is still held out, and with a sigh, I grab it and let myself be hauled upright. "You'll like the garden."

Verrel leads the way downstairs and out to one of the houses farther down the Claw. This one can barely be considered a house, being little more than beams lashed together to stop them from blowing away into the sea. Someone has built a series of wooden platforms on what's left of the roof, and we have to climb up a rickety ladder to reach them. Verrel slings Kirren under one arm and the dog allows this with a long-suffering expression that tells of many such trips.

The platforms are covered with planters made out of every conceivable type of junk. The tubs and wooden crates are overflowing with greenery, the first sprouts waving new fronds in the sea breeze. Here and there rough-made screens channel the wind away from the young plants.

There are no other houses to impede the view, and the sea is stretched out behind the garden, bronze and gold and red as the sun sinks lower in the sky.

"Welcome to Verrel's masterpiece," says Dash as he sits down on the edge of the platform.

"It's amazing," I say, and, really, it is. Come late summer, this will be a paradise, full of food for the Whelk Streeters. When I was just a girl, I kept a botanical sketchbook with pains-takingly inked plants, their parts neatly labeled. For all my skill with a brush, when it came to actually growing anything I was black thumbed. Ilven once gave me a little violet love-in-hiding for my windowsill, and there it languished. I managed to wither a plant that not even the harsh cliffside weather could kill. I look up at Verrel. "Truly beautiful."

Verrel grins and flushes, brushing one hand through his messy hair.

Lils and Nala have joined Dash on the platform's edge, their feet dangling over the mudflats. Verrel quickly takes a seat, and I see that there is only one place left for me to sit: on Dash's right. I sigh inwardly.

When I'm settled, Dash grins at me and hands me the vai bottle.

Together, the five of us—six with Kirren—are bathed in the last ruddy light as the sun dips below the horizon. We watch in silence, passing the bottle back and forth, and as the sun slides lower, the tide rises, and beneath us the wavelets lap at the house's foundation.

"How many bodies?" Lils asks as she watches over the waves. I have no idea what she's talking about, but there's a tightness in her voice that makes me peer sidelong at her. Her face is stern, dark eyes shaded by her hand. "Before the boggert's done here."

Whatever they were trying to keep from me earlier, it

seems the vai has loosened their tongues and smudged their memories. I stay quiet, plucking what I can from their conversation.

Dash drinks from the bottle, the vai spilling over his chin and dampening his shirtfront. "Four," he says as he lowers the vai.

"I don't like this."

"We all have to do things that we don't like sometimes."

"This is different, Dash. We're not talking about robbing a market barrow or hustling 'ink. You can stop this before it goes further, tell the boggert it's dead. You said you know where—"

"I said I *think* I know where it is. That's different."

"Then you could try to stop it," she says.

"Perhaps." He takes another gulp. "But I'm not going to. We need that power, Lils."

My head is spinning, and I can barely piece the fragments together. It makes no sense. The rest of the Whelk Streeters are also quiet—whether because they agree with Lils or would rather not get involved in the argument, I don't know.

"If you really mean to do this, then I just hope you know what you're doing," Lils says.

"Oh I do," he says. "Don't you worry yourself about that."

WHEN IT STARTS TO GET DARK, we all traipse giddily back home where we carry on drinking in the common room. Every time I look up, Dash is watching me or pouring me another drink. His fingers brush mine as he hands me a bowl filled to the brim with the spice-sharp liquor. It spills over my skin, and I suck my fingers without thinking.

The edges of things are going blurry, colors bleeding into each other. I think it's the poisonink in the tea that's making me react so badly.

"I'm going to bed," I mumble.

"All alone?" says Dash.

I wave off his lecherous comment. "Oh hush, you. No, really, I need to sleep."

"No head for vai," says Lils, who has become more and more companionably intertwined with Nala as the night has settled in. "None at all."

"Poor thing," agrees Nala, and licks Lils just behind the ear.

I watch them kiss in the fatcandle-lit room, distantly jealous.

Dash catches my eye and leans back on his elbows. "Sure you ain't gonna stay up for one more drink?"

"No." I shake my head, and the room swims alarmingly. I must be slightly tipsy, because in the half-light, Dash looks almost pretty. Definitely a sign that this night has gone on long enough. I stumble away from the others, and I'm barely able to unlace my boots before I collapse on my bed.

The soft sound of their voices carries me into sleep.

A FEW HOURS LATER I'm awoken when someone trips over my nest of blankets and lands next to me, laughing and cursing.

"This," Dash points out, "ain't my bed."

"Rather." I shove him with one hand, hoping that he'll roll off the bed and, if I'm lucky, down the stairs too.

"Don' be so pushy, kitty-girl," he says. "I'm trying to get some shut-eye here." He's mumbling and drunk and I do not have time for this. Tomorrow morning I have to be at the Crake by six.

"Gris! Can't you go sleep in your own bed?"

He's already snoring. I sigh, give him a final shove for good measure, turn on my side away from him, and try to get back to sleep.

DASH WAKES ME AGAIN, in the early morning. Only this time it's by nuzzling at my neck. He's thrown one arm over me and pulled himself close during the night. I suppose I should be grateful that he's still wearing his clothes.

"Are you drunk?" I ask loudly.

He stops nuzzling but doesn't pull away. "No. Are you?"

"I'd have to be far drunker than I was last night to want to take you to my bed."

Dash pulls his hand away and half sits up. "It can be arranged," he says, but he's laughing, and for some reason I laugh too.

"Go away," I say, and cover my head with my coat, trying to burrow away from the light.

"Ah, you can't mean that." He sounds like he's amused by me.

"Yes I do. You're pretty and vain, and you think you can get anyone to do what you want. I'm not interested in people like that."

"Pretty?"

"And vain. Don't forget vain."

"I'll do my best not to."

Outside, the terns and the sea mews are calling. It's still quiet though, just the soft rumble of the surf. Pelimburg is asleep. Faint gray light threads through a gap in my curtain and Dash drops back down again.

He's warm.

Would it be so bad to indulge him, to tie myself deeper into the Whelk Streeters? I shiver as he brushes a tendril of hair away from my neck and kisses the skin there. A thread coils through me making me warm and cold all at the same time. I turn over, and he curls one arm under me, sliding his palm down my back. His weight is half on me, and I feel smothered, scared. My breathing speeds up.

I can't tell if I'm nervous.

He kisses down my throat, and the kisses are hot against my skin like sparks blown from a fire. I feel like I'm going to have burns all down my neck, and then those same spots turn cold as he moves farther down. Dash pulls away, easing off me as if he knows that if he doesn't I'll just stop breathing from the sheer overwhelming need that's rising in me.

"You don't have to," he says. "Do anything you don't want, I mean."

But I don't know what it is I want. "I have to get to work," I whisper.

The warmth leaves me as Dash sits up. "Go on," he says. "Get dressed."

The curtain swishes softly behind him as he leaves.

I roll flat onto my back and take a deep gasping breath. Wonderful. It takes a few minutes before I can calm the strange flutter of my heart, and then I head to the little tiled washroom to scrub myself clean in cold water and change into my new blue dress.

When I've untangled my hair sufficiently and brushed it back into a bun, dressed in clean clothes, rubbed skin grease into my chapped hands, and rinsed out my mouth, I feel almost able to face the day. Through the small high window I can just see the sun rising, casting a pale pink glow over the cloudless sky.

To my surprise, when I tiptoe into the common room I find Dash sitting, waiting for me, two steaming bowls of tea in front of him on a cloth-covered crate. He's also toasted some heels of stale bread over the fire and set them on a plate.

"Sorry there's nothing to go with them," he says, gesturing at the chipped plate. "I thought you'd need a bite before you go to work."

"Oh." I sit down, and stare at the plate and bowl. "Thank you."

The tea is chamomile, and Dash and I sit in comfortable silence, drinking our tea and listening to the birds that wheel and dip outside the house. A sea mew lands on a windowsill looking for a handout, and I throw him the last of my crust.

"Now you'll have the whole lot of them here begging," Dash says. He throws a scrap out through the window and the bird catches it in mid-flight.

I leave the house feeling oddly light. Even the prospect of a day filled with washing dishes can't bring me down.

11

WORK IS EQUAL PARTS dull and busy. I wash dishes and dream of sunsets. I think about what happened, playing every word, every touch, over in my head. Can I trust Dash?

I doubt it. And now I have a new worry—what if he finds out about this *thing* I'm meant to go to with the bat Jannik? Gris-damn it all, then he'll really believe I'm some kind of kitty-girl, that I'm selling myself. *He can't find out.* I press my water-wrinkled hands to my forehead and damn myself for a fool. It's too late now to get out of this.

The day stretches on, long and longer, brown-stained teabowl after teabowl. My legs ache from standing, the small of my back throbs in dull agony, and I keep having to stop and press my fists against the hollow there, as if somehow I can knuckle the pain out of my body.

I want to sleep, to go lie down and wake up in my turret room, the servants bringing me tea in bed, warm blankets, goose-feather pillows. I want to be clean, to wear clothes that aren't wrinkled and stained, that don't smell like cheap soap and sweat and tea and fish and grease.

I want to tell Owen that I'll do as he says, marry whoever he wants, as long as I can still have scriv.

Then I think of Ilven's pale face, her hands as she played with that thin ring. In a way, I've done this for her. If I go back now with my tail tucked like a beaten dog and take whatever punishment they give me, whatever husband will have me with my honor in shreds, then Ilven's perfect leap means nothing.

Perhaps what I really want to do is go home to Lils and Nala, to the Whelk Streeters.

Not that I'll be leaving the shop anytime soon since the evening-shift girl is late. Mrs. Danningbread has no one to pick up the slack, and so I have to stay until the flustered girl finally runs into the scullery almost three hours late.

I'm practically crying with hunger. All I've had to eat the whole day is the toast Dash gave me this morning and endless cups of tea. The tea is my attempt to fill the hollow space inside me, and it works. For a short time anyway.

Mrs. Danningbread has left for the evening, but her daughter-in-law, Stella, takes one look at me and sits me down by the tearoom counter. The waiters are clearing a space in the corner of the shop and laying down wooden pallets to make a low stage. I watch them without any real interest, my head cradled in my arms.

"Eat this," Stella says, and puts a plate loaded with scones and gooseberry jam before me. The scones are dry and the jam a little badly set but I don't care. I wolf the scones down so fast that I feel like I've stuffed my stomach with chalk.

Finally, when I've gorged myself so much that I don't think I'll be able to stand, let alone walk back home, I take a look around the emptying tearoom, half hoping that I'll see Jannik scribbling away, his dark head bent over a book. But the poets are gone, most of them, and a younger, smarter, brighter crowd is taking their place.

They remind me a lot of Dash. They are low-Lams, Hobs, and half-breeds, but they carry themselves with a gallant swish, their coats are deep navy or black, and they wear crisp white shirts that wouldn't look out of place in a House wardrobe. Their waistcoats are jewel bright, and some are heavily embroidered with delicate patterns. They're none of them well-bred though, for all their finery. They laugh loudly and shove at each other's shoulders as they tell ribald jokes and off-color anecdotes. They slap the thighs of their tight dark trousers and stamp their high boots.

"What's going on?" I ask Stella as I push my empty plate away. With one finger I press at the crumbs, wanting to prolong the sweetness.

"It's the night crowd," she says, and measures poisonink leaves into an urn. "They're always a bit boisterous on a music night."

The small stage suddenly makes sense. I wonder what kind of music they play—if it's going to be like the street-theater musicals. Curiosity makes me linger. Already it's growing dark out, and the thought of running through Old

Town in the night isn't exactly appealing. Stella shoves a cup of the poisonink tea across the counter toward me and I sip it, watching the crowd.

I'm about to get up to leave before the last light is gone when Nala comes bounding through the door, her red hair in a frizzy cloud around her shoulders. She's wearing a loose dress of faded purple and, as usual, not a stitch on her feet. They are gray with mud splatters.

The boys who greet her with wild hugs and plant overenthusiastic kisses on her cheeks don't seem to mind. She waves them off, still laughing, and then spots me.

"Firell!" She dances through the crowd and takes my hands in hers. "I didn't know that you'd be coming tonight."

"Neither did I," I say.

"Verrel is coming later with Esta and Lils." She claps her hands. "It'll be good, all of us, just the thing to keep Esta from thinking too much."

"And Dash?" *Felicita, you idiot.* I can't believe I'm even asking. My heart speeds up. Too much tea, obviously.

Nala gives me a sidelong look. "Of course he'll be here. We better snag good seats." She grabs my arm and maneuvers me to a table near the stage. I sit down and I relax and let myself forget about Jannik and his stupid intrusion into my life. I'll go to his little party, and then never think of it again.

Charl is working the night shift and he ducks and weaves among the patrons, filling tea orders and selling bottles of brown ale from under the counter. He grins at me and touches my shoulder as he passes.

The Crake is filling up quickly, and Nala stands on her chair to wave Verrel, Lils, and Esta over. Esta is still expressionless, but she allows Verrel to order her tea while the others get ale.

Night falls, and the flickering glow from the outside lamps and the fatcandles on the tables casts everything in oily yellow light. Faces are in shadow, and as I drink the last cold drops of my 'ink-laced tea, I find myself staring at the door, watching for a familiar head of tousled dark hair to appear. The places where he kissed my throat feel branded.

Stop it. Stop looking.

Lils scowls at me and shakes her head. I look down at my empty teabowl instead and let the thrum of noise and voices lull me. I won't look up again, I tell myself.

But, of course, I do.

I can't help myself.

"Another round?" says Verrel as he stands, and I murmur assent along with the others. He flags Charl down, and the sweating low-Lammer nods, tallying the order in his head. When he leaves, Verrel pulls a half-jack of vai from his pocket and grins at us. "Drop of the blood?"

Dash arrives after a long, uncomfortable hour with us squashed together at the table. Esta is still drinking straight tea, but Verrel is happily tipping cheap vai into our empty bowls and bottles when I spot Dash talking to one of his compatriots at the door.

He sees me and raises a hand in greeting, then saunters over to our table. The crowd parts easily before him, and he never has to ask anyone to step out of his way. Sometimes I have to wonder if perhaps Hobs really do have magic of their own.

Nala stands, sending her chair tipping backward. "Look." She points at the knot of people by the makeshift stage. "They're here."

The band sets up, tapping drums and tuning fiddles. A tall, nervous boy is crouched on a stool, bent over his kitaar and strumming it while he fiddles with the ivory tuning nuts. A short girl with dirty-blond hair is sitting on a tall barstool on the stage and drumming her heels against the struts, her right hand shimmering a tambourine against her thigh.

"Have you heard them before?" Dash asks as he squeezes into the tiny gap between me and Lils.

I shake my head.

"They're very good, but I don't think they'll be to your taste."

"What does that mean?"

He leans closer so that his breath is tickling my ear. "Just that it's not the sort of thing you'll find in the ballrooms of House Malker."

"So?" I shrug. "I'm always open to new experiences."

At that he laughs and puts his arm loosely behind me.

I'm not really sure what I'm supposed to do, but no one seems to notice his actions, or they put it down to the room being crowded and not to some strange idea of courtship that Dash—uncultured clot that he is—feels is appropriate. So I settle back with my heavily laced tea and wait as the crowd slowly quiets. His arm is a strange weight, uncomfortable and pleasant at the same time. I round my shoulders and try to concentrate on the band.

The girl on the stage is still gently rattling her tambourine and it fills the suddenly silent tearoom with an expectant hiss. The fiddler raises his fiddle and draws his bow across the strings. The music is slow, sad.

Then the drums come in and the tempo picks up, and the melody becomes a rousing, stomping whirl.

It slows again, and the girl begins to sing. Her voice is soft and the tearoom is quiet quiet quiet. Her voice wavers, then strengthens.

She's singing a song about goodbyes and sunlight. The drummer joins his voice to hers, and they sing the chorus louder, the words strong and no longer sad.

Faster and faster the song goes, and I realize it's about more than what it first appeared. It's about wealth and poverty and injustice, and the tearoom crowd knows the chorus and with each verse more and more of the crowd begins to sing, until everyone is hollering around me and thundering their boots against the wooden floors, making the tables shiver, the teabowls dance.

The words seem familiar, as if I've heard them in a dream and then forgotten them.

Inside me, the scriv from the vai dances too, and the whisper of magic runs through my veins. I shiver. *Gris*, I need this. Even this pale imitation of a scriv-high is enough to make me weep with frustration. The little relief it gives is not a salve, it's a lure.

Dash is pouring straight shots of vai, no longer even pretending to hide the illicit drinking. No one cares or notices. The vai calls to me, pregnant with scriv, promising me power.

I down my shot and Dash pours me another, and another. I lose myself in the swirl of sound, in the headiness of the music and the crowd's reaction. The only thing I wish is that I could hear the singing girl clearly—half her vocals are drowned in the hubbub.

There is a way, of course, and the more I think about it, the better the idea sounds. It's only the smallest of magics, using no heat, and I've enough scriv in my system to do it. I can be subtle—they'll never know it was anything more than the art of the musicians, the strength of the music itself. I look quickly around me, at the rapt faces, everyone singing and cheering. They are focused on the stage.

Satisfied that I'll attract no attention, I reach out with invisible hands and shape the air, making the particles vibrate against one another, and gradually the music grows louder and louder, until the chatter of the crowd is lost under the surge.

The band members exchange confused looks but carry on playing, and the crowd just cheers more, singing until they are breathless. Dash hugs me closer to him with one hand and I hear the whisper in my head like an echo.

"Oh, you are an interesting one, little House Lammer," he says, and I smile dreamily.

Magic.

12

GIDDY WITH VAI AND MAGIC AND MUSIC we spill out into the streets. The night is starry but the streets are wet. A squall must have blown over while we danced and sang inside the Crake. The moon grins down on us, and the stars flash and glitter. Silver light makes the windows gleam, and the shadows are strange and shifting.

Music booms and echoes in my head, although it's been a while since the band played their final encore and bowed to rapturous applause. The buzz of conversation seems stuck in my ears, and the ground feels too rubbery to walk on.

Someone catches my hand as I stumble.

"You all right there?" Dash says, and the laughter bubbles through his voice like sugar melting on a stove.

"I am perfectly," I tell him as I summon deep reserves of dignity, "*perfectly* all right, thank you very much." The words seem to take forever to draw out of my mouth, and I find myself getting bored with the sounds I'm making. With a supreme effort, I concentrate on stopping the buildings from spinning about me and focus on the other Whelk Streeters instead. At least they're *supposed* to be moving.

Lils and Nala are skipping ahead of us. Well, Nala is skipping and tugging Lils along with her. Finally Lils takes a few reluctant, experimental gallops, and the sound of their giggling echoes off the shuttered shops.

At the noise, Esta whoops, and the windows bounce her shout down the narrow alleys. She's smiling and Verrel is hovering around her like a protective older brother. He's nearly twice her height and they make an amusing spectacle.

Dash still has my hand, and he pulls me back to a slow amble so that we fall far behind the rest. "So just what was that in there, darling?"

"Don't know what you mean." The words trip and stumble all over each other, and this makes me laugh again. I imagine each word as a juggler or an acrobat, leapfrogging down my tongue. The rubbish in the gutter bounds, mimicking the thoughts in my head. A crumpled paper ball leaps over a mud-laced leaflet. The leaflet stands on one corner and after a few staggering steps pirouettes after it. Accidental magic. *Just how much vai did I drink?* The papers collapse back into the muck and I frown. Not enough obviously. *I wonder if Dash has any more on him?*

"No, I don't. You drank at least half a bottle," he says.

Oops. Possibly, just possibly, I'm thinking out loud.

"Just possibly," he confirms. Dash stops, and I jerk to a halt. At first I can't quite work out why I've also stopped moving until I notice my hand in his and put two and two together. Happy with my sudden flash of genius, I smile up at him. "I am very drunk," I inform him, just in case he hasn't noticed. "Therefore you must not take advantage of me, because that would be awfully ungentlemanly . . . and . . . and . . . stuff." I wave one hand to indicate the importance of said stuff.

"Hmm," he says, then leans forward and kisses me.

I have never been kissed like this by a boy before. It's different and strange and rather enjoyable. Of course, my only comparison is Ilven and that was tentative and wet. I pull away. The memory of Ilven is salt against my raw skin, and I blink furiously, pushing the image of her white face and the soft brush of her mouth away. There is only Dash here.

"You're not a gentleman," I tell him as solemnly as I can. This is very serious.

"I never said I was, darling."

Oh, right. He's telling the truth. I decide that he can't be all that dreadful if he's honest, and I kiss him back.

I shouldn't be doing this. The ghost of Ilven watches, her face drawn in sadness, her leaf hairpin glinting under the starlight. I pull back from Dash and turn to her. "Go away," I say. She just stares. "Go on! Shoo!" I flap my hands at her memory, and the image dissolves into the faint mist that's creeping in off the ocean. She wasn't really there. I rub my hands over my face, scrubbing the vision away.

Dash is looking at me, head cocked. "And that?"

"Nothing," I mumble, and hug myself against his chest. "Just stupid memories."

"Ah. Those." He nods. "Nothing quite like ghosts for making you feel guilty."

I pull back from him to stare at his face. He is serious, not mocking me at all. Eternity passes. Dash might be fickle, deep and treacherous as the Casabi, but he's also someone who takes care of his own.

This time it's me who presses in for a kiss.

The mist roils up, thick and white, spreading through the streets like a low, clinging ocean of ghosts. It swirls around our legs, making us a little skerry in the street.

"Look," I say as I pull away. The air is cold and smells of salt and fish, but it's a clean smell.

Dash looks down. "There's a tale," he says, "that the whalers tell, about how sea-mist that comes in this far is all the spirits of the dead, looking for the ones they left behind."

I shiver. "Old sea stories." But it's sucked the beauty out of the scene, and now all I feel is cold and wet. There are other stories about mists like this, about how they're portents of the Red Death. "Let's go home."

"I ain't arguing with that idea." He's grinning, the little lech.

We take a very long time to walk back to Whelk Street, kissing all the way, and the others are already asleep by the time we crawl up the stairs, laughing and shushing each other. Dash takes me through to his side of the house, and I realize that although his bed is narrow, you don't need all that much space to do what we do. There are moments when I think I should worry more, or hurt more, but then I touch skin and taste sweat and forget.

I jerk out of my strange hallucinatory world when my fingers brush over a deep gash on Dash's thigh. "What's this?" I ask him. There is blood there, tacky still.

"Nothing." He moves my hand away. "Accident at work." Or at least whatever scheme currently passes for employment in Dash's world. I wonder what tricks and deals he was organizing this time. And when exactly he's going to fall foul of the sharif.

Not long after that, I'm curled up so close to him that we might as well be one person instead of two, and I fall asleep.

"You're going to be late for work," Nala says, far too loudly.

My head aches and my mouth tastes like marsh-rat fur. I sit up and blink in the unexpected light. Belatedly, I realize two things: one, I am completely naked, and two, I am not in my own bed.

"Oh Gris!" I pull the blanket up to my shoulders and look around. Dash's bed, Dash's room. No sign of Dash. A feeling rather like nausea fills my belly, and my face heats. I am revolting.

Nala taps her foot, then her face softens. "You don't take Rake's parsley, do you?"

Gris. No. Another wave of something halfway between shame and terror swamps me, and I feel like crying, only my eyes are too dry and itchy to produce even the smallest teardrop. I huddle deeper into the blankets and wonder if you can fall pregnant your first time, if, on top of everything else

I've managed to do, I'm going to end up like one of those
Hob girls who stand on the side of the road with some scruffy
woebegone brat in tow, begging for a meal. I close my eyes in
horror. "No," I whisper, and feel even stupider for it.

She lets out a long sigh. "And we don't have none. Lils and
I don't hardly need it." Nala holds out a bowl of tea, long
since cooled by the look of it. "Dash left that for you. Drink
up, and then you best run as fast as your legs'll take you before Mrs. Danningbread gets it in her mind to let you go."

A cold wave courses through my body, leaving my skin
tingling.

The tea is lukewarm, and I swallow it as quickly as possible—
anything to kill the taste in my mouth—and then dig through
the debris of Dash's bed for my clothes. I pull my shift over
my head, then pause to survey his domain.

There's still a single book lying near the bed. Curious, I
pick it up. It's an old copy of Prines's *Mapping the Dream*, so
old that the red cover has faded to a dull brownish pink. *The
Dream* is famous, and Prines has the dubious honor of being
a crake worth studying, especially because of his historical
connection to Mallen Gris. But why a Hob would be reading
verse detailing the poet's obsessive and ultimately erotic en-
counters with his House Master's son is beyond me. The language is archaic, couched in layers and layers of metaphor, as
impenetrable as a snarl of fishing line.

I lift the book, and a small folded note drops from the
pages. Dash's name is written on the outside in a neat slanted

hand. An educated hand. I pause, feeling the crinkled edge against my fingertips. *Dare I?*

Perhaps it's some girlfriend; perhaps I am just one of many. I unfold the letter. It's short, merely stating a time and date, and ending with the word *yours*. A jealous heat crawls through me, and the taste of bile fills my mouth.

Hastily, I shove the note back, hoping that Dash won't notice. I need to leave his room.

I've never scrubbed and dressed and brushed powder over my teeth as fast as I do now.

I arrive at the Crake almost a quarter hour late, but Mrs. Danningbread does nothing more than raise one gray eyebrow at me in disapproval. "Get to work," she says, and I slink into the scullery, feeling very achy and miserable and sorry for myself. I keep wanting to spin around and dance, and then five minutes later I want to hurl crockery across the little room. Or do both at the same time. My face is being pulled in two directions: mouth wanting to laugh, eyes burning because I need to cry and I can't.

My head is a giant ball of pain and even though I drink cup after cup of water, I still feel like a sea-sponge left in the afternoon sun.

Who is she? Every Hob girl I've ever seen becomes my rival in his affections. Then again, it need not be a Hob. The writing was educated—perhaps I am not the first high-Lammer to sleep in that room.

The whole morning I try to quash these contradictory

feelings. And I don't know if I want to vomit because I'm hungover like a street-Hob or if it's because I've fallen in some kind of love with one.

The dishes pile up, and I lean against the wall and press the wet cloth to my head. For a moment, my eyes are soothed, and the coolness masks my headache. Except then I'm able to think, and I really don't want to do that.

I drop the cloth. Across from me the whitewashed wall is pitted where the plaster has fallen out in chunks. The brick underneath is cheap red clay. *What am I doing here?* I look down at the cloth, at my hands wringing it over and over. These are not my hands. *This is not my life.*

But it's what you have, a resolute voice says, echoing in my apparently empty skull, *and you'd best make the most of it.*

IT'S JUST AFTER THE ELEVENSES CROWD and before the lunch rush, and I'm slowly cleaning the last of the morning's dishes, when Mrs. Danningbread sticks her head into the back room. "Firell?"

I look up from my dishwater and wipe the hair from my face with raw fingers.

"There's someone up front who wants a word with you."

My heart does a giddy flip, and my skin goes icy. *Jannik.* Gris, I'd forgotten I was supposed to meet him tonight. The last five days have passed in a blur.

Then I shake my head. It can't be that damn bat—he said eight in the evening, and by no stretch of the imagination could late morning qualify.

After drying my hands, I peer tentatively around the doorway. The Crake is fairly quiet at the moment—a welcome lull in the general routine of rushed panic—and my visitor is immediately apparent. Sitting at a table, surrounded by the dragon-dogs she's paid to exercise, is Nala. Esta is with her.

In a way, Nala reminds me of a Lammic version of the dragon-dogs: they are both impossibly thin and long-legged, with long noses and a hunched look to their shoulders. Nala's carroty hair is a bit more orange than the deep chestnut of the dragon-dogs' silky ears, but it's still uncanny. Next to these pale slender creatures, Esta looks dark and out of place. She's lighting matches and watching me with a sullen air as she flicks one after the other onto the tabletop where they smolder out, trailing smoke to the ceiling.

Nala waves at me, as if it is somehow possible that I didn't notice her, and Esta rolls her eyes in exasperation. A day spent in Nala's permanently jubilant company must be rather trying, I imagine, and I give her a sympathetic smile.

Esta sucks her teeth in response and rolls her eyes again.

Fine. I'm not here to make the little brat like me, anyway. "You've come for tea?"

"No, no." Nala swings her dog-walking satchel onto her lap and digs through it. It's stuffed with scraps of paper, nubs of chalk that cover everything with colored dust, various strange shells, a withered stick that looks like it came from a flowering irthe tree, and a large bone with meat scraps still attached. She rummages until she finds what she's looking for, beams at me again, and pulls out a carefully folded fat paper envelope.

"Uh, yes?" I stare at it as she waves it between us.

"For you."

I take it. "Thanks."

Nala looks at me expectantly.

"What is it?"

"Rake's parsley. You'll need to take a double measure every day until you bleed and from then on a single teaspoon every morning. Mind you, it tastes like the back end of a dog." She says this so cheerfully that I can't help but stare at her. "Make a tea, hot as you can, and swallow it fast."

I've heard of Rake's parsley, of course, but have never actually seen it before—why would I have? I can feel my cheeks burning, the blood rushing to my face. Quick as I can, I shove the envelope into my apron pocket.

Nala seems oblivious. "It's just enough for a week, and it's fair brass so that's all I bought. I got it from the apothecary down on Richmond. She's the best for this sort of thing."

I thank her again, the words sticking on my tongue. I am thoroughly embarrassed. Then I wonder—since Nala seems to be somewhat more in tune with all things feminine—if she could help me with one other problem.

"Do you know where I could borrow a good dress, something fashionable but not too expensive?" I blurt out.

"What would you want one of them for?" She squints at me. "Trying to impress His Flashness?"

"No." I twist my hands. "I have to attend a, well, a party tonight, you see, and I need something to wear . . ."

"A party. What kind of party?" She draws her brows together.

How do I explain this one. "A b-bat party." I say the words fast, swallowing them under, hoping Nala doesn't really hear me.

She does. "Oh. You won't need tat too fancy for one of them," she says as she wrinkles her long narrow nose. "I might have something at home that you can use for the night." She gives me a flat look. "Did Dash tell you to go to this?"

Why would Dash send me to a bat party? The question is so unexpected that for a moment I am thrown. The silence is dragging on too long, and anything I say will sound like a lie. "No, um, I was invited."

She shrugs. "Your business then, but I daresay I wouldn't have picked you for one of them."

One of them who? I want to ask her but she's standing now, and the dogs whine and press their long heads against her hands, eager to be gone. Esta flings the last burned match down and follows the pack as the dogs flow out the door in a river of silky white and red fur.

EVEN WITH THREE SPOONFULS OF SUGAR, I can't disguise the bitterness of the Rake's parsley in my tea. Nala assured me that it's best drunk fast and so hot that you burn your tongue. It leaves me feeling even more nauseated and shaky.

Wonderful.

Perhaps there's a way for me to get out of Jannik's party tonight. The last thing I feel like doing now is prancing off with a bat to some demented vampiric shindy.

The fear that he will go to my mother if I refuse overrides

the pain. Above and beyond the shock, the humiliation would destroy her: House daughters do *not* run away, and they especially do not fake their own suicides and then go live with Hobs and half-breeds in filthy squats out on the Claw.

And they never bed Hobs.

Of course, it's something of a lie. I know well enough that the men of the Houses take Hob women sometimes. There are enough of their bastard spawn littering Pelimburg.

I shove my aches and tiredness down into a ball at the pit of my stomach along with the ever-present craving for scriv, and when the second-shift scullery girl comes in, I head home at a slow angry trudge.

Nala's still not back when I get there, but Lils is waiting.

Her face is set in a grim mask, angrier than her standard expression of general irritation at the world. "You're a fool," she says when she sees me. "And you're not the first."

"Explain." I dump my bag down on the floor and go to pour myself a bowl of whatever blended tea is Lils's special for the day. She's got a pot on the boil, and there are tea eggs rolling at the bottom of the murky water. The thought of biting down into an egg just about has me running for the little balcony so that I can throw up. The taste of Rake's parsley wars with the dregs of my hangover. *Never again.*

Lils sighs and shakes her head. "You don't know what you're doing," she says. "Don't be a fool when it comes to Dash."

"I'll thank you to keep your advice to yourself." Anger burns, choking me, and I think about how if I just had the slightest bit of scriv in me, I'd pin her against the wall, let her feel the slow crush of what a War-Singer can do when riled.

"All I'm saying is, don't lose your head or worse over him." Lils pushes past me to check on her eggs. "You don't have the foggiest when it comes to that lad and what he'll use you for."

I take a deep breath. "Your concern is noted." I think of Dash's letter, of how I am far from the first, but I won't let Lils see my fears.

"Don't you get all fancy-Lam on me." She snorts. "It won't stir me none. Don't go thinking you're his and he's yours. There's things you don't know—" Footsteps sound on the stairs and she falls silent. She turns her attention back to her pots and prods the eggs with a wooden spoon.

Nala and Esta are chattering on the stairs. Or, at least, Nala is talking, and Esta is presumably listening. I back away from Lils to go scrub myself clean and await whatever dress Nala has tucked away.

I'm hiding in the washroom when Nala peers around the door. "Do you want to have a look at it?"

I nod. Whatever it is can't be worse than the tat I'm wearing.

It turns out to be a high-waisted crimson gown. Very last season, and the hem is a little ragged. It's been re-dyed at least once but the faint stains won't be visible at night or by fatcandle-light. It's obviously meant for someone a little more bosomy than me, but it's a good enough fit, and at least I have a clean pair of cream-colored stockings to wear with it.

Nala paces before me, looking at me from every angle.

"And?"

"It'll do."

"Now I really feel like a kitty-girl." I look down at the rather-too-gappy bodice.

"Well you're just about halfway there," Nala says. "What about shoes?"

I don't, however, have anything remotely resembling suitable footwear. One glance at Nala's muddied feet tells me that there's no point asking her if she has any shoes that I could borrow.

"Your new boots will do then," she says. "You won't see them under all that material."

The knowledge that I'll be wearing heavy leather lace-up boots with an evening gown of MallenIve silk is somewhat irksome. I don't know what I was hoping for—perhaps my pair of embroidered slippers to rise with the tide and wash up at the doorstep.

I tie my hair up, pinning it in place as best I can. My mouth is full of hairpins, and my speckled reflection looks sallow and ratlike. Before, I would have been powdered and perfumed, my hair done in an elaborate style by the patient fingers of servants. The household crake would have written lines in my honor, my dress would have been new, and I would have been as beautifully turned out as a glass sculpture from House Canroth. And as empty. I jab the last pin in place, stick out my tongue at my reflection, and set to cleaning the grime out from under my fingernails with a splinter of wood. My hands are red, chapped. They smell faintly of hard soap. The creams and unguents in my bathroom back in my mother's house are like phantasmagorical things, little jewel-glass bottles, worth a month's pay for a Hob out here on Whelk Street.

Perfumes and pretty things. I'm reduced to nothing without them. Is that all I am, all I ever wanted for myself? I face the wretch that glares back at me from the mirror. I am more than my wardrobe, more than my family name, more than my mother's aspirations, more than a toy for my brother's whims. The girl gives me a haughty look; it is one I recognize even without kohl and reddened cheeks. It is the look of self-possession. I smile slightly and nod back.

Nala also loans me a black lace shawl. I cover my shoulders and head downstairs looking completely out of place on Whelk Street. The few Hobs I pass whistle and jeer, but I keep my head high and ignore them. It's a good walk back to the Crake, and I'm in a mood halfway between anger and tears when I finally pull up a free chair next to a wild-eyed crake and wait for the Gris-damned bat to arrive. The outside tables have all been lit by fatcandles in little glass cages, and warm orange firelight blossoms over the polished wooden tabletops. Some of the crakes are wearing wide-brimmed hats set with small candles that gutter out in the wind then promptly relight themselves. In this strange fluttering of light and poetry, I wait.

A snatch of rhyme drifts down from a high window. It's the skip-rope song the Hoblings in the street are so fond of singing while they play. Mostly I barely hear the words these days, the taunts slipping over me as smoothly as the finest silk from MallenIve. This time though, they've added a new verse.

> A *corpse for a corpse, the sea-witch said,*
> A *hand for a hand, a head for a head.*
> *Pelim rose and Pelim fell,*
> A *death for a death to end the spell.*

The words are meaningless—children's gibberish—but I shiver anyway, hoping for Jannik to arrive soon so I can leave this place.

The faint chimes of the tower bell are calling out the hour when I spot a black coach rounding the corner of the cobbled street. The six unis pulling it are soot black, their backward-sweeping horns crystal and silver. Even the most demented crake stops whispering to himself when House Sandwalker's coach comes to a halt. I die inside. Everyone is watching, and for days after this they'll be gossiping about some tarted-up kitty-girl getting into a bat coach. I pull my shawl tighter and try to pretend that everything is normal as I rise and walk over to where the coachman is holding the door open for me.

"Are you trying to get me noticed?" I whisper to the dark figure inside. "People will talk."

He smiles in answer, fang tips flashing. "Get in, and then you can berate me to your heart's content."

Impossible damned bat. I sit opposite him, and the coach sets off with a jerk, bouncing so hard over the cobblestones that I'm certain that any moment I'm going to be violently ill. If I am, I shall aim in Jannik's direction. Serve the insolent, grinning fool right.

"Are you feeling poorly?"

I glare at him. House Sandwalker is up in New Town, a hillside villa, so I have at least a good half hour of bone-rattling traveling to endure before we get there. I am not in the mood for conversation. I perch on the edge of my seat and make sure my feet are tucked away under my dress. The only thing remotely comforting about this nighttime ramble through the city streets is the faint tickle of magic that brushes my face. I'm almost tempted to lean closer to him just to feel more of it. *Idiot.* I concentrate on glaring harder instead.

He sighs and leans back against his seat. "It's not that bad."

"And I have only your word on that."

"Come now, Feli—Firell, it's a party, there'll be wine and food and music. Nothing you haven't faced before."

"And if someone recognizes me?"

"The only people who will recognize you are unlikely to care."

A tendril of worry winds its way up my spine. "How do you mean?"

He sighs again and looks out the black window. Vague shapes flit past us, ghost houses and lights. "You'll see."

13

THE SANDWALKER HOUSE CROUCHES high on the slopes of a hillside, looking down over New Town. The stone building faces directly onto the street, and a wide flight of stairs sweeps up to the grand doorway. The marble steps are opalescent, smooth as a fish's eye.

It's vaguely reminiscent of the university entrance, albeit on a smaller scale. Moonvines are growing rampant over the face of the building, although this early in the season the flowers are nothing more than tight green promises.

I imagine that when the vines flower, the whole façade will look like a painting done in a palette of whites and greens. There's an air of cool serenity to it that I would never have associated with the bats.

Then again, what do I really know about them? In Mal-lenIve they are considered lower than gutter-trash, but thanks to the wealth of the three families here, they've been granted citizenship in Pelimburg. It's a cheap, dishonest freedom. All it really means is that the bat House Heads—all three of them—are on the city council and that they and their families no longer have to carry pass-letters and are free to travel at night. Mostly Pelimburg just ignores them, pretending that they are a distant joke told at someone else's expense. The Haner Street Agreement supposedly gives them freedom, but all it really does is make it plain that the bats keep to their own and know their place. Not so very different from before. I suppose we all take what little freedoms we can get. At least now it's an offense to stake a bat for no reason.

"Here we are," Jannik says.

"So I see."

The carriage door swings open to give me a clearer view of the house. I step down, and the house looms over me.

I try to raise my hem as little as possible as I climb the marble steps. Vanity, I know, but I'm inordinately embarrassed by my boots. Another manservant—also a bat, I notice—opens the doors wide as we approach and Jannik ushers me in ahead of himself.

The entrance hall is the exact opposite of the one at House Pelim. Ours is dark and stuffy, but still homey, with umbrellas leaning in muddy piles against the wall and the collection of leashes and rain boots and other tack that seems to accumulate whenever my brother is home making the house smell of leather and wildness. The serving Hobs do clean up quickly, but the house always feels lived in, like a real home.

This place is cold and clean. The walls gleam, and the only items to greet a visitor are a slender plinth displaying a small silver card tray and a pale minimalist flower display. It all seems rather bleak. Jannik leads me quickly from the room, as if he too finds the atmosphere chilly, and we go through a series of rooms and passageways to an enclosed garden. The scent of forced flowers, thin and sweet, drifts on the cool evening breeze.

Distant murmured conversations hum over a sweep of music I vaguely recognize. I think I last heard this piece with my mother when I accompanied her on one of her rare outings to a performance at the Pelim Civic. All I remember was boredom, and a certain resentment at her for paying all her attention to Owen. It was the night he told us that his quiet little wife was with child. A new Pelim heir on its way.

Now the music sounds sublime, seawater rushing over me after a hard day's work. I let it drown me and then realize with a start that Jannik is laughing. I open my eyes.

"All there?"

I don't even know what he just asked me. "So what can I expect at a ba"—I swallow the word—"vampire party?" I probably don't want to know. He did make it quite plain that there would be no other Lammer Houses attending.

"It'll be easier to show you than to tell you," Jannik says, and leads me past a bed of flourishing greenery, down a small stone path to where the party is in progress.

A quartet is performing unobtrusively on a raised stage, and in the clearing, several long couches have been positioned, draped with lush materials. People mill about, dressed in somber finery. Here and there a flash of jewel-bright silk adds a high note.

It takes me a moment to realize that the crowd is all, or mostly, river-Hobs. A few pale-skinned vampires move between them like predators. There's not a single Lammer in sight. I'm the only one here. As I take this in, it becomes apparent that the Hob fashions are rather like my own. They are out-of-date, overdyed to fit the season or to cover fading and wear.

My gaze falls on the occupants of one couch. A bat is feeding off a Hob, drinking from her brown wrist.

No. My stomach turns and I whirl around to face Jannik. "You bloodsucking sack of filth!" It seems that I am learning well from my Whelk Street compatriots.

Jannik closes his eyes. "I didn't bring you here for that," he says without looking at me. His tone is slow and patient, and that only infuriates me all the more. "I have other sources for blood."

"Bats are supposed to feed only on nilly blood—that's part of the Haner Street Agreement."

"*And* any willing donor."

"Semantics—there's no such thing."

"Obviously, your experience of poverty has been cushioned somewhat," he says. "There are many who when offered enough coin will do such things that you would find . . . unpalatable."

Maybe he's right, but how desperate do you have to be to let a bat drink your blood? It's revolting, and my stomach won't settle. It's—it's not allowed, I keep telling myself, even as I remember the Hob girl who dyed my hair. Anja. She had wounds on her throat. And the blood on Dash's thigh. *Dash—*

Bile creeps up my throat and I swallow convulsively. I keep my eyes on my feet, not wanting to look at the scene. If I don't look, I can pretend it's not real.

Jannik sighs. "Would you like a drink?"

Ugh, after last night I really don't think so. "Water," I say. "Please."

"We do have wine. For the Hobs."

"Strangely, I have no desire to drink some barrel leavings you've deemed bad enough to waste on a pack of starving Hobs."

The sound of his laughter makes me look up. "You really know nothing," he says. "My mother would never feed a meal badly. Besides, we own a vineyard in Samar."

Some of the very best wines come from Samar. I'm quietly impressed, not that I tell Jannik. "Perhaps I might have a glass."

Jannik signals to a gray-coated servant, and we are promptly served two glasses of red wine. The color is deep, almost black, like the sea roses that bloom in summer in my mother's garden. I can taste raspberry and sour fig and sorrow. Like the music that swells around us, this wine makes me think of home. My real home.

"So." The wine gives me brittle courage. "If you didn't bring me here to be a meal, why exactly did you invite me?"

Before he can answer, another bat glides up to us. She's tall, and although she looks a little like Jannik, the lines of her face are softer, less angular. She stares at me.

My heart drums faster, and I can hear the blood in my ears. At any moment, she will recognize me the way I have her, and my game will be up. But Roisin merely flicks me a look of bored disinterest, then turns to Jannik. "Moving on, are we?"

"Something like that," he says with a pained smile.

"Mother will be so pleased," she says. "It was an embarrassment seeing you get so pathetically involved with that—"

"Not as pleased as she'd be if you started showing some sign that you were indeed born into the Sandwalker line." He says it acidly, and it is the first time I have heard hatred in his voice. "You can't hope to impress her with nothing more than your talent for perfumes."

While I can still feel the delicate feather brush of Jannik's strange magic, his sister, Roisin, is as dull as a piece of driftwood. It must be a humiliation to both her and her mother, that this exalted daughter is weaker in power than her unwanted brother. That is, if I understand the hierarchy correctly.

Roisin blinks very slowly, and I am reminded of my mother's old cat. I fully expect to see Roisin lashing the tip of a gray tail and flexing her claws. "Enjoy your meal," she says. And then to me, "Perhaps a low-Lammer will be more to his taste."

She leaves us with an imperious sweep of her long skirts, and I turn to Jannik. "She seemed to think you brought me for a reason. So if it's not food, what is it?"

Jannik looks nervous, then tries to disguise it by flicking his long black hair back from his face. "I wanted to talk to you. Since that day we met on the promenade, I've been . . ."—he trails off, looking even more uncertain than ever—". . . in-trigued."

I laugh, and a pained expression flashes across his thin face. "Intrigued?" I take an unladylike gulp of wine to cover my confusion and vague horror. Sweet Gris. What does he mean by that? Surely he doesn't think—

Please not.

"Come," he says, and crooks his arm. "I'd like to show you something."

After a moment's hesitation, I slip my arm through his, and immediately I'm struck again by the peculiar prickling fever of the bat magic. I squint at him, but he doesn't seem to be aware of the connection.

We go back inside, and the music and faint burble of talk fades until we are enveloped in a mausoleum of silence. He leads me into another white hallway, at the center of which stands a huge glass prism lit by fatcandles. Inside is something white draped over a wooden cross. There's a shimmering qual-ity to it and I can't help but feel curious as we draw nearer.

It's a shapeless long-sleeved robe. It looks rough, woven of hair or wool. The shimmer is in the cream threads, some-thing about the way the light catches them.

"Do you know what this is?"

Not a clue. "Am I supposed to recognize it?" I ask him slowly.

"No." He drops my arm. "My mother is one of the most powerful vampires in our race, and her line is the ruling one. This was my grandmother's robe. She was the daughter of a queen, but she had to leave the city of Urlin. There is no robe like this in all of Pelimburg. My mother has it on display here because she likes to remind visitors of exactly who we are."

I knew none of this. To be honest, I didn't even know that the vampires had any kind of culture. I knew they had a city, even half remembered the name. But that was all.

"And despite that," he says, "I am nothing. My brothers are nothing. In Urlin, perhaps I wouldn't have noticed it, would have been content to be just another wray, told what to do, where to go. Perhaps there I would have had a chance to be married off to a lower-ranked feyn." He touches his fingers to the glass. "Here, there's no chance. There are only three Houses, and I am the youngest son. There is nothing for me here."

"You mean what? That you can't marry? If it's so important can't you just ship some feyn or whatever from MallenIve? I'm sure the bats—sorry, vampires—there would leave that swill-pit in exchange for this." I indicate the room with a sweep of one arm.

He shakes his head. "No feyn of available age. Believe me, we have looked into it—searched all the rookeries. Would you like more wine?"

My glass is empty, and I barely remember drinking it. I nod dumbly and set the glass down. We leave the glittering robe behind. "What about . . . Urlin, is it? Couldn't you go there?"

"Without getting into detail, let us just say that with my family name, going back to Urlin could be somewhat problematic."

"So what are you planning to do?"

"Planning?" Jannik raises one eyebrow. "I'm not planning anything. Just like you didn't plan on running away from home and pretending to be dead."

"But I did plan—oh." I touch my fingers to my lower lip. "Is that what you're going to do?"

He laughs. "Hardly. I've no desire to go slumming. As far as my family is concerned, I'm going to stay here and be nothing more than a servant to my sister when she comes into power. I'll age and fade and one day die." He fixes me with a look. "But you have made me think, and like you, I am going to do what I want."

"And what exactly does that entail?"

He shrugs. "Going against my mother, a frightening enough thought in itself—"

A sudden pressure fills the room, like a giant hand has grasped me tight and is squeezing the very breath from my body and turning my bones to a pulpy mass. My hands fly to my skull as if somehow I can press back against the pain building there.

"Jannik." A voice as cold and clean as the house cuts across the room, and we both whirl to face an imposing older woman. Jannik's mother.

The pain drops, and the magic around her becomes tight and controlled. Even so, it feels like the air is trembling against my face, and the hairs on my arms rise. My whole body tingles. I have never felt anything remotely close to this, and wonder and fear make me gasp.

The woman is slender and tall, with thick black hair pulled back in an elaborate fall of pins and curls. Like Jannik's, her nose is sharp and large, but for all that she is a handsome woman, and she stalks forward with the predatory grace of a hunting sphynx. Her white silk dress whispers as she moves. Even though she's not touching me, I can still feel the pulse of her magic hammering against my skin.

Jannik said his mother was powerful, but I had no idea that this was what he meant. Roisin has not the faintest flicker of magic. His mother is a different beast entirely. My heart flutters, and my breath is knife cold. If anyone knew the feyn were like this, the bats would be as good as dead. This is why no one has ever seen the matriarch of House Sandwalker out in Pelimburg. Why all the business is conducted through Jannik's father.

"I've just had a most interesting conversation with my daughter," she says.

Jannik pales. "I meant no insult."

She ignores him, raising one hand for silence. "You would have made me far happier had you been born a girl," his mother says with a distant sigh. "But you were not, and instead I have the shame of a daughter who is barely worthy of the title of our House. And I do not like being reminded of her failings. You will refrain from speaking to your sister again, in public or in private. You will not flaunt your own power in the face of her lack. Is that clear?"

"Quite, Mother," he says, his head bowed so that he will not have to make eye contact with her.

She softens and then for the first time seems to notice me by his side. The ice in her voice thaws. "I'm relieved that you finally deigned to follow my advice, Jannik, dearest, and dropped that little Hob of yours." She puts one hand against his cheek. "It doesn't do to get too attached to a donor. There are consequences. We may not be in MallenIve—"

"I know that," he says. His voice is strained. He grabs my hand, and I can feel the dampness of his palms. Jannik is scared of his own mother. It's not at all reassuring. "If you'll excuse us," he says. "I believe I would like to make sure that my guest is . . . comfortable."

She laughs. "An excellent idea." She drops her hand and Jannik dips a short bow, then pulls me away from her. We leave the room, but I can feel her gimlet stare raking my back as we exit.

"I was rather hoping to avoid her."

"She is somewhat"—I search for an appropriate response—"imposing."

"I think you mean terrifying."

"That too."

Jannik places his hand against an oak door and pushes it open. The room on the other side is small and dark. And occupied. A Hob girl is stretched out naked on a couch, and there's a bat kneeling on the floor, bent over her as he feeds at a bite on her inner thigh. She's particularly beautiful, with a face like an oil painting, all perfect proportions, her skin smooth and shining with a golden warmth. Her hands are

dyed red. She's murmuring a name—the bat's, I presume—
and her crimson fingers are caught in his hair, as if she's trying to bind the two of them together for all eternity.

She opens her eyes, raises her head, and we stare at each
other for one drawn-out second. Her hair is in long thin
braids, her eyes are winter storms. In an instant, we recognize
each other. She's Anja, the Hob who told me to go to Dash.
My mother-of-pearl necklace glimmers on her pale brown
chest.

Before she can say anything, Jannik rushes us out into a
long hallway and up a flight of stairs. I try to stop him, clutching at his sleeve. "I know her," I say.

"So do I. What of it?" He says it in a bitter, angry way, full
of a strange jealousy that I can't place.

I've forced him to stop. Jannik pulls his sleeve out of my
grasp and cradles his wrist against his chest as if he's burned
it. "She's my brother's—" He stops, sighs. "She's not supposed to be here. Mother's told him to—" He shakes his
head and bites down on whatever else he was going to say. "It
doesn't do to get attached," he says, like he's quoting something that has been said to him a million times. He continues walking.

I'm cold, trembling. "Where are we going?"

"Away from the others," Jannik says, then pauses on the
stairs and looks down at me. "No one will come to my room,"
he says. "And I promise you that I will do nothing to you. You
can trust me."

"Like I can trust you not to blackmail me into coming here in the first place?"

He clutches the banister tightly and doesn't look me in the eyes. "You're right." Jannik takes a deep breath, then lets it out slowly. "I'm sorry for that."

"Are you now?" I say archly, but the idiot actually does look fairly contrite and woebegone, like a kicked dog. I follow him up to the landing and down another long passage. We see no one, but it doesn't help. I still have in my mind the image of the naked Hob, back arched, as Jannik's brother fed off her. She knew me. She saw me and she will remember having dyed my hair. My only hope is that she hasn't thought to connect me with the suicide of . . . well, of my former self. Of the daughter of House Pelim. I shake my head and follow Jannik into what must be his room.

He lights fatcandles, and they smoke as they catch. The smoke drifts in oily curls up to the high ceiling then fades. Whatever I expected a bat's room to look like, I don't think I was prepared for how normal it is.

Jannik watches me warily as I look around. I catch his eye and try to reassure him with a smile.

I know that most of the legends about the bats are false. They're as mortal as we are, for a start. The butchering on Haner Street proved that. And the sun won't kill them, although eyewitness reports from that terrible day talk of the staked bats' skin blistering enough to permanently disfigure them.

They've been our monsters in the dark, threats to keep small children on their best behavior. *If you don't do as Mother says, then the bats will steal you in the night and drain you dry.* They are not like us, we say.

But here in this room, I see books I've read and loved and a wide bed so much like my own that I feel the urge to flop belly-down on the covers and breathe in the smell of the sheets and pillows. A feeling of intense homesickness sweeps through me. Longing drags me toward the bookshelf. The nearest book is a fat red-bound edition of Traget's *Melancholy Raven*, a book I can almost recite at will, and next to that is a cloth-covered collection of Aren's *Tales for Children*, the spine worn from countless openings. I reach for it, feel the familiar frayed edges, and pull it out almost without thinking. The book falls open to the story of the little selkie who traded her skin for the chance to be with the Lammer she loved. It's not my favorite—that honor goes to the story about the necklace made of spiders who grew fat on the deaths of the High Lady's lovers—but I smile anyway, to think that perhaps I've stumbled on some secret of Jannik's. That the bat is a romantic.

My mother's voice is in my ears, soft and lullaby soothing, and as I run my fingers under the opening words, I am swept back to a time when my hands were small and my hopes were high and childish. *Once upon a time, there lived a seal-girl. She was the youngest daughter of the king of the Beren Sea . . .*

"Would you still like some more wine?"

I snap back to the here and now. Jannik is holding a glass out for me. I close the book and carefully return it to the shelf. "Why did you bring me here?" I say even though it hurts to squeeze the words out. I want to cry. "Why?"

He sits down on the edge of the bed. "I wanted to talk to someone who wasn't food or family." There's no humor in his thin smile. "I wanted to talk to someone who had enough courage to take what she wanted."

"It wasn't courage that made me run away." I sit down next to him and take the offered glass. How do I explain to a bat that what I've done is so dishonorable that I might as well have truly thrown myself from Pelim's Leap? "It was desperation. I had a vision of a future before me that I couldn't face."

"I do too," Jannik says, and takes a small sip of his watered-down wine. It's like he's trying to compose himself. "And look where I am—too frightened of my mother's anger to even run." He downs the glass. "What is it about you that made you so different from me that you could take that leap and I can't?"

There's no answer to that. "Take me home," I say.

He shakes his head. "I can't now. It's late and I'll have to rouse the hostlers, have them organize a coach and unis."

I frown. I've never given a moment's thought to waking servants at any hour of the night.

"Just sleep here." At my sharp look he laughs. "I'll take the floor, and I'll get you to your job on time. I promise."

"You're full of promises." But the thought of sleeping in a soft bed with warm blankets is appealing. And I understand Jannik now. I'm his symbol of hope, his reason to believe that one day he too can throw off the shackles of his family. "Fine."

He leaves me alone to change into a man's nightshirt that he loans me. While he's gone, I crawl up to the windowsill that runs along the bed and stare down at the empty street. Moonlight thin and weak makes the paved rows look slick. I wonder what Dash is doing now. Is he home? Has Nala told him where I've gone? My body feels empty, achy, and I hug myself tight.

Perhaps he doesn't even notice that I'm not there. Perhaps instead Dash is passing his time with some other.

A sudden flicker of movement in the shadows makes me start. There's someone down there, watching the window. I draw back. "Jannik?"

He peers around the door. "Yes?"

"I—" I wave him over to the windowsill. "Look."

The bat crosses the room, stares out the window. He swallows once, loudly. "Did he see you?"

"I've no idea." Jannik's tone warns me to ask nothing more. He knows who is hiding in the shadows and watching these rooms. Sweat dampens my brow. Could there be sharif watching here? Has Jannik sold me out despite his word?

"Stay here," he says. "I won't be but a moment." He strides from the room.

After a few seconds, I sidle back to the windowsill and peep slyly through the curtains. It isn't long before I see Jannik trot down the wide steps and across the deserted road to where the stranger hides in the long black shadows.

A slender shape moves. The grayness blankets him, making it impossible to see his features, and in the darkness all color is leached from his clothes, his hair, his face. I squint. Jannik is talking, moving his hands. The stranger just stands, slouched against the opposite wall, his hands shoved into his jacket pockets.

Jannik takes a step closer, and then I can see nothing at all of the stranger, hidden now behind Jannik's long coat.

What secrets are they sharing, that they must talk so close?

Finally, their two shadows peel apart, and the stranger walks off. Jannik stands for a while, perfectly still, watching him leave, a slim package clutched in his hands.

I pray that the stranger was no sharif spy.

Before Jannik can return I slip down from the window and tuck my feet under the bedcovers, reveling in the smooth feel of the material against my legs.

Outside, I hear Jannik coming down the hall.

I pull the covers up around my shoulders. The material is soft, and the blanket is stuffed with goose feathers. I feel like I'm being wrapped in safety. This is nothing like my nest of ragged blankets and sacking in Whelk Street. "And?" I say when he enters.

"Nothing."

"Truly?" I can't hide the trembling of my voice.

He looks at me queerly, then shakes his head. "A business deal gone sour," he says, but his face twists, and I don't need to be a Reader high on scriv to catch the lie in his voice. "It's really nothing to worry about." The thin package turns out to be a book, and he slips it casually into the bookshelf.

I watch while he unrolls some winter-weight blankets onto the floor. He leaves the room to change and comes back wearing a nightshirt almost as white as he is. I smile because it looks so normal, so utterly mundane. And then I remember the boggert-soft caress of his strange magic. Jannik is not a Lammer, and he is nothing like me.

I lean forward and pull out the book he returned, as if this will somehow distract me. Or perhaps I just want to see if he will stop me. "You like Prines?" I'm not familiar with it beyond the most superficial level even though it's his most famous work. Indeed, I mostly ignored it because the only people I met who ever liked this particular slim volume seemed to be about one hundred years old. The cover has long since faded from its original red. I flick through the pages. *Mapping the Dream.* I shake my head. Dash has a copy of this. A copy so very similar I could almost mistake it for the same book. I flick through it, looking for a telltale letter.

Jannik winces. "If you'd just be a little more careful," he says softly. "That's a first edition."

I pause with my finger against a page browning with age. The script is ornate, and I realize that this must have been printed on the original House Mallen press. "Oh." I suck in a deep breath. "I'm so sorry." Carefully, I shut it and run my palm ever so gently across the fraying material of the cover.

"I shouldn't have it anyway," he says. "It belongs to my mother."

"So why did you loan it to someone else?"

"I needed to show him something." He laughs at himself.

"You could have used a copy."

"I could have, at that." His face goes calm, and he smiles ruefully. "There's a dedication on the first page."

I open the book, and there, in an elegant sloping hand, is a dedication, a date. It's in a strange language, although as I trace the words, I note a slight similarity to High Old Lammic.

"My father gave that to my mother as a wedding gift."

There's some significance here that I'm not getting.

Jannik sighs and holds out his hand. I pass the book back. "It's priceless," he says. "My father bought it himself."

I shake my head. "I don't get it."

"He was the first wray in his family to buy something with money he'd earned for himself," he says. "It's symbolic."

"So why give it to her?"

He cocks his head. "You don't understand much about people. You just think you do."

"And if you're just going to be insulting, then I'm going to sleep." I huff and drop down, pulling the covers tighter about me.

There's a lengthy pause while I wait for him to say something back, to draw me out, but instead all I hear is the rustling of the leaves outside.

"Good night," he says as I'm about to apologize, and he blows the fatcandles out. The room plunges into an inky blackness.

After a while, when I'm safe under the blankets and the room is filled only with the very faint sound of his breathing, I ask him: "That couple that we saw . . . ?" I hope he knows who I mean, I've no wish to spell out the details. "Is that common? Does that always happen?"

"Are you asking me if I fuck my food?" The words sound overly harsh in the darkness.

"I suppose I am."

The night feels blacker and emptier and he says nothing. The bat is not going to answer me. I turn on my side and pull the pillows into a more comfortable position. The nightshirt and the linens smell like him—it's not unpleasant.

"If I do," Jannik says, "it's only when he asks."

"How reassuring." I'm tired and I speak without thinking. "I hope you pay him extra for it."

There is only silence.

14

THE HARSH *CAWS* of a passing flock of ibis break the morning stillness. I kneel on the bed to get a better look out of Jannik's wide window. In the dawn light I can see over the slate roofs of the houses, all the way to the Levelling Bridge and the wide brown smear of the Casabi. The sky is gray and cool, and there are no clouds. Last night would have been a good night on the boats, and Lils will already be dockside, unloading the day's catch and taking it to market.

"It's early still," Jannik says from the floor. "If you want I can have a servant draw you a bath and find you some suitable clothing."

I can hardly arrive at the Crake to wash dishes in Nala's borrowed dress. "That would be kind of you." The awkwardness from last night is gone. I feel like Jannik is an extension of me, the part of me that stayed home and just dreamed about running away. I peer over the edge of the bed and smile down at him. Amazing what sleeping in a decent bed does for my mood.

"You're entirely too happy in the morning," he says. "I'm afraid it would never work between us. I'm just going to have to deny you your dream."

He's joking, of course, and I lean on my elbows and stare at him. "Heartbreaker."

Jannik closes his eyes. "I know. I'm terrible for it. I do hope you can find it in yourself to one day forgive me."

"Forgive you! Please, I've already moved on. I'm seeing someone."

At that he blinks and sits up. In the early light his eyes are a gray violet, the color of the sea under the moon. "Are you really? Callous little flick."

I GET HIM TO STOP HIS CARRIAGE a few blocks from the Crake. It's not that I'm embarrassed to be seen with him, more that I don't need people asking me uncomfortable questions. Despite that, I get more than a few raised eyebrows when I walk into work.

"Bats, eh?" Charl shakes his head, laughing.

I draw up and begin to answer him stiffly. "It's not what you think—"

But he waves my protests down. "Leave it," he says. "You're not the first to need extra coin, and you won't be the last neither."

None of them will believe me. I drop any attempt to explain myself and just gracefully accept that people are going to make assumptions and that the more I argue, the more it'll look like I'm trying to hide something. It's annoying, but

I picture myself in their places—seeing me leave last night in a bat's carriage—and think about what conclusions they would have drawn. It makes me want to laugh at how stupid I am. Instead, I grit my teeth and head through to the scullery, my joints already aching at the thought of spending all day with my hands in sudsy water.

Gris, this dress. It's stiff against my skin and scratches at the seams. Nala's gown is folded up and stashed away in my bag. There's no way I would have worn it here.

I'm itchy and it takes me a while to realize that it's probably from the starch. This dress must belong to some maid who has long since outworn it. The red dye has faded to brown, and the hem has been let down till it's nothing more than the narrowest seam of material. The bodice is tight and uncomfortable but I'd rather be wearing this than one of Jannik's original offers. Better to wear a maid's tat than to be squeezed into one of Roisin's castoffs and not only look out of place but be reminded of everything I have thrown away.

After lunch, Charl heads through the scullery to stand at the back door and smoke a 'grit in peace, away from the eyes of customers. "You hear about the tide?"

The heel of my hand is rough against my eyebrow as I rub at an annoying itch. There's always tide talk in Old Town, where fortunes and lives depend on the sea. Mostly I barely listen. It was Owen who paid attention to tide talk, who lived his life by the rise and fall of the ocean. "What's it this time?" I ask, only half interested.

"Red Death."

The teabowl shatters against the edge of the stone sink as I jerk back. It's the Red Death that almost wiped out my family's fortunes not that many decades ago. Red Death could bring Pelimburg to its knees. Fish will die, seabirds will die, the tiny creatures that fill the rock pools will die. Everywhere there will be the stink of rot unless the tide moves quickly past. "How bad does it look?"

Charl puffs on his hand-rolled 'grit and frowns. "Not good. It's a big one, and it's set to be a sitter."

Gris damn it all. What use are our few Saints if their Visions can't warn people long before the Red Death comes?

"It's because of those idiot House girls," Charl says. "Suicides and boggerts sucking bodies dry. Red Death means a sea-witch is coming, and all the magic in Pelimburg's not gonna stop that."

"Rubbish," I snap. "Magic is what keeps Pelimburg running."

He laughs. "No one but a high-Lammer would say that. It's fish and copper and tea. Magic just makes things easier."

Carefully, I run my fingers across the bottom of the sink, searching for the broken shards in the gray water. "Without magic, Pelimburg would be nothing but a beach where seals come to pup."

"And mayhap it would have been better that way."

And maybe he's right.

"Do you really think that this means a sea-witch is rising?" I hate believing Hob superstition, but I find myself infected anyway.

"'Course," he says.

"And if magic can't stop a sea-witch, then what can?"

Charl stares at me queerly. "Ah, everyone knows that, girl."

Everyone except me, apparently. "Humor me," I say as I carefully wrap the shattered pieces of bowl in some old *Courants* I find stuffed behind a crate.

"Well, they go as soon as they get what was promised to them. And to do that, you need to speak to the boggert and get it to give you a sign."

I pause, my fingers pressed on the sharp edge of a piece of pottery. "What do you mean?" My breath whistles.

"Sea-witches need sacrifices. That's why they follow boggerts around. They feed on the bodies the boggerts leave behind. But you can get a sea-witch to do what you want provided you give it something in return. Whatever it is you offer has to be marked by a boggert-sign."

"Something—what kind of something?" The words are hard to get out. In the old days, before the Hobs were brought to heel, they used to give the sea a girl and a boy every decade. Maybe they knew something we didn't.

A corpse for a corpse.

Charl stubs out the last little twist of his 'grit. "Tell Dash we're ready," he says. "And all of the Fourth, and Jaxon's pack too. He just has to give the word." He stands and heads past me, back to work.

"I'm not a bloody messenger service," I mumble as he leaves.

Ready for what? I push aside the slow creep of nervous sickness in my stomach. It's probably another episode like the 'ink—sorting and bottling the herb to sell it.

His plan to destroy Pelimburg, of course.

Something's far from right, and it has to do with my House, with Dash, and with magic the high-Lammers cannot control. Fear crackles through me. I shake my head. I'm grabbing at shadows and fancies. Dash is no destroyer of cities. He's a street Hob who sells himself to bats.

I LEAVE WORK LONGING to somehow find an excuse to go back to Jannik's bed. Of all the things I miss, why is a warm, soft mattress so high on the list? After everything that's changed in me, am I still so selfish and so utterly *House Lammer* that I would sell my honor for a chance to return home to my pampered little cage? Guilt floods me, and I try to sublimate the shadowed vision of my mother's face gone gaunt with worry. It stays, so I force myself to think of Dash instead. A thrill of excitement twines itself with suspicions and guilt. My face flushes and sweat dampens my palms. I no longer know what I'm feeling. His Hob smirk fades, is replaced by Jannik's smile, Dash's sallow skin painted over with boggert-white, his gray-green eyes turned indigo and darker than ink.

I laugh bitterly at myself and kick the dry circles of sand on the promenade so that dust puffs up around me.

Go home, Felicita. Stop playing this stupid childish game where you pretend to be something you're not. My family needs me. Surely they will forgive me, erase my disgrace? Things have changed now. If the Red Death is coming, it will cripple House Pelim again, and what will my little blot of dishonor be against that dark mark? They will need me, to sell me off for whatever they can to recoup their losses. The turning of the tide brings a change in all our fortunes, and it's too big a thought for me to face.

I dare a glance at the sea, and sure enough, it's a strange dull color, coppery as blood spilled in a water bowl. The beaches are black with dead fish, and despite my revulsion, I hop down over the wall and onto the flats.

Oh Gris. Already this bad? The air stinks, and the huge sand flies are thick on the fish corpses.

More than a few people are standing about staring at the carnage. The Red Death seems to have caught a shoal of the little spiny puffer fish; they lie on the mud in ranks, like a deflated army.

The mass of the Red Death is coming along the warm Beren current, and it hasn't reached Lambs' Island yet. Maybe it'll break up before it hits the really good fishing grounds out past the island. It's not moving fast, after all.

And perhaps instead the Red Death will poison the city and my family will fall and I will return to them like a portent of change, of good fortune.

And perhaps scriven dust will fall like rain, and we will no longer be at the heel of MallenIve and its mines. I snort and shake my head at my own foolishness.

A group of Hobs are huddled together, whispering. A

snatch of their conversation blows to me on the wind that whips about us.

"—sea-witch."

Of course they'd blame all this on a sea-witch.

"—found another body, caught it in one of the nets—"

Oh. I pick my way past the puffers and the occasional rubbery splat of a dead jellyfish and try to hear more.

"Was clear as glass," says the tallest Hob, her hair ripped out of its bun by the rising wind. Dark curls hide her face. "Some Hobling what got lost in the marshes. Poor mite."

"It's a bad business," says another. He's old, world-weary.

"Damn those stupid Lammer bitches and their fucking Leap." This one's young and fiery, snappy as Dash, as Jaxon, as Charl. "Bringing all their bad luck down on us like a storm."

"True enough," the woman says.

"They'll get as they deserve, you'll see," the young man says, with a harsh fervor that makes the others laugh.

"Oh, what, you've had yourself a Vision have you?" the woman says. "Leave that mucking guesswork to the House Lammers."

The Hob shakes his head. "No guesses," he says. "*I know.*"

I take a deep breath, turn away from the mass of dead fish, and head back home.

THREE DAYS HAVE PASSED since I spent the night at Jannik's house. There's been no sign of Dash, although I passed Charl's message on to Lils, who took it with a grim-faced nod.

I pass my time working. The shop is quiet as the city

holds its breath, watching the Red Death crawl up Pelimburg's beaches.

Whispers are everywhere, passing among the Hobs and low-Lammers and spreading a net of rumors. Sea-witches and sacrifices. The skip-rope chants around the city grow more menacing, more superstitious. If I see Hoblings at play, jumping in time to their songs, I detour to not hear what fresh insult they've added to their list against my House.

I've heard nothing from Jannik, and he and Dash war in my mind, their faces overlapping. Which of them can I trust? Both? Neither? As I dawdle home from the Crake I think of the bat feeding on the Hob, of her legs splayed, and of my late-night conversation with Jannik.

It's hard to picture him doing that. He seems so . . . controlled, studious. I have an easier time imagining him filling in account ledgers than giving in to any kind of passion. Maybe he was just trying to shock me. Testing our boundaries. I shake my head. No, Jannik doesn't . . . do that with his food. He can't. I will it not to be.

A wind comes off the ocean, heavy with the smell of decay. The heat is rising, and it isn't long before the beached fish and dolphins go off. Some ill-dressed Hobs are trying to scavenge what's washed up—they're desperate.

I walk faster and keep my eyes down, not wanting to look at the miasma of sand flies cloaking the carcasses down on the flats.

Quickly, I turn onto Whelk Street, and relief sweeps through me as I enter the familiar front door. From the bottom of the steps, I can hear raised voices and a strange, repetitive thumping. Frowning, I put one hand to the rickety banister and make my way up.

My heart skips. It's his voice. A flush of terrified excitement fills me, even though I try to tamp it down with my anger. I can't. *What about the letter-writer, Felicita? Stop this, stop acting like a lovesick nilly.* I want to see him, and only now do I realize just how worried I've been. I bound up the last few steps, trying to stop the stupid smile that I'm certain must be plastered all over my face.

Dash is lying on the floor of the common room, giving orders to the rest of the Whelk Street crew, Kirren curled against his chest and licking his face.

The floor is covered with planks of wood, smelling of sawdust and sweet sap. It's a fortune in building supplies, and Lils, Esta, and Verrel are building partitions across the rooms to replace the makeshift curtains. Verrel is working with a speedy assurance, hammering joins together with hardened wooden pegs. The other two are holding what they're told to hold and generally just being the dogsbodies.

"What's going on?" I hiss at Lils as I dump my shoulder bag in a mostly clear corner.

"Dash wants the building fixed before it falls down on our heads," she says with a shrug. "Wants to protect us or some rubbish like that."

"Protect us from what?"

"That I'd love to know. But the daft wanker seems to think that if he's not here every moment of the day, then the whole lot of us will just wither up and die without his flash presence. Thinks we don't know how to take care of ourselves." She glares in his direction and then passes a handful of sharpened pegs to Verrel, who pounds them into a nearby beam. "I'll show him someone who can't tell his arse from his elbow, I will," she mutters.

Dash seems oblivious to our conversation, his face slack. He looks dreadful. I kneel down next to him and cock my head until he focuses on my face. There are dried stains on his collar and vest, and he stinks of sweat and must. Blood and 'ink.

"Dash?" It's been so long since I've said his name aloud, it feels awkward on my tongue. "What—are you all right?"

"Hello, love," Dash says when he finally sees me. I twist my hands. He's never called me that. It's always "darling," or my false name said with an ironic grin.

His eyes are glitter bright. "You can start on the tea so our hard workers here can have a bite of summat soon as they're done, yeah." He lifts his hand and tries to stroke Kirren's ears but his coordination is nonexistent, and he misses the dog and hits himself in the face instead. "There's a good lass," he mumbles as I shake my head in exasperation and go to fill the tea urn.

He's either very drunk or very high. Or possibly both. Whatever it is, I decide that there's no way I'm putting any poisonink in the tea, and instead I brew up a mix of dried chamomile flowers, redbush, and honeybush.

"That's as much as we can get done today," Dash says, still

lying on the floor. "The light's failing." Lils helps me sit him up against the wall and we hold his teabowl for him until we're certain he's actually going to get the tea in his mouth. Then I pull her into the washroom.

"What's going on?"

Lils twists her fingers. "Came home like this 'bout an hour ago. Wasted." She lowers her voice. "Crying too. Got him cleaned up a bit before Charl and his lads came through with all their wood and whatnot. Can't have them seeing him that mucked." She looks furious for a moment. "Don't know what His Flashness is thinking, wasting brass like that."

By now, of course, I have an inkling of an idea concerning where Dash goes to get his seemingly limitless funding. I have a vision of him lying naked under a bat while it feeds, and I shake my head. I can't be totally sure of that.

The getting drunk part isn't *completely* unheard of.

"Crying?" I ask. "Is—is that normal for him?"

She shakes her head and chews at her bottom lip. "I don't like this none," she says in her dark growl. "Never ever seen him this bad. If I din't know better . . ."

"What?"

Lils shakes her head again. "He's acting like a girl what's been thrown over by her boy," she says. "And that's not like him. Not at all."

We go back into the main room. If he really was crying earlier, there's no sign of it now. Kirren is curled on his lap, tail thumping against his thigh, and Dash is drinking the tea with a steady concentration.

Nala has returned from work, and she's sitting next to him, playing with the dog's ears. She looks up as Lils and I enter the room. "Dash says we're none of us to go into work tomorrow."

"Does he now?" Lils walks over to the tea urn and pours Nala a bowl. "Why's that?"

"Because," he slurs, "I have plans."

"What kind of plans?"

"Surprise ones." He shoves the dog off his lap and tries to stand, clutching at the wall. "Another body went and washed up on Harriers Beach, just past the point."

I clench my fists. That makes three now: Rin, the marsh Hobling, and this latest one. And the Red Death has brought fishing to a standstill. Anything that can get out of the water is moving onto the land. There's a glut of crayfish on the fish markets, and the selkies have disappeared, headed out for clean water, distant beaches. House Pelim, with its—*our*— reliance on fleets and fishing, is one of the hardest hit.

"Another body?" Esta drops her bowl. "Like Rin?"

Dash nods, still leaning against the wall. He looks like he's about to fall over. That or be violently ill. "And the look-fars have seen sea-drakes," he says. "Ill current is bringing them to the city."

Not a good sign. Not at all. They can't be too close to shore, otherwise the alarm horns would have been blown, but it's still worrying.

"How many?" I ask.

He shrugs and almost topples to the floor.

"Come, you." Lils grabs his arm. "Nala, give me a hand here, will you, love?" She turns her attention back to Dash. "You're going to go sleep this off," she says. "And that's a Gris-damned order."

He doesn't argue, just lets the two girls walk him to his room. From behind the new wooden wall I hear him say, "I mean it, girls. Every one of yer is coming with me tomorrer."

I glance across at Verrel, who merely shrugs in his un-hurried way. "We do what he says."

"Do we?"

"Some of us owe him a little more loyalty than you do." He leans back with a sigh, and I wonder what exactly it is that Dash is up to.

Should I have offered to help him to his room? I don't truly know my place in this world, and sometimes when it seems I'm standing on solid ground, I sink into marsh mud and have no idea what I'm supposed to do.

I step toward the makeshift door, meaning to go after them, but then Nala and Lils are already out of Dash's room.

"Here," says Lils, grabbing my wrist and stopping me from going in. "Let's make a bite to eat. You must be starving."

"She's not the only one," Verrel says.

They close around me, dragging me to the little stove and its boiling water.

"Tea eggs," says Lils. "That's all I've got the energy for after dealing with that mucker."

I glance back at Dash's door. "Is he going to be all right?"

Lils pauses and gives me a strange, soft look, full of pity.

"Don't you worry about him," she says, then looks at the floor. She shakes her head. "You poor daft girl." The words are whispered, exasperated.

My cheeks burn, and I bite the tip of my tongue. That look—her eyes are too full of knowledge that I don't have—and the weight of her pity smothers me. I go help with the eggs and say nothing more.

I'M AWOKEN BY A FAMILIAR HAND on my shoulder and the smell of fresh tea and toast. "Rise and shine, darling," Dash says. I'm still grumbling into my thin pillow when the rough blanket lifts and cold air blows across me. A moment later, the cold is replaced by the warmth of a body pressing against mine. Dash kisses up my neck, pulling my hair back and coiling it loosely in his fist. Sleepily, I turn and kiss him back. He's clean, smelling of the hard green soap we all share. His hair is still wet, fine drops dripping from his curls. I let him push up my night dress, and I cup my hands around his face.

Dash tastes like tea and tooth powder, and his tongue is soft against mine, making me moan in sleepy happiness. His body shifts and I feel his full weight on me. As I run my hands down his face and neck so that I can unbutton his shirt, he catches my fingers in his.

Bite marks.

"It's nothing," he says.

He tries for nonchalance, but it's too late. I've already felt the scabbed-over gashes at his throat where some vampire has bitten into him. So now I know for certain. Like me,

Dash has gone to one of Jannik's parties. Unlike me, he's let one of them feed off him for a handful of brass. These are new, the scabs still pink and soft.

"Who?" I manage to ask. The heat in my belly slips away, replaced by a cold liquid knowledge. I know the why of it—it's about coin, as Jannik so clearly pointed out to me that night.

He pushes himself up on his palms and squints at me. "Does it matter?" he asks me softly, after a long pause filled only with the distant soughing of the waves.

I nod, not trusting my voice.

He settles back down, burying his face against my neck. I wait, still holding him lightly. Eventually he says, "No one you know," and I make a choking noise, half sob, half laugh.

I picture Jannik. "When?"

He shrugs. "What does it matter?"

I turn my head, pull away from him, and press one fingernail against the fresh scabs so that they break and a trickle of blood runs down his neck. He doesn't flinch when I do this. Instead he laughs.

"It was a goodbye present," he says, but he's not talking to me.

I watch the blood run thinly across his skin and try not to think.

"I have to go wake the others," he says, and the warmth leaves me. After he's gone, I lie in bed watching the spiders on the ceiling while my tea cools. It's before dawn, and the room is shadowed with blue and gray. Outside my little nook,

I hear the grumbling of the others as they wake, the clink of teabowls, and the ever-present screaming of the sea mews.

With a reluctant sigh, I push off the covers and rise to meet the day.

The others are bleary eyed, and I stumble past them and help myself to more tea, avoiding all eye contact with Dash. For some reason I feel embarrassed by their knowledge of my relationship with him.

"So what's your grand plan then, master Dash?" says Lils. We're eating a quick breakfast of eggs and toast, and the sun is just beginning to tinge the horizon. I lean back and set my teabowl down. I'm rather interested in the answer myself. It had better be good if there's a chance I'm going to get fired over it.

Dash catches my look of irritation and winks. "Well," he says, and straightens his waistcoat, "it's a spring low, so we can mostly walk to Lambs' Island."

Everyone is silent, then Lils says to him, "You're a right mucking chancer, you know that? What if we're caught? You got a taste for iron pliers all of a sudden?"

"No one will be caught. I've paid off the look-fars." He stands. "Now, everyone get a move on. We need to bring back as many mussels as we can carry before the Red Death hits the island."

Lambs' Island is forbidden. Once, years ago when we still traded with the Mekekana nation, it was the only place that they were allowed to land their bug-ships. Since the war, and since the War-Singers of MallenIve and Pelimburg stood together to destroy an attacking Meke fleet, we've seen not a breath of them. Lambs' Island has been abandoned, the old iron warehouses crumbling into the sea and the traders' villas left to the lizards and the seabirds. No one goes there. We are magic, and the Meke are not; our worlds will not meet on friendly terms again.

On days when the tide is at its lowest, there's a broken causeway that extends from the tip of the Claw all the way to Lambs' Landing. Parts of it are difficult to cross, and you're bound to reach your destination wet, but that's not what keeps people away.

"What about the Meke ghosts?" I ask.

Dash just laughs at me. "That's a rumor spread by the Houses. There are no ghosts on Lambs' Island."

"How do you know?"

"We've been there before," Lils answers for Dash. "He's right. There ain't nothing there but broken-down buildings and blue mussels as fat as your fist. We bring enough of those back, we'll make a mint at the market. Especially now."

The others nod. Shellfish are scarce now with the bad tide, and they seem to think the rewards outweigh any risk.

Faced with their certainty and the knowledge that, thanks to Dash's connections and vai, the House look-fars in the towers won't report us to the sharif, I take the tightly woven straw bag that Nala holds out to me. The other Whelk Streeters trip downstairs, chattering softly to one another as they go. Kirren runs under feet and between legs, making even sullen little Esta laugh. Dash stays at my side, keeping pace with me as we make our way to the rubble-built causeway.

THE SUN IS WELL OVER THE HORIZON by the time we reach the island. Kirren is wet and happy, bounding along the sandy beaches before racing back to Dash's heels. The air is clean, unspoiled by coal fires or fish markets or the mess of city stink that infuses everything in Pelimburg. I take a deep breath, filling my lungs with the sharp taste of it. The sea here is still green and gray, untouched by the distant spreading mass of the Red Death.

"Here's a good lot!" Lils yells from one of the tide pools. I join her and Nala, pulling the fat mussels from the rocks. Tugging them free is hard work, and sweat trickles down my brow and back. It doesn't take us long to fill all the sacks we've brought, and then we tie them tightly and set them in a shallow tide pool to keep the mussels alive.

As I'm tying my hair back again after it's come loose in the wind, I spot Dash climbing the rise of the hill to where the Meke's long-abandoned lighthouse stands. It's weather crumbled and stained white with guano. Scores of birds are wheeling around the tower. Among them are the large black-winged shapes of the sooty albatross; I've heard enough Hob talk to know they believe that these birds are the ghosts of the drowned.

No they're not, I tell myself firmly. They are birds. Live birds, who squabble over the fish guts sailors throw overboard.

Silently, I follow Dash up the low hill, keeping him just in sight. The air has chilled, and I shiver in the breeze whipping off the ocean. Maybe Lambs' Island really is the home of ghosts. If there's a boggert feeding off the Hobs, then perhaps it's here now, watching us.

Dash disappears over the crest of the hill. I lift my sodden skirts and climb faster.

At the rise, I pause and look down. He's making his way to a protected little bay, just a narrow tongue of sand between black rocks. The sun bites into my eyes and I squint and shade them so I can see better. A few minutes later he's crouched on the sand as if he's waiting for something.

The sea laps at his feet. His mouth is moving, but I can hear nothing.

He's been still so long that eventually I tire and sit down cross-legged among the wax-berries and aloes and the ubiquitous sea roses that shed their wide black petals like old blood. I should leave him to whatever he's doing and head back to the others, but something keeps me watching.

And I am rewarded.

A sleek head rises from the waves, her blond hair plastered back. There's something familiar there, but I'm too far away to see the face clearly. The girl, pale and silvery as a fish, stays in the shallows, the foam swirling about her feet. She takes Dash's hand, and he talks.

I want to know what it is he's saying, but there's no way for me to move closer without him noticing me.

The girl listens and then nods, but she doesn't let go of

Dash's hand. He has to pull himself free. She bows her head, her fingers tearing something from her hair. It flashes silver and green, bright as new leaves, and she holds it out for a moment before dropping it in the sand at Dash's feet. It blinks there.

She says something more, then lets the tide pull her back out into the water, back under. Dash watches her sink before he bends to pick up the thing on the sand. Quickly, he tucks it into his pocket and stands.

I crawl backward, out of sight, and run down the hill before he can see me.

Lils, Nala, Verrel, and Esta are lying stretched out in the sun like basking seals. Esta gets up as I approach and toes Verrel in the ribs until he rises and follows her off across the sand. Lils props herself up on one elbow and scowls at me. In contrast, Nala laughs and pokes Lils in the side.

It doesn't take long for Dash to join us. I pretend to have seen nothing.

We lie on the beach near the shadow of the old lighthouse, watching the clouds scud across the sky and the little pale crabs ghost-walk between strands of the beached seaweed. Dash pulls a bottle of vai from his leather rucksack, and that elicits a ragged cheer from the others. My body is dry for magic, begging me to indulge once again despite my last hangover.

"Not for me, thanks." I push the bottle gently away, hard as it is to resist its allure.

"You should, you know."

"Should what? Get drunk on a beach just before walking

back in time to beat the tide?" I laugh and throw a piece of driftwood for Kirren. He brings it back to me, his hot breath warming my fingers as he snuffles the bleached wood into my hand. I scratch behind his ears and throw the stick again.

"I promise you, it'll make the return journey much more interesting."

"I'll just bet."

Nala takes the bottle from Dash and swallows deeply before handing it to Lils. They're drinking fast, giggling and leaning against each other. Off in the distance, Verrel is helping Esta build a bonfire on the beach.

"What is it with Esta and fire, anyway?" I ask. "One day that girl is going to burn us all while we sleep."

"Well, we won't be the first," Dash says. He grabs the bottle back from Nala and drinks. This time I give in and take it when he offers. As he passes it over, I spot an opalescent mark on the palm of his hand. The skin looks puckered and tender.

"What do you mean?" I shiver even though it's warm here in the spring sunshine. Esta whoops as the dry branches catch.

"Our dear little Esta and her brother escaped from their father by tying him to the bed and setting him on fire one night."

I'm horrified. I stare at her. She's so small, delicate-looking, and with her selkie-dark skin she looks like a fragile sculpture carved from the glassy black rocks that sometimes wash down the Casabi. "And her mother?"

"Her mother was a selkie. She got back her skin while her husband burned and headed straight for the sea."

And here I am, feeling sorry for myself because of the choices I've made. An angry guilt moves me, and I drink deeply. The strong spice washes the sour sick taste from my mouth, and already I can feel the scriv drifting through my veins. So very little, but it's a drug, and my nerves are screaming for more.

Something must show on my face because Dash is looking at me queerly. "He was a hard bastard, their father. And I know the type, my own da was the same." He shrugs. "There's some who deserve to live and some who don't. The world wasn't going to miss him. Esta did what everyone else in her family was too damn scared to do." He sounds like he respects her ruthlessness. "She did what was right."

"Verrel said that he brought her and Rin to you."

"About three years back now. Lils was less than impressed at the time."

"Shut up," says Lils. "You didn't give me no warning. It was you I was pissed at, not the mites." She looks at me. "You never saw children so angry and scared. Gris knows what their da did to them, and there was no way they could follow their mam into the sea." She shakes her head. "Half-breeds, always getting the worst of both. Took months for the bruises and burns to fade."

"And the sharif were looking for them," Nala says softly, drawing shapes in the sand with her finger. "That was a bad year. I don't think they left Whelk Street for that whole time. Dash was always bringing them back treats, and Verrel would try to cheer them up with his stupid songs."

"And half our money went to paying off the bloody sharif," Lils says. "And hiring chirurgeons. And then paying them off so they wouldn't talk none."

Dash shrugs. "It was worth it."

"For Esta and Rin?" Lils says. "Or for you?"

"Oh, always for me, of course." Dash grins. "All my love for my fellow man is long since used up."

Lils snorts and drinks deeply. "Wasted it, did you?"

"You bled me dry."

"Shut up, you."

"Tossing me aside for some skinny redhead . . ." He's still grinning, and I take this to be some kind of long-running joke between them.

Nala punches him in the arm. "Skinny redhead? I'll show you skinny redhead," she says, then collapses against him in a fit of giggles. She looks up, squinting against the sun. "Weather's going to change soon," she says. "Best get this over with." Nala clambers to her feet and waits.

Lils says nothing. Instead, she traces the edges of the picture Nala has drawn in the damp sand. With her dark expression gone tight and a little frightened, she allows Nala to pull her up.

"We're going to go swim," Nala says, tugging on her lover's hand.

There's no need to talk. I sit next to Dash, drinking with him while we watch the two girls pull off their dresses and wade out into the shallows wearing nothing but their bloomers and shifts.

"How far are they going?"

Dash moves closer to me to take the bottle. "Until it's safe." Heat radiates from him, and he smells like salt and dune sage.

I frown. The two girls are far out now so that just their heads are bobbing at the surface. Lils's is dark and small, with the bun pinned tightly at the base of her skull, and Nala's wild cloud of hair is slicked back with seawater into bloodred tendrils. For a moment, she reminds me of the pale girl in the water—they have the same fine bone structure, the cheeks and jawline of House daughters. She reaches out with her pale hands and undoes Lils's bun.

The wind changes and I feel a shiver of terror, remembering:

the bat feeding at the Hob's thigh Jannik's mother pulsing with stomach-churning power the long giddy drop down Pelim's Leap as I tossed my shawl and shoes into the surf Ilven's face white and pinched the last time I saw her after her mother had announced her betrothal the taste of her breath in my mouth, sweet with sugar and scriv and fear

Then the visions fade as Lils leans back and lets the water cover her hair.

"What—?"

Dash grimaces. "That's our Lils. It's only safe for her to let down her hair where there's no people, and where there's salt water to wash all the nightmares out."

"What are you talking about?"

He looks at me sidelong. "Lils is a throwback, a Hob with magic. She can trace her family line back to MallenIve, and to the opening of the Well."

The Well: root of all the magical disasters that befell our country. The magic unleashed by House Mallen that day warped the living things around it. There were patches of fallout that made Hobs and Lammers and animals of all kinds turn strange, some bodily, others magically. Most of the tainted survivors were killed, although some escaped—like the unicorns and the sphinxes who took to the red sands of the deep desert. Even the nixes and selkies fled for the safety of the sea and the treacherous Casabi. Few magical Hobs managed to evade the later purges led by the Great Houses.

Dash carries on talking with a kind of fierce wistfulness. "As long as her hair is coiled up tight the nightmares stay where they are. Her family was able to hide the children who were born with the nightmares by catching them young and keeping their braids tight. No one ever caught one of the dream-children."

I stare at Lils with faint horror. "If the sharif find out about her, they'll have her destroyed."

Hob magic—like all things from the Well—is too un-predictable. Dangerous.

We do not allow it.

I take another gulp of vai from the almost-empty bottle.

"The sharif won't find out," he says.

"You're going to make sure it never happens, I take it?"

Dash nods, then throws a handful of sand at me. Without thinking, I let the scriv boil up through my center, turning the air solid and thick, leaving the sand hanging in a shimmering curtain between us.

"Shit." I let the sand drop and it hisses as the grains land. Cold rushes over my skin.

"Got you," he says. "There's no denying that little game." Dash grabs my upper arm and tugs me closer to him. "What House, Lammer? And the truth this time."

I swallow hard. "Pelim."

He lets go of me. "So you're the other dead girl."

There is nothing I can say. He's going to send me away, send me back to my family. I can't face that, and my throat goes thick with tears. What will they do when I arrive on the doorstep, stinking of Hob and sweat and tea eggs? I should have stayed, should have taken the bit like a well-trained uni and let them marry me off to whomever they liked. At least I'd still have a home and a future, even if I had no dignity.

The last thing Dash will want in his life is someone like me. Or worse—now that I know about Lils and her illegal magic, he could kill me and bury my body here where no one will ever find it. It's not like anyone will be looking for me.

Fear makes it impossible for me to face Dash. All I can think of is the ways he could destroy me.

So I'm not expecting it when he leans in, tilts my chin up, and presses his mouth against mine. It's a very gentle kiss, soft and sweet. He pulls away. "You can trust me, Firell," he says. "I keep all the secrets for everyone."

"It's Felicita."

"Not anymore."

The cold leaves my skin, the fear dissipates. I'm his, part of the Whelk Streeters, and nothing will ever break that. My past slips from me like a shawl in a strong wind.

A shout from the water makes us both turn. Circling Nala and Lils is a group of bobbing heads. Esta shrieks, drops the stick she's using to prod at her fire, and runs fully clothed into the ocean.

"Selkies," I whisper. They tend to keep to the deeper waters or to only come ashore as seals. It's too risky for them to show their true selves. The selkies come up out of the waves, slender and dark and beautiful.

"Sweet Gris." I've never seen a selkie up close before, but the legends are true. A man could lose his heart and head over them. Then one bows down to hug Esta close. Even from where I sit I can see the way the selkie's grief twists her face. Esta is crying too, great sobs that rack her slight body. It's as if all her sorrow for Rin is finally being unleashed. When she's done, I think she will be left as light as a rag.

"You knew they'd be here. We didn't come here for mussels or—" *The girl in the water.*

Dash shrugs again. "I knew there'd be a chance," he says. "The look-fars told me that they'd spotted selkies out past the island."

The selkies crowd around Esta, enveloping her, touching her short hair and stroking her face. I may not have known Rin, but the sight of their sorrow punches me, and I choke down my sadness. If all I can feel is the very fraying edge of their grief, then I do not want to think how dark the center must be. It makes me think of how my own mother must be mourning me.

Nala and Lils skirt the selkies and come to join us, Lils busy pinning her dripping hair back up in a tight coil. Before she does, I can see that it hangs almost to her hips and I wonder what would happen if she had to cut it off:

Would the dreams inside her be free to touch all of Pelimburg and drive the city mad?

15

WE RETURN FROM LAMBS' ISLAND, sacks heavy, sand in our hair, vai on our breath. Esta is dancing along the causeway rocks with no care for the slippery seaweed or the crunch of periwinkles under her bare feet.

I've never seen her so happy. For the first time, she looks her age and not like a dour little midget. Dash holds my hand the whole way back, and Lils and Nala help each other over the rocks, laughing as the wind whips their wet shifts around their legs and snags at the finest tendrils of hair worked loose from their buns. The tickle of dream-miasma from Lils's few loose coils is barely a feather brush against my thoughts, lending the day a hallucinatory feeling, like I've been drinking 'ink-laced vai by the gallon.

"You'd best watch that hair, Lils, darling," Dash yells at the two girls. "It's drying."

Lils pauses to twist the stray wisps into thin braids, and Nala helps her pin them tightly into her bun. They look like ghost girls on the rocks, with the sun low on the horizon and the Red Death staining the far waters behind them.

I turn my body closer to Dash and let his warmth soak against me. He makes a very comfortable windbreak, and I smile as he hugs me tighter against him. He's keeping his wounded hand tucked close against his side, and I keep pushing down the questions I want to ask him. Something's not sitting right, but the thought in my head is too crazy, too huge and ugly for me to face.

She looked like Ilven. Just for a moment. For one stupid terrible moment, I thought Ilven was alive.

But she's not, and the only way I would see her now is if she were some shade from nightmare memory. Ghosts are lonely creatures, sometimes merely echoes, but other times they are more willfully destructive—stupid things clinging to life, filled with refusal to accept death. Ilven would never be so gauche.

By the time we reach home, the vai and the dreams and the exertion have taken their toll, and it's all I can do to get undressed and curl up in my bed before I fall over.

As I battle to keep my heavy eyelids open, Dash kisses my shoulders and tells me to trust him.

IT'S EARLY MORNING, and the others are still sleeping off their hangovers. We're standing on the little balcony among the buckets of cold rainwater, just the two of us.

"Morning," he whispers to me, as if we had just met on

the street. Then he grins. It's very awkward and shy—so very un-Dash-like. "There's something I want to see," Dash says.

In answer I pull my blanket around my shoulders and hop from one painfully icy bare foot to the other. "I'm freezing to death," I point out through chattering teeth.

"Unlikely weather this time of year. Cold winds coming off Lambs' Island." He frowns.

A shudder runs down my spine. "You dragged me out here at dawn to chat about the weather?"

"Not at all." Dash squats down by a bucket of water and stirs it thoughtfully with one finger. Then he reaches into his jacket pocket and draws out a folded paper packet. "Take it," he says. "But be careful."

The paper is tightly twisted at both ends and smaller than a package of headache powder. With shaking fingers I un-screw one end. A fine smear of grayish powder is gathered in the crease. Longing courses through me in a wave of heat, unexpected and strangely welcome. "Where did you get this?"

"I have contacts. Take it."

"Now?" I can't believe that it's actually there. It must have cost Dash a fortune. Just the bribes alone he would have had to pay the dealers to convince them to sell to him . . . I take a deep shuddering breath.

"That's what we're here for." He sits down cross-legged, his back against the house, and watches me.

I take the pinch of scriv and breathe it deep. Instantly, I

feel whole, Lammer, myself. Magic snaps around me, the call of power. This is more scriv than I've taken since I left home. A glass—even a bottle—of vai pales in comparison.

For this, I would go back. I swallow and close my eyes, letting my body remember the balance, finding the scriv-tripped center within me. No more thoughts of going home. I concentrate instead on feeling the scriv activate my magic.

There. I open my eyes and the whole world is clearer, sharper. Dash is somehow more real, and around us the air is a living thing, a veil for me to manipulate.

"Working?"

"Yes." I breathe the word out.

"Good." He folds his hands and says nothing for a while, just watches me, crake-curious. "You control the air, you can harden or soften it at will. Heat it? Cool it?"

It's a rather Hob way of looking at the process. War-Singers control the molecules. We can manipulate the energy: increase density here, and the air becomes hard; push the molecules someplace else, and you can suffocate a person in a little private vacuum. "Essentially," I say.

"And you can move things about using that control over air?"

"You know I can."

"Good." He stands, shoves his hands in his jacket pockets, and leans back against the balcony rail, as casual as can be. The sky is pinking. The look-fars on the cliffs are calling the alarm for the Red Death. It's still there, tainting the ocean. "I want you to pull water up out of this bucket"—his chin jerks—"and make a wall of water between us."

One deep breath to focus, and then I am doing as he asks, pulling the water, using the air to bring it toward me. Then I press it flat between two hardened layers of air, almost like holding the water between plates of glass.

"Pretty," says Dash.

It is. The water ripples and shimmers between us like an antique glass windowpane, distorting his features.

"You can let it go now," he says softly, and the water falls to the ground, soaking the hem of my shift, splashing across Dash's boots. The scriv fades from my system, and a pang of loss rocks me so hard I almost drop to my knees.

"Very good," he says. "You'll do." He steps closer to me and kisses me once, then pulls away. "Looks like all my bargains are going to pay off."

My heart goes tight, warmth flares all down my back, then leaves me cold again. I'm feverish.

"As it is," he says as he steps away, heading back into the house, "I'm just Gris-damned lucky."

16

"AND WHAT MAKES YOU THINK you still work here, eh?" Danningbread glares from behind the counter. The door *snicks* closed behind me, and I can feel how the other staff stop to watch. I swallow, about to make my excuses for not being at work yesterday, when Mrs. Danningbread waves her hands at me. "Into the back with you," she says. "I've no time to listen to whatever lies Dash has told you I'll swallow."

Relieved, I rush through to the scullery. As it stands, Dash hadn't even thought to give me a lie. Perhaps he'd just assumed it wouldn't matter.

Everyone seems nervous, on edge, and even the poets are quieter than normal. In fact, they are bizarrely so, their quills flying over their paper. The only noise comes from the scritching of nibs and the scratching of paper against wood.

It's eerie. I wash almost no bowls—their tea stands cold and forgotten at their elbows.

Finally, bored, I go to stand in the doorway of the scullery and stare at the bowed heads of the crakes. Mrs. Danningbread eyes me narrowly but doesn't scold me for coming out. The vast copper kettle steams, but no orders are being placed, and she flexes her arthritic fingers on the counter, watching over the crakes in their crow-black coats.

The door is closed against the wind, and I can just make out the faint rattling of the Crake's sign banging against a wooden beam. In the silence, the tearoom feels oppressive, too hot, and smelling of sweet aloe and poisonink and damp wool.

The quills fly faster.

"What's going on?" I whisper as I sidle up to Mrs. Danningbread. She shakes her head, her mouth firmly pressed into a bitter little line. Charl is leaning against the front doorframe, and he looks for all the world like a guard, barring the way.

A thin figure appears, hazy through the thick glass, and Charl straightens to open the door for this guest. A sharp wind shrieks through the tearoom, sending the crunched-up wads of paper on the floor scuttling into the far corners and under the tables and counter.

The stench of sea-rot replaces the smell of teas and herbs. There is a girl in the doorway, a familiar girl with fine braided hair and almond eyes and red-stained hands. She sees me and her eyes widen, her mouth twitches, as if she's trying not to give herself away. The door slams closed behind her as she steps into the room and the wind falls.

At the banging of the door, half a dozen crakes look up and gather their papers. One by one they stand, bringing their work to Charl. He flicks through the quire of paper, barely glancing at whatever is written there, then nods and hands the papers to Anja. She stares at me for a moment longer, her handful of poetry trembling, before she runs back out into the street.

The waiting poets gather about Charl, and brass clinks against brass.

"Excuse me," I say as I edge past the crakes who are now returning to their seats. Charl's face goes pale as I approach. "What's happening?"

"Nothing." He shakes his head and leans back against the doorframe, his arms folded across his chest.

"Really?" I turn and snatch a sheet out from under the fingers of a surprised crake. My gaze darts across the rhyme, down to the long smear of blotched ink at the end. It's a simple thing. I might see no point to poetry and I might consider all of it a waste of time and awful to boot, but I can still recognize that even the worst crake would never be caught dead penning his name to such trite verse. My House name glares out at me. My fingers tighten, crinkling the paper.

Murderer. Destroyer. Rapist. A lord criminal who hides behind his power, his House. A villain untouchable.

Until now.

The wet ink smears, and my brother's name is obliterated.

"What. Is. This?" I hiss at Charl, who merely shakes his head. I drop the paper back onto the crake's table, and he pulls it closer to him, pressing it flat again. The mess where his hastily penned rhyme was written glints up at me, a slick black eye.

"Are you all writing this—this rubbish?" I ask, and my voice is oddly clear and loud. The crakes shuffle, do not answer. "And the brass. Who's paying for your time?" But I know. I know.

I know someone who has the money to destroy Pelimburg. At least that's what I was led to believe. Only now I wonder if perhaps it was never about destroying the city, but about bringing the ruling Houses to their knees. The Hobs know where power lies—it's not in magic anymore. It's in coin and property and secrets.

If I run, I can still catch up with Anja. She sent me to Dash; she knows. I don't even bother going back to the scullery for my shawl or asking Mrs. Danningbread for permission to leave. Charl tries to block my way for a moment, then seems to think better of it and lets me out into the rising wind. The air is thick with fine white sand that grazes every piece of my exposed skin, cuts into my eyes. I squint, scanning the streets.

There.

Anja's braids whip about her head. She's already at the top of the road, about to turn the corner. I gather my skirts and run after her, my boots thudding and skidding on the cobblestones. Most of the vendors have packed up because of the wind, and only a few stalls stand, desperate, against the stinging sand. Despite the wind and the closed shops, the streets themselves are far from empty.

Hordes of scruffy Hobling gangs are gathered, their thin clothes ragged around skinny legs and arms. Older Hobs stand with them, reading something out from papers. I want to stop, to find out what's going on, but I don't want to lose Anja. My feet fly over the black stones, my breath whistling in tune with the sea-wind.

When I reach the top of the road, Anja has disappeared into the crowd. For a moment I stand on the rise of the hill, looking down at the mingling Hobs and low-Lammers. There's no sign of the thin braids among them.

I trudge back to work.

A few of the little Hobling packs have broken off to play skip rope, and the familiar rhymes pulse through the street. The words battle with the wind, with the rising stench coming from the Red Death.

New words about my brother, about our House, and about Malker, Eline, Evanist, Skellig—a host of Houses great and minor and all the blame Dash has laid upon them.

The Houses fall with falling girls, says one rhyme, in reference to Ilven and me. Another spins together her death and the red water on our shores, the magic of the meeting between sea and suicide. One chant laments the sailors on the whaling ships who never returned, their families compensated with a handful of coins.

There is accusation and judgment in every line.

> *You will not pay us off with silver,*
> *You will not pay us off with brass.*
> *Sailors lost rise from the river,*
> *You will not pay the dead with glass.*

The Hoblings are all chanting in time, whole packs of them, each taking up a new refrain and adding to the din.

I pause, and the wind slaps my skirts about my ankles, spits grit against my cheeks.

> *Pelim will fall and Pelim will fall.*
> *The heir must answer the witch's call.*

My hands shake as I reach out for the Crake's door handle. With all the force I can muster, I slam the door shut behind me, cutting off the rising chant.

Now that I think of the nonsense rhymes I've been half hearing over the last few days, I realize that there is a message: they're warnings.

Mrs. Danningbread says nothing and I stand there, immobile. "Charl?"

The low-Lammer boy cocks his head, waits.

"What is it—what does Dash want?"

He puffs, as if he is considering what to tell me. "Ask him yerself."

"Maybe I will." But I don't move. I don't want to know. Swallowing hurts.

Charl opens the door again for me, and the wind brings in chanting and stink. The whole world smells like rotting fish.

It's time to go.

* * *

THE HOUSE ON WHELK STREET is echo-empty. I slam my knuckles on Dash's freshly built wall, but there's no answer.

Bastard.

I'm alone here. With my hands shaking, I open the door to his realm and step inside. There are wads of bunched-up paper scattered over the floor, and an upturned ink-pot has left a virulent bluish-black stain. The ink has settled into the scarred wood and dried. A quill lies on the floor, the sharpened nib split where Dash ground it against the old floorboards. He was writing something.

Perhaps he was trying to explain to me. I pause only briefly before I grab the nearest ball of paper and carefully smooth it open.

Whatever he wrote there is obliterated, scratched through so hard that in some places the ink-heavy nib has torn through the paper. I drop it, pick up the next one. It is the same.

The salutation—just two words—scratched out and blotted.

A word that looks like it could have been *please*.

Another that asks why.

They are all variations on a theme, and if any of them were ever written to me, I cannot tell.

Finally, I throw the last letter down and walk out to the main room.

Anger makes me feel like my skin is too small, crushing me. That Dash could say such filth about my brother. We may never have been close, but Owen is a respectable member of House society, married to a woman from another

House of reputation. There's just no way that what Dash says is true.

Owen was ten when I was born, and not many years later, our father died from a common Hob disease. It's almost unheard of for House Lammers to catch the Lung, let alone die from it, but there it is. And there lay the seeds of my mother's eventual mania. I was a lonely child: my mother was in mourning, and my brother was thirteen. I barely remember those years, but I have a faint memory of being older, six perhaps, and trying to follow Owen as he raced off over the downs that sweep out to the forest, riding his shaggy gray nilly with dragon-dogs at his side.

Mostly, I don't think he even meant to be cruel to me. Just that for him I barely existed. In the grand scheme of things, his cruelty was meaningless.

I hate this life.

The sky is gray and a veil of drizzle falls around me when I leave. Tears prick at my eyes. I feel betrayed. More so than when I found the letter in Dash's room.

Everywhere I go, I hear snatches of rhyme, skip-rope slander. And now it's more than the rhymes; they were merely a catalyst. People stand on street corners or by market barrows and talk. With each telling, Dash's lies take on more flame, fanning the crowd to a slow seething anger.

Other people add the fuel of their stories, their rumors and mean-minded gossip, and the fire grows.

The street theaters are all showing bizarre tales. Gone are the stories of old heroes, of Mallen Gris and Ives Verrel, of the fall of House Mallen. Instead, there are a bare handful of scenes repeated.

A girl in white with kelp knotted into her hair who presses her palm against a man's chest. Her face is painted silver, and she has a fey look. Her red underskirts trail far behind her, almost off the stage. She is death come as a sea-witch. The man is dressed as my brother, in an imitation of Pelim finery.

I watch Owen fall again and again.

When I see a familiar street-theater wagon, I race up to it and corner Verrel.

"Tell me about this," I demand, one hand sweeping in the damning scene.

Verrel looks surprised to see me.

"What is the truth?" I can hear the edge in my voice, the razor-glass anger.

"All of it," he says.

"What about the shit he's spreading about Pelim Owen?" Murders, cruelties small and large. They're saying he killed Hob girls, servants unfortunate enough to swell with bastard Pelims, that he had a rival suitor drowned, that he ordered the burning of a section of Stilt City to flush out a thief. Accusation on accusation. If even half of it were true then my brother would be a monster beyond all imagining.

"True. Everyone knows that."

"Not everyone." A deep breath. "I know it's all lies."

Verrel frowns and turns away so he can crank a lever up; curtains fall, and the opening scene is prepared again. A Hob mummer with a pillow stuffed under her dress waddles onto the stage, taking her place opposite Owen. "You're not one of us," Verrel says. "Not really. You don't understand."

"So explain it to me!"

He pulls out his bag of tobacco and his rolling papers. "When I first moved into Whelk Street, Dash's sister used to come visit us on her occasional day off." He half smiles, his eyes far away as he lights the 'grit. "I used to have something of a crush on her, though she was older than me. She was a pretty girl, and bright. Then she fell pregnant, and no amount of Rake's parsley was going to make that go away. She was strangled."

"Strangled." Even the word chokes if you say it hard enough.

On the makeshift stage, my brother's fingers are on the girl's neck. As if my brother would have sullied his hands when he could have used scriv. The thought makes me ill— it's a lie and here I am almost believing it. He used nothing. Owen did not kill this girl. He did not kill the others. I look away.

Verrel's expression goes hard and he blows smoke. "There's your answer."

"You're telling me that my—that Pelim Owen killed Dash's sister because, what, because she was some easy little Hob lay?"

"You may want to watch where you're going with that thought," Verrel says. "And because I like you, I'm going to pretend I didn't hear it neither."

I feel suddenly small and empty. I don't know what is true anymore. If I ask Dash, ask him right out, I'll know if he's lying. I'll see it in his eyes. "Where's Dash?"

"Off organizing something or other."

"You're not going to tell me, are you?"

Verrel shakes his head.

"Fine. I'll find him myself."

The wind has finally dropped, and night is falling with the rain. Everything is drawn in shades of gray and charcoal dust. Rather aimlessly, I head back toward the Crake, where Dash seemed to know the nighttime crowd.

I hear the music before I turn down the familiar road. There are people standing in the shadows, and buttery light spills from the Crake's open door. As I walk, I stare at the figures around me, wondering if any of them is going to be Dash. It's mostly couples, hands under shirts, skirts and dresses raised around hips, mouths locked. I look away quickly until I spot someone I recognize, her back to the wall.

Anja looks at me blankly. Her eyes are the wide black pits of an 'ink-high, and her mouth moves, whispering secrets. It has been only a few hours since she last saw me, and yet she is so far gone into her 'ink-trance that she does not know me. I'd be surprised if she remembers her own name, the musty smell of poisonink is so strong. Her cheeks shine under the lights, tears like gold leaf on her skin. I remember her naked and moaning as the bat fed off her. Now she has her red-dyed arms around someone else, her stained hands resting loosely on his shoulders. She's sobbing, her body lurching, as her partner offers her what comfort he can.

She sent me to Dash.

Anja turns her head toward me and her eyes narrow. "Clear off," she says. "Fucking Lammer. You take everything from us."

Her partner turns to face me, and I feel my heart stop. My ribs still rise and fall as I try to draw breath, but I am certain that I am already dead.

"It's not what you think," Dash says, and lets go of Anja. "Firell!" he yells after me, but I am already running into the night.

DON'T LOSE YOUR HEAD *or worse over him,* Lils said. Because she knew. I race through the streets, my boots slamming against the stone. Mud and grime spray up and soak my dress. *Idiot. Idiot. Idiot. Why didn't I listen to her?*

I'm blinded by the rain, by something that feels almost like anger, only rawer and bloodier. I run so hard that every breath is bloodied, that the muscles in my legs ache and still I push myself on. Perhaps this is how the little hares felt when Owen used to set the dragon-dogs on them.

Owen. Owen makes me think of Dash, and I bow my head, grit my teeth, and push myself harder.

I don't even know where I'm running, and when I am finally brought to a halt by a stitch under my ribs, I realize that I've crossed the Levelling Bridge and am in New Town. The only places here that I am familiar with are House apartments and offices. Somehow, I don't think any of those will be viable options to go crawling to for help. I stand bent as I gasp for breath. My side feels like someone has struck it with an iron ax, and I press one hand to my ribs, digging the fingers between the bones to tear the pain out. The heat in my cheeks fades, and the rasp of my harsh breathing subsides, giving way to the drumming of the rain against the slate and ceramic roofs.

It's coming down harder now, and the wind is back, blowing in off the sea. A sure warning that another storm is building up out over the waves. It won't take long for it to come into Pelimburg and I don't want to be caught outside when it does.

There's only one place I can think of where I might possibly be welcome now: House Sandwalker. I try to orient myself. The bat House was one of the hillside villas. I stare up through the misted rain wondering if I can spot the building from here. The only one that really stands out is the massive marble rectangle of the university.

Another symbol of how far my House has fallen. That was ours once.

I bow my head and trudge up the street, hoping to spot something familiar soon.

Jannik and I traveled through here by coach, and on foot and in the rain everything appears different, so I'm slightly startled when I recognize the white façade with its moonvines and marble steps. My feet are aching in my boots, I'm soaked through, and now that I'm finally at his door, I wonder if this is such a good idea.

What do I say to him? And worse, what if I have to try to explain myself to his mother or some other family member.

It's useless. And I feel like an even bigger fool for having come here like a beggar.

I'm turning to leave when the door above me swings open and a familiar voice calls out. "Felicita?" He sounds uncertain, like he thinks I'm just a boggert haunting the steps.

Maybe I am. I don't even have the energy to correct him. Who cares what he calls me now. I nod. Jannik takes the stairs two by two. "I thought it was you," he says. "I saw you from my window."

The rain is almost horizontal now, and my wet petticoats and dress slap against my legs, whipping me toward him.

"Get in out of the cold," Jannik says. "I'll find you something dry to wear."

The door shuts. In the sudden quiet, I can hear my teeth chattering. My tears are warmer than the rain, and now I can feel the difference and I hate knowing that I'm crying over Dash.

"Your lips are blue."

I'm not really surprised. By now I'm certain that every extremity is blue. Hugging myself for warmth, I follow Jannik up to his rooms, where he gives me a thick warm towel to dry myself and a long cotton nightshirt. The nightshirt is soft as a kitten's fur and faded to a dull gray. It must be his, a favorite. The kind of sleepwear you keep because it feels safe.

He leads me to a washroom and gestures for me to change. When I'm alone, I peer into the oval mirror above the porcelain basin. The rain has plastered my hair against my head, and my eyes are puffy and red. It's obvious that I've been crying. With a sniff, I rub the towel over my face and hair, as if I could scrub all the misery away with the rain-water. Then I strip out of my wet clothes and dry myself with a numb ferocity. I want to punish my skin.

Finally dressed, I glare at the mirror. Now I look like a child with my face pinked and the old nightshirt softening my body. And I want that—I want to go back to childish things and start over again.

Jannik is waiting for me outside. "Better?" he whispers.

I nod.

We go to his bedroom, padding as quietly as we can on the thick-carpeted floors.

"Do you want to tell me what happened?"

We're sitting on his bed, me cross-legged and him with his legs stretched out. His feet are bare, and his shirt is buttoned askew. He must have been in his nightshirt when he saw me, and dressed quickly. His feet are chalk white and narrow. Elegant. He notices me looking at them and shifts so that he's mirroring me, cross-legged, his feet tucked under his knees.

"Nothing happened," I say.

He stares down at his lap, at his interlaced hands. "So what are you running from?"

"I'm not running from anything," I snap back. I can feel the burn of tears threatening to spill over. I will not cry over that useless manipulative shit.

"From who then?"

"Oh Gris." I bury my face in my hands and take a shuddering breath, trying to stop the tears from falling. It works, mostly, and I wipe the moisture from my face and blink. "Nothing happened. I thought I was . . . well . . . involved with someone. Turns out that I'm not." Anja was crying too, I remember, and guilt threads through my belly, stitching the ache deep. Dash said it wasn't what I thought.

I snap the silk thread. Dash hates me, hates my family. I can't trust what he says.

"Oh."

"Yes, *oh*." I manage a twitchy almost-smile. "It doesn't matter. It wasn't that serious." These are the things I need to tell myself. It means nothing that he was my first—someone had to be. "And I really didn't know him as well as I'd hoped."

"You'll meet someone else," Jannik says. "Someone who'll treat you better."

I want to laugh hysterically at the bat's inane platitudes. "Oh, and just who exactly? I've destroyed my life. I can never go back home. I'll probably end up living in Stilt City married to a drunken river-Hob and producing half-breeds like maggots."

"Charming." He shifts so that he can lean back against the wall. He's sitting kitty-corner to me now, and he's not looking directly at me. It means I can study him. In profile, he's awkward, his nose too long and straight for his face. But other than that, he's handsome enough. If he wasn't a bat, he'd be plain. It's the coal-dark hair and the pallor of his skin that make him so striking. So interesting to look at.

I used to think he was ugly.

He turns, and our eyes meet. The unearthly indigo is the color of the sky as the first stars rise, and my heart stutters for an instant. This is not the sea green and coppice brown of Hobs and Lammers. It is something wild and strange and subtle. For that one lost heartbeat, I see Jannik as he is.

"What about you?" I say. "What's going to happen to you?"

Jannik laughs. "I've no idea, but I'm quite certain that it's not what I want."

"What's that then?"

"The usual. Meet a nice girl, fall in love, have two children, keep the books balanced, perhaps publish some small collections of verse."

"That's horrifically dull," I say, when in fact I am oddly entranced by this marriage of poetry and mathematics and the contradictions it implies. "Why two?"

"It's neat. Orderly."

"I always wanted six."

That makes him turn to face me. "Are you insane? Why would anyone want six children? It's like a bloody litter of dragon-dogs."

His expression—part genuine shock and part curiosity—surprises a laugh out of me. "Because I grew up practically an only child, and I always wished for more brothers and sisters to play with. I thought it would have been wonderful. We could have had all these adventures . . ." I smile, remembering my childhood, playing games with the imaginary family I created for myself. Poor Ilven, constantly having to remember all the names of my vast, nonexistent clan of playmates.

"It's really not all that wonderful. I'm the youngest of four, and I don't think I've ever exchanged more than a sentence or two at a time with either of my brothers. And my sister barely speaks to us. Just because you are family doesn't guarantee you'll be friends."

I don't want to talk about family.

The room is very still, and the smell of the leaves outside the window, clean and green, mingles with the distant ocean musk. This far up, I can't smell the rot. I close my eyes. Like this, with everything calm and quiet, I can feel Jannik's magic filling the space around me. It is insubstantial as mist, and just when I think I have a lock on it, it thins and disappears. "You're magic," I say softly into the dark, finally acknowledging why he fascinates me.

I can hear him shifting, feel the way the air is displaced, and a fresh wash of the strange power laps against my skin.

"In a manner of speaking," he says.

My eyes flick open. The room is layered in grays and blues. Across from me Jannik is staring narrowly.

"What's that supposed to mean?" When he doesn't answer I press on. "It's illegal. Only the high-Lammers are allowed magic, the sharif could have you killed—"

"We can do nothing with it," he says. "Do you kill the unicorns because they are magical? The sphynxes? No." He shakes his head, a very controlled movement, barely there at all. "We're just animals, after all."

"You're telling me that you have all this magic inside you, and you can't access it?" It sounds eerily like the high-Lammers. "There must be a way to tap it—scriv, perhaps?"

"No." He leans back, away from me, forcing a physical distance between us. "There are a handful of feyn—women in our family line—who can use magic, but as for the rest of us . . ." Jannik's staring at me again, a careful look. "Think of us as carriers of a disease."

"So that's why the women are more important," I say. "You're just—"

"Breeding stock." He grins, flashing his sharp teeth. "I come from a powerful line, but even that's not enough. There are too many wray for it to matter."

"So you'll just end up"—I wave my hands in the air, skimming for some kind way to put it—"as some kind of glorified servant?"

"Essentially." His grin hasn't slipped. "Mother will keep me in reserve."

"Alone."

He nods.

I feel awful. I wonder which is worse, being condemned to a marriage you don't want or being forced into solitude in case your bloodline is ever needed.

"In MallenIve, most of the wray are indentured whores," Jannik says. "So I shouldn't complain."

"There are free vampires there," I argue. "There's even a

marriage between one and House Guyin. It can't be as bad as people say."

He stares at me unblinking.

"So run away." I feel like I've made up my mind on his behalf. I grab at his wrist and hold fast despite the sharp prickle of magic. "Do something—"

"And what then?" He pulls his arm free and with a quick twist catches my own. His thumb is against the blue vein on the inside of my wrist, pressing down on my pulse. I feel sudden warmth, my skin throbbing in time with my speeding heartbeat. "What am I supposed to do out there?" He nods at the window, at Pelimburg slumbering. "I'd be even more alone. You know nothing about us, your people are scared of us."

"I'm not scared."

His grip tightens on my wrist, and I force myself to not pull away. "Yes, you are," Jannik says, and he lets go. "You still think I'm going to bleed you dry." His head is lowered now, he's refusing to look at me. "And I wouldn't do that. When we hunt, we feed off nillies. Feeding from people is different, it's not really about food."

"So explain it to me."

"No."

Impossible damn bat. I shiver and hug my knees. I think I've overexerted myself tonight and that's good because maybe I can sleep and not think about Dash, not think about Anja, who was crying against him. I can forget about his hatred for my family. I've decided it's all lies, that everything that came out of his mouth was meant to wound. He does everything with a reason, and he made me trust him just so he could break me harder.

He's worse than my brother.

Jannik's voice intrudes, disrupting my thoughts. "What if I told you that there is a bond in blood, that it's more than a Lammer's paper marriage, that it's about magic and death?"

I sigh. "I'd say you were being overly dramatic and that you should take up a permanent table at the Crake."

"If I feed too long from one person, after a while I start to know where he is. Then I know what he's feeling—"

"I'm tired."

"And then what he's thinking."

"Jannik, I don't want to hear this." I rub my knuckles into my eyes. Maybe if I don't look at Jannik, I can pretend that what he's saying has no relevance.

"Go to sleep," he says after a while. "I'll take the floor again."

"You don't have to." My eyes are still shut tight so I can't see his expression, but the air in the room feels different, almost expectant. "It's a big bed. We can both sleep in it and barely know the other one is there."

"All right," he says carefully. "If you're certain."

I'm really tired now, so I grunt noncommittally and crawl under the duvet. After a few minutes the weight on the end of the bed shifts and I can feel Jannik leave. He must have gone to sleep on the floor.

Then the covers lift and I realize that he's changed out of his clothes and taken up my generous offer of allowing him to sleep in his own bed. He's far from me, careful that we do not touch.

"Good night," he whispers, and I manage to pull myself out of my half sleep enough to murmur something back. Then the night closes in on me, blanking out my memories.

17

My arm is curled loosely around a warm body, my face against his neck. His hair is tickling my nose.

At first I think I have woken up in Dash's room—that last night never happened—and then magic flutters against my cheeks. I lie perfectly still, feeling the insect tickle as the glamour tracks across my skin. It's nervous. Uncertain. My breath is held; I did not think magic was sentient.

There is an ache in my chest, so sharp and hard, so tight and cold.

The patter stops, and I let my breath out in a soft *whoosh*. The bat magic isn't alive any more than scriv-fueled Lammer magic is. They are so very different in feel though, and I put it down to bats' magic being organic, part of them, the way a uni's is. It's addictive though, this brush of the *other*. Why don't I feel disgusted lying next to a bat, its magic crawling over me? I should feel filthy, should want to scrub the touch of it from my skin. Instead, I brush my fingers along Jannik's shoulder and feel the faint pulse of the magic through the cotton of his nightshirt. The thrill that shudders through me is not from his magic but from something warmer, something more real and *now*. I keep my fingers resting against his back, not wanting to break this illicit contact. The longer I stay like that, the harder it is for me to pull away. I study the curve of his ear, the line of his cheek. A lock of dark hair is tucked behind his ear, the black tip like an ink brush drawing shadows across the white of the pillowcase.

This is wrong.

I swallow and draw my hand back. Clutch it between my breasts and wait for the rhythm of my heart to return to normal.

Careful not to wake him, I roll away. The sheets here are cold, chilling my skin and dragging me to the present.

Last night comes back to me: the look on Dash's face when I saw him, the feel of the rain beating against my skin like tiny silver-cold hammers. I bite my lip. *Stop it, Felicita. Don't think about it.*

"You're awake?" Jannik says, his voice muffled by the pillow. He doesn't turn to face me.

I wonder how long he has been lying there, listening to me breathe, feeling my fingertips against the sweep of his shoulder blade.

Through the window the sun is bright, and the birdsong coming from the branches of the stately oaks planted along the avenues is loud. I'll be late for my shift at the Crake. If I even still have a job there. And I don't care. I stretch my arms above my head and point my toes, feeling tired muscles crack and ease.

"I'm . . . here," I answer. And I am. I'm me again. I'm the daughter of a Great House, and I will not be brought down by the infidelity of Hobs. I'm going to find a way to go back home with my honor intact. Leave Dash and his flunkies for good.

Then I think of my mother dealing with the inevitable mockery, her already brittle relationship with me shattering. My brother's scorn and disgust. They'll know I lived with the Hobs, they'll assume I bedded down with them. Nothing I can say will make that better. Perhaps I could run to MallenIve, and from there begin a correspondence. We have apartments, holdings. I could oversee our assets there . . . and who would be stupid enough to marry me? In MallenIve there's a chance that they would at least do business with a woman, unlike in Pelimburg. But I am not one for figures and accounts. I have never had a head for business. Oh, I could make deals and be the face of our House, but how would I know to choose one offer over another? Or when to hold out for a more fair transaction? I need a business partner, and I can think of no one I trust.

So I will face this day like any other. With a sigh, I roll over and scoot off the edge of the bed. Jannik is looking at me, only one eye visible. I give him a slightly embarrassed wave and tiptoe through to the bathroom.

My clothes, despite the fact that I wrung them out and hung them over the bath to drip-dry, are still damp. Jannik's nightshirt is so warm and comfortable that I have to fight myself to take it off and get dressed in the cold layers.

Everything feels too tight against my skin, and I'm horribly uncomfortable. I hope my clothes will dry as I walk to work— the sun is out and the storm has swept past Pelimburg.

When I get back to his room, Jannik has dressed in a plain black suit; the only hint of color is in his dark olive necktie. He looks pale and sickly, and I wonder if part of the disgust we feel for the bats comes from the way they remind us of illness and death. Well, that and the fact that they feed on blood.

Unbidden, the nightmare memory of Anja at the bat party rises again. I wonder if Dash knows that just a few nights ago she was stretched out naked under a bat and probably begged him to bed her afterward. Of course, I suppose he's done much the same. Let them comfort each other, then. I swallow down my revulsion and shiver.

"You're leaving already?" Jannik says.

I nod. "I'm late. Even if I run I won't make it there on time."

"Oh. I assumed you'd be riding with me." He stumbles over the words and a faint frown puckers his brow.

"I'm sorry, what?"

"I have to go to our buildings by the docks. New stock of rockrose and sandalwood is coming in from MallenIve today, and I need to check the quality and see if we should place more orders." He cocks his head slightly. "It wouldn't be that much trouble to take you to the Crake."

It would certainly help, and it's not like I haven't ridden in a carriage with him before. Or, I muse, shared his bed. I flush at the memory of magic caressing me, wrapping me up in a shroud of windle-silk. It's better that I concentrate on his magic than remember watching him sleep and thinking him strange and beautiful.

We walk through a house just rising, and servants bow or curtsey as Jannik passes. They ignore me in my drab work clothes. I pull my mostly dry shawl tighter around my shoulders and dip my head so that I don't have to look into their eyes and see the thoughts there.

Lammer-whore.

I am not this thing. I raise my head sharply, and with my chin jutted out I walk alongside Jannik, willing these Gris-damned bats to say something, *anything*. The anger waits inside me, cold and ready. Even I know it's just a façade. I'm so scared now that I have nowhere left to go. My armor is frost thin and just as useful.

Nothing happens, no one breaks my meager defenses.

Instead, Jannik takes my arm and we walk down the steps to the waiting carriage.

THE COACH RATTLES and jolts across the bridge. By now I'm strangely calm inside, as if last night happened to some other person. Both of us sit in comfortable silence, and I watch the buildings flicker past us and let the rocking carriage soothe away my thoughts until I am empty. The faint reflection of my face is laid out on the glass, like a ghost over the city. I look wan, tired.

"I—I'd like to see you again, if that's possible," Jannik says.

The words break into my cocoon, pull it apart. I stare at him in confusion. He is frowning slightly, not really looking up at me. He pulls a monogrammed handkerchief from his pocket and twists it around his fingers. "There's a new tearoom that's opened on Fletcher Street. I—p-perhaps," he stutters. Then he lets the last words free in a rush, "Perhaps you could join me there tonight? Or tomorrow or . . ."

I have no idea how to answer. What could I possibly have said that would make him think there could ever be something between us? After all, there is no precedent in Pelimburg for a relationship between a vampire and a high-Lammer. While I'm wondering what to say to him to let him down as gently as I can without making some kind of fuss, all expression slides from his face. He leans back and looks past me, through me, and the white eyelids flick down and cover his pupils.

"I apologize," he says. "You need time to get over your previous relationship."

It's a convenient out for both of us. I nod and look away from him, stare instead at my hands, curled up in a tight ball on my lap.

I want to say something to him, to tell him that it's all right, but my words are dead. "It's not about you being a—" I begin, but he saves me the trouble of my little fabrication by cutting me off.

"I understand." His voice is brittle. The magic around him is thickening, twisting in on itself. It's almost as if I can see it turning the air dark. My breath catches and he must hear the soft gasp, for the magic stills, goes quiet.

What does it taste like, this magic of his. Would it be

scriven-sharp and sweet or would it run like blood across my tongue. I push the thought back. What am I thinking? To grind up his bones into dust like desperate high-Lammers do with uni-horn when they can't get scriv?

The carriage jerks to a halt and I look up. The Crake is already open, the tables set up on the wide gray sidewalk.

But nothing is normal.

Dash is standing there, arms folded, waiting. Behind him are the other Whelk Streeters, looking defiant and angry.

They're far from alone. A crowd is slowly gathering, people spilling in from the alleyways and side streets. The snatches of ever-present skip-rope songs are gone, their message relayed, their role played.

"What's going on?"

Jannik shakes his head. "I've no more idea than you."

The vampire coachman opens the door. I'm supposed to get out. Forcing my feet to step forward, I allow the coachman to take my hand and help me down from the shining black carriage. Dash is already striding forward, but he stops in confusion when he sees me.

"Tell the bat to go play with his numbers down in the Old Town warehouses. He has no place here with us," he says. He sounds angry, but under that is a constricting fear, so dense that it is palpable.

Fear for himself or for Jannik?

I turn and look over my shoulder. Jannik is enveloped in darkness and shadows.

He sighs. "I heard."

"I mean it," Dash says. "Tell him to get the fuck out, now. There's nothing here that needs his attention."

Jannik frowns. He's heard the same note of urgency that I have.

"You were to stay out of New Town today, you idiot bat. I told you when I saw you last—keep the fuck out!" The fear has given way to anger. Dash pushes past me as if he barely even sees me and grabs the coach's doorframe. The anger drops, and his words are rushed and desperate. "I meant to send you a letter," he says to Jannik. "There wasn't time." He edges closer in so that I can't see his face. "Whatever happens, you need to keep away from the New Town warehouses near the Great House holdings, trust me."

I stare at him. The liar. He wrote those letters. He wrote them over and over and over and they ended up on his floor, destroyed. Why is he lying to Jannik about it? The realization comes like the snapping of a silk thread. The two of them are locked into a silent argument so full of recrimination and anger and hurt that it makes the very air between them feel charged with static.

The bites on Dash's neck. The stranger in the shadows, watching Jannik's window. Even that stupid Prines book— Jannik's, loaned to Dash, then returned like a lover's letter. I shake my head. Not true.

And still he expects us to trust him. Just because he's Dash.

I'm about to tell Jannik that whatever the malignant little Hob spawn says, he'd best do the opposite, when I catch the look on Jannik's face. He's moved out of the shadows, his magic swirling around him. His eyes are blank and white, but there is no disguising the way his mouth is slightly open or the tightness around his eyes.

"Please," says Dash.

Jannik nods at the coachman. "Do as he says. Take me away."

I step down completely and watch as the coachman scrambles up to his seat and *clicks* the skittish unicorns into action. The coach rattles off, then turns up a side road, and the hoofbeats and the sound of the wheels on the stones change timbre and fade.

Dash looks at me. "So now we know where you spend your nights."

"Same place you do, apparently," I say as I step forward and press my fingers to his shirt collar. Press them into the hidden bites on Dash's throat. He was never mine, and Lils knew why. She was trying to protect me from this.

He winces and shoves my hand away. "Never thought you'd be whoring yourself out for a few pieces of brass though, did I, kitty?"

"I don't—" I pause. "Forget it. Why are you here? What's going on?" I jerk my chin toward the gathering crowd. "Are you starting your little revolution today?"

"Funny you should say that." He grins, and for a moment, the flash of his white teeth and his cocksure arrogance strike right at my heart.

Instead of clinging to him, I press my palms against my dress and take a long calming breath. "What do you mean?"

"Esta's already starting fires."

I glance at the crowd. Sure enough, there is no sign of Esta. I wonder how long it will be before the smoke starts blowing over the city.

"You're going to burn down Pelimburg." It's hard to get the words out, they catch like tiny barbs.

"Not at all." He grins. "I'm merely going to punish a few of her citizens." Dash shrugs one shoulder. "The fires just add to the whole atmosphere of our little performance."

I grab his shoulder, anger making me feel like I'm made of burning iron. "You're mad. You have some . . . some *pointless* vendetta against my brother, and so you want to destroy the city. People are going to die."

"Never pointless," he hisses.

And then I see it. The truth is in his eyes: the pain and the fury and the self-hatred and the knowledge that everything he does now still won't bring her back. I know these feelings well. They are mine, and I face them every night when I think of how I failed Ilven, was useless in the face of my best friend's fears and pain. I drop my hand and stare at him. "No." I shake my head. "No, no, no."

He shrugs again, but this time it lacks his casual arrogance. "I need you," he says. There's a resigned desperation there, something I would never have associated with Dash.

"What?" I'm startled out of my despair.

Dash grabs my wrist and forces my palm open. Before I can protest he drops a small pouch into my hand. "In a few minutes, Lils is going to untie her hair and we are going to drown Pelimburg in madness." He drops his voice and uncurls his fingers to show me the mark on his palm. It's bigger now, jellied and pale. The bones show through the translucent flesh. "And I'm going to call the sea-witch. The nightmares and the destruction will bring the high-Lammers out of their Houses, and I can mark the sacrifice," he says. "Your job is to keep the Hobs on our side of the river safe."

"What are you talking about?" He's marked, boggert-touched, and still alive. "What is this?" I do not touch the mark on his palm, but he knows what I'm talking about.

"A promise," he says. "Now, you need to do what I ask."

My hands shake. It's a barge day, when the biggest ship-ments come down from MallenIve, and New Town will be full of people, of House Lammers down to run through led-gers and oversee stock handling. The warehouses that line the loading docks on the Casabi will be full of new shipments of silk and scriv and glasswork. Everyone will be there, from the wherrymen guiding their barges like recalcitrant unis to the Heads of Houses overseeing stock. The low to the high and everyone between, all the dockworkers and factory girls, the mail runners and *Courant* readers. Everyone. He can't be serious—he can't be meaning to call up the sea-witch. Some-thing Dash said flashes through my mind: the sea-witch fol-lows the boggert but requires four deaths.

"There were only three bodies—"

"Four now." Dash raises his hand, and I want to vomit.

He's twisting everything. He's killing himself, killing in-nocents so that he can have his Gris-damned revenge on my brother. "This isn't about saving the Hobs," I hiss at him. "And it never was."

"No," he says, and he grins. His eyes are frightened, giving the lie to his cheer. "But I did always love a good spectacle."

The crowd begins to move forward. I look down at the little pouch in my palm and smell the citrus musk that leaks from it. Scriven.

My hand closes around the pouch. I know that whatever it takes, I need to try to do something to stop Dash. I look at the crowd. The people seethe, anger making them blind and ugly. They still believe in him, haven't seen that he's playing on their anger in order to fuel his own revenge. If I do anything obvious to stop Dash, they will tear me apart. The best I can hope for is to keep as many people safe as I can. I want to cry at the injustice of it all.

"They deserve it," Dash says to me. Or maybe he's saying it to himself, still trying to convince this angry vengeful side of him that what he's doing is right. Then louder, harsher. "They deserve it."

"Do they really?" My voice is thick, barely sounding like my own at all.

His eyes are beautiful close up, threaded with gray and olive and gold and black. "This is a judgment."

"Justice," I whisper back, "and with you the judge."

"The dead are the judges," he says, and folds his boggert-marked hand tightly over mine, forcing me to feel the tiny grains of scriv moving under the leather of the pouch. "Not me. I'm just the person bringing in the executioner."

I search his face for truth and find belief, find conviction. These are truths of their own, I suppose. I bow my neck and take a shuddering breath.

What choice do I really have?

Dash takes my elbow and steers me along with the crowd. Ahead of us, Lils is hand in hand with Nala, and the mass of people is eerily silent. The dockyards and the fisheries and the tanneries and the teahouses must be empty. Even the crakes walk with the crowd, their tongues stilled for perhaps the first time in their lives.

WITH DASH'S HAND CLAMPED ON MY ARM, we march through Old Town, gathering followers as we draw nearer and nearer to the Levelling Bridge. My arm begins to ache, and I'm certain that when this day is over I will see bruises on my skin. The scriv pouch is held tightly in my free hand, and I squeeze it harder, as if somehow I could magic it away and with it this whole dreadful farce.

The first turrets of smoke are rising in the air over the warehouses, and the distant clanging of the city's tower bells fills the morning with a cold precise chant. In New Town, House heirs will be rushing to their burning warehouses, watching as their fortunes go up in flames. My brother will be there.

Those who can will waste their precious scriv containing the fires.

We reach the bridge, and the crowd stops.

"What now?" I pull my arm free.

"We wait." Dash watches the bridge with a fierceness I'm unused to. He hugs himself, and I realize then that he's shaking. His hands are trembling, and he held me so tightly to disguise his own weakness.

Next to us, Nala and Lils are standing with their arms around each other, watching the people panicking on the bridge: some are running for New Town, others have seen the crowd and come down to join us, their faces grim and bright at the same time. This is no ordinary riot. This is a jury, watching the execution. The sentence has long since been passed.

"What happens after all this?" I ask, fighting to keep my voice level. "The sharif will hunt Lils down, hunt Nala down."

"No they won't."

"And how can you be so Gris-damned certain!"

Dash ignores me, his gaze sweeping the bridge. He lifts his head and looks up. The sky is a perfect cerulean dome, washed clean by last night's rain. "Because I made sure," he whispers.

We will none of us be safe after today, it doesn't matter how many people he's bribed this time. "Where's Verrel?" I know I saw him with us earlier, but now I've lost him in the mass of people.

"I'm more worried about Esta," Dash says. "She should be back with us by now."

"She's setting more fires," a voice says behind us. I am startled and relieved at the same time: Verrel. He points to where more smoke is climbing into the pale blue sky. The wisps are faint and white, but even as we watch, the columns grow thicker. There are no warehouses on the hillside. Esta's burning the family homes.

"Shit and bugger," says Dash. "She was only supposed to burn the warehouses down by the docks, not the bloody mansions too." He takes a step toward the bridge, then jerks still. The expression on his face is torn. "Idiot," he says under his breath, and I'm not sure whether he means her or himself. "What's she thinking?"

"We need to stop her," Verrel says.

Dash whirls around to face him. "I bloody know that," he says. "But it's too late—I can't leave this now." He sweeps one hand out to encompass the crowd, their murmurs growing as they wait to see Dash destroy Pelimburg's old order.

Verrel stares at him, then swallows, the lump in his throat bobbing. Fear radiates off him. "I'll go fetch her," he says softly.

"We don't have time." Dash nods to Lils. "We need to get started before the House Lammers reach the bridge." Desperation has given his voice an edge. Things are not going according to his grand plan.

Verrel doesn't seem to have noticed Dash's rising panic. "So you were just going to leave her?"

"I wouldn't have to if she'd bloody gone and done as I told her!"

"Fine." Verrel strides past us and toward the bridge.

"You are not one of the heroes in your fucking street operas," Dash shouts, his voice strangled. "You're not."

Verrel pauses and looks back. "And neither are you."

"I never bloody claimed to be."

"That's not what your little mob is going to say after this day ends."

"No." Dash shakes his head. "I can't let you go after her, it's too dangerous." He grabs at Verrel's arm and catches the low-Lammer's sleeve.

Calmly, Verrel pries Dash's fingers off and pulls himself free. "It's not really up to you." His voice is as low and soft as morning surf. "You don't own us, Dash."

At that, Dash steps back. We watch Verrel cross onto the bridge. Dash stares, his mouth hard, then shouts after him, "I can't push the timing back, Verrel!"

Verrel pauses and half turns to look at us. "Dash," he says quietly, "whatever nightmares Lils calls up, none will be as bad as the ones I'll have if I leave Esta to face that alone. Or did you forget what memories she carries? They'll tear her apart."

"Do you think I don't care what happens to her?"

He shakes his head. "No. I just think that you've forgotten what it's like to have a friend instead of an agenda."

"Fuck off then," Dash says. His anger is back, controlled, focused. "I hope you find her, but if you don't, I won't mourn either of you."

"I never expected it." Verrel's mouth twists in an awful parody of a smile. "I hope your scheme works, Dash, and that you get whatever it is you want."

"I'm not doing this for me," Dash says. "I'm doing this for everyone who's suffered under the high-Lammers."

We watch Verrel walk across the bridge until the shadows of the Houses swallow him up. Black smoke is pouring from several locations around New Town, and the air is turning storm dark, thick with the smell of burning and ash.

"You'd best take your scriv now, darling," Dash says. "If you're to hold back Lils's dreams." He glances down at the wide brown Casabi, its water choked with weeds and silt.

He has to be joking. But one look at the set of his jaw and the iron in his eyes and I realize he isn't. Every muscle in my body has gone tense. "I can't hold it all back," I whisper to him. "I can't." I'd need to pull a bubble of protection over the whole of Old Town. Perhaps if I'd been trained at university—Gris knows I have the natural talent.

"You can and you will." He turns to face me. "If you don't, all these people will suffer." He spreads out one arm, showing me the massed crowd behind us, the silent witnesses.

"And the ones in New Town?"

Dash looks across the bridge. "Only our enemies wait there."

"Our enemies? There's no *our* in this. *Your* enemies. My brother is there, my mother, Esta and Verrel." I look at the tall buildings that rise up the hillside. "Innocent people, Dash!"

"No one is ever innocent. All the Houses," he says, "not just Pelim, the whole lot, and everyone who stands with them." He raises his chin. "Lils!" He's going to make the workers suffer too, the ones who haven't heard the message to clear out of New Town, the unlucky ones who don't pay any attention to skip-rope rhymes. And he doesn't even care.

Lils and Nala turn at his call, stepping out onto the center of the bridge. Nala lifts her hands to her lover's braid to undo the little black ribbons that keep Lils's dream-hair knotted back, that keep the nightmares trapped. They must hate so very fiercely to be willing to unleash that on Pelimburg. How many others are so deeply indebted to Dash, or feel that they are, that they're ready to do anything at his command?

Lils's hair is a tangled coil of tight curls. Pin by pin, ribbon by ribbon, the waves come loose, and the first faint flurry of dream-images tickles along my vision, rustling through my memories like a playful wind through fallen leaves. Nala brushes her fingers through the sticky curls, and the wind picks up, stirring the nightmares lying under the drifts.

"We're waiting, *Felicita*," Dash says.

I'll do this now, and afterward Dash better run, because I will string that little Hob bastard up by his fancy necktie.

He grins at me as if to say *I know, darling, and I don't care.* I suppose he doesn't. After today, he's dead anyway, final victim to the boggert. But there's something plaguing me, a niggling detail. I recall a conversation with Charl.

"Who are you giving to the sea-witch?" I say. "What did you promise her?"

He narrows his eyes. "A life for a life, of course."

"Who?" I can barely whisper it, although I know the answer.

"It could have been a sister for a sister," he says. "But I liked you too much for that."

He's going to kill my brother. All this suffering handed out to the Houses and their retainers just so he can feed Owen to a sea-witch. Dash might hate the high-Lammers with an indiscriminate passion, but when it comes to Pelim, his loathing takes on a personal tone. He wants them all to pay but it is my brother he will make an example of.

Dash pulls something small and silver bright from his pocket: a hairpin, picked out with the emerald leaves of House Malker's crest. I have seen this particular trinket many times, holding back hair straight and pale. It's Ilven's. "I have the boggert-sign," he says. "All I need to do is mark the right person, and the sea-witch will come for him."

Ilven. A name hooked on kisses and secrets. The pin flashes, and I remember running my fingers through her hair and using this pin to hold the twist of her loose bun in place. The smell of her neck, like sea salt and citrus.

The boggert-sign. My heart curls small, a little animal, terrified at this realization.

"And if you don't?" My hand jerks, wanting to knock the offending item from his fingers.

"Then the sea-witch will rise and kill, and keep killing. Without a marked sacrifice, she'll not return to the water." He closes his fist. "Someone has to die, Felicita, darling. Or are you going to step up in his place?"

Fear comes first, followed by guilt. I don't deserve to die, I think, and I realize I am a coward. That he has made me into one. "You utter bastard," I say. "You're no better than my bloody brother."

He laughs in a desperate way.

I open the pouch and take a healthy pinch of scriv. One deep breath, and I can taste oranges in the back of my throat. Magic boils in my veins. I will make him pay. Pay for using me, for using my friend's death, and for twisting her ghost to his stupid, stupid cause.

"Look on the bright side," Dash says. "After I'm dead, the boggert will be gone too. Malker Ilven will be just a memory."

"I hate you."

"Save it for later," he says. "You've got bigger things to deal with now. Quick, girl, or there'll be more deaths than you want weighing you down."

And I hate him even more for being right.

Nala is holding Lils tight, and there's a physical wind around them now. They are caught in a private storm that tears at their hair, at their clothes, and Nala buries her face against Lils's neck and her cloud of carroty frizz tangles up in Lils's dark serpentine mass and the dreams spill faster. The first drops of water rise from the Casabi as I coax them up.

"Whenever you're ready." Dash picks at his teeth with a splinter of wood. He's trying for nonchalant, but I can see faint beads of sweat popping up on his forehead.

And it comes to me in a flash: crime and punishment. Maybe he's already dead, but I can make him suffer. Because Dash has severely underestimated me.

I raise a solid wall of water around myself, around the crowd, like a curtain across Pelimburg, separating Old Town from New, curving it up and over our heads in a protective bubble. The probing dreams cease, like dead moths falling to the ground. Behind me comes a collective sigh as the crowd is freed from the nightmare visions.

And then I very carefully twine that curtain of magic-controlled water so that Dash is on the wrong side of it.

18

It takes only a split second for Dash to realize exactly what I've done. He reaches his partially translucent palm toward me and touches the shimmering wall that I've brought down between us.

He stares at me. Then he drops his hand and smiles. His teeth are so white in his brown face, so startling. His mouth moves, but I have no idea what he's saying.

My heart feels like it's trying to crawl out of place. I strengthen the wall. More water boils up from the river, thickening the barrier. At least this way I can concentrate on something that isn't the sour taste of betrayal. I swing my gaze away from Dash, determined not to look at him. I'm a coward. A high-Lammer. Just what Dash thinks all high-Lammers are like. My stomach clenches and I swallow convulsively.

Lils and Nala are wrapped in a cocoon of hair, protected from the dreams. They are caught up in a little bubble of safety, and they neither notice nor heed Dash's presence. In New Town, it won't take long for the War-Singers to get to their scriv and shore up their defenses, but until then, the city is going to be a chaos of flames and nightmare visions. People will die—throw themselves from buildings, drown themselves in the silt-brown Casabi. How long before my brother comes down to the source of the nightmares, trying to control his losses? How long will Lils's magic last before the dreams fade?

Dash has to mark my brother—mark *someone*—before the sea-witch rises. How is he going to do that after he's been weakened by the insanity of the nightmare visions? I didn't think, and now more people are going to suffer. For the first time since running away I am almost eager to see my brother. I scan the crowd hoping to spot him among the screaming faces. Dash should have been on this side, ready to give whatever signal he devised to stop Lils's nightmares. He must have had some plan in mind for after he'd lured Owen into the open. It was not one he shared with me. I'm a traitor, and I am a fool.

Verrel and Esta are also out there. I can't do this—even Dash doesn't deserve my disloyalty.

Unless there's some way I can find the others, bring Dash back to this side, and keep them safe. I press forward tentatively, but the fragile magic can't take the strain of my losing focus, and I feel it tear, spilling water across my hand. It drips down my arm. An insect-legged flicker of a memory I had thought was buried worms toward me:

my brother's face as he locks me in a wardrobe to stop me from following him I'm four he left me there for

the afternoon it was only when dinner was served that
he remembered to free me smell of feces and urine and
the snot-stickiness of my skin the burn of thirst and
hunger and over it all the black terror the fear that I
would be there forever

Shaking, I step back and take another pinch of scriv even
though my fingers are trembling so hard that I almost lose
the precious dust. My magic bounds up again, and I knit the
dream-wall closed. Finally, I force myself to really look at
Dash, trapped there in the nightmares. Through the veil of
water everything seems distant and unreal, and I can almost
persuade myself that it is truly not happening.

How long before the sea-witch comes? I want to scream.

Dash is sitting on the bridge with his knees drawn up to
his face. His eyes are blank, and he doesn't see me at all. Gris
knows what horrors live inside his head. The taste of bile is so
thick in my mouth that I have to lean over, clutching at
a post, so that I can spit on the ground. My skin is ice-cold.
Sweat soaks my clothes. If I really needed to punish Dash,
I could have waited for a better time.

And now there's no way for me to open the wall and drag
him back—I'll be overwhelmed.

And if the wall falls . . . I glance behind me at the crowd, at
their pale, strained faces. I wonder if any of them realize that
I've purposefully cut Dash off, that this was not part of the deal.

The crowd has been almost eerily silent up until now.
From New Town there is nothing—the wall has killed all

sound. Even if Dash could pull himself together long enough to speak, he wouldn't be able to tell them what happened or beg me to bring him back across.

"Oi!" someone yells, and then they begin. Someone's pointed out that Dash is caught on the wrong side of the wall. They jostle, they shout, and through gritted teeth I say over and over, "It was a mistake."

But no matter how many times I repeat it I will never make myself believe it. Bodies crush around me, and the air is forced out of my lungs. I send the scriv-magic harder outward and upward, siphoning even more water from the river and strengthening the bubble arching over us. I may be able to do nothing for those I have betrayed, but I can still protect the ones I haven't.

On the other side of the wall, the smoke is turning thick and black, pouring down the alleyways, winding around the houses. The first wave of people run up against the wall, beating their hands against it, bloodying their faces as they smash their heads over and over, as if this time they will get free. They scratch their fingers raw. They turn on one another like animals. I catch a glimpse of Dash, still curled in on himself, before he is lost, trampled under the maelstrom of flesh and fear. Then the area clears, and he is gone. There is no body there, and I cannot see his face in the crowd. Another mass of people rush up to the wall.

The only two people who remain untouched are Nala and Lils, caught up in their own world. They are pale skin and brown, dark hair and red. A tangled geometry of flesh. Is that love? Is that what love can do? Save you from all the horror the world has to give?

The girls spin, a slow intricate dance between the hordes.

The bridge is soon clotted with gore, the cobblestones gleaming with blood. The sky is no longer blue, but orange and black from the fires, and I see people fall from buildings, their bodies nothing more than flaming cinders.

I realize I've bitten the inside of my cheek when I taste blood in my mouth. How long before the Houses rally themselves, rise against this attack? How long before the nightmares caught in Lils's hair are all gone?

Still no sign of Owen. What made Dash think that my brother would come down to the docks and waste magic on protecting the warehouse servants? He should have known better.

My face stings, and I take more scriv.

When the sea-witch finally rises from the Casabi—woken by boggert-deaths and drawn to the shore by the concentration of terror and blood—I stand still. Hold the wall. Her hair is Red Death, her skin and flesh spume and spray.

I witness.

It is the very least I can do.

She walks out of the mingled waters of the river and the ocean tracking black kelp behind her.

Then she is gone, into the nightmares.

MY SCRIV-MAGIC IS FADING. I haven't moved. I'm as parched and as dry as if I had just crawled across the red desert outside of MallenIve. The wind, finally able to penetrate the fragile bubble of magic, begins to tug at my hair.

I can feel, just faintly, other walls that have sprung up all over Pelimburg as the House War-Singers have protected their own as best they can. I wonder if it will be enough to protect them from Dash's vengeance. Perhaps. But what little I saw of the violence unleashed by the nightmares does not fill me with much hope for my fellow high-Lammers.

My brother, my mother. Are they safe or is Owen already dead?

The water drops with a sudden crash as the last of my scriv runs out. Brine sloshes across the Levelling Bridge, soaking the people, the bodies, rinsing blood from the wounded and the dead.

I can't bring myself to care. Inside me is a pit of blackness and it sucks at every emotion that tries to flutter upward.

Nala and Lils break apart, blinking. Nala drops the barest brush of a kiss against Lils's forehead before gently turning her around and braiding up the mass of dark hair. Moans carry faintly on the breeze coming down the mountain, and the smell of burned flesh, wood, and something sickeningly sweet is carried with it.

My hand is on my mouth. I don't remember moving it there. The skin is dry, flaked with the ash that is falling faint as a fine rain.

The sound is back. I'm going to be drowned by the screams and panic. I'm free though, I tell myself, I'm free to go look for the others among the bodies. I need to find Dash and see what damage the sea-witch has done.

My legs ache but I don't let that stop me. I walk straight past the two girls, stepping over the bodies nearest me, and then pick my way through the worst of the slick filth on the ground. No matter where I look, there is no sign of a familiar face. Black kelp ribbons about the bodies, and here and there the eyes of the dead are plucked out, filled with sand and broken shells. This is the way she came. These are her dead. I follow the trail of sea-witch-tainted bodies, hoping that they will become fewer, that the trail will end. Even if that means finding my brother's corpse.

It does not. All around me people gibber, moan. They've seen her walking, spreading the Red Death inland, although the Hobs and Lammers who were caught on this side of the bridge have yet to realize that she is not merely another nightmare.

I walk until I can't take a single step more and then sit down on a low stone curb and cradle my head in my hands. My tongue feels thick and huge.

So I don't see him, don't hear him until his boots are right next to mine and he says "Felicita" in a tone that is heavy with exhaustion and guilt.

I raise my head, dragging my gaze away from those polished black boots, gray now with ash and muck, and up to Jannik's drawn face. His cheeks are thinner. He looks older. His pale skin is marred by red streaks.

He crouches. Balances his hands on his knees. "What are you doing here?"

"And I should ask you the same thing." My words have no bite to them, even though I clearly remember Dash telling Jannik to stay in Old Town.

"I'm doing what I can." He rocks a little, exhaustion almost overwhelming him. "Everyone is. Even my mother stepped out of our house to do what she was able."

Around us, people are passing, some carrying the injured, the dead. Others already with wood and stone in their hands to shore up the worst of the crumbling buildings.

"The bridge and the docks were hardest hit," he says. "Seems the dream-fever didn't reach all the way to the Tooth." His eyes are darker than I've ever seen them. "So *certain* Houses suffered hardly at all."

He doesn't know that my brother is a marked man.

"Good for them," I say dully. "Wait." I stare into those indigo-dark eyes and he flicks the membrane down, hiding his thoughts. "How do you know it was dream-fever? You were on our side of the river. There was no way for you to feel that."

"People are talking about it." But there's something there in his face that even his slicked-over eyes can't hide. Pain and suffering.

I stand. He doesn't. We stare at each other, and I know what he's keeping from me. "I need to find Dash."

"And you think I know where he is." Jannik looks at his hands instead of my face.

I remember something he told me last night, and the pieces click, fall into place. Jannik and Dash, and the things Jannik has been carefully not telling me. Why his mother was so determined he stop feeding off one particular Hob. "I know that you do." I bend down to touch his face so that he cannot lie to me by looking away.

His third lids are still down, and the day's sunlight has left a fine blistered rash over his skin. Jannik draws a deep shuddering breath. "Follow me."

Together we make our way back toward the riverside warehouses, and this time I cannot pretend that there are fewer bodies. The sea-witch is taking them indiscriminately—old and young, Hob and Lammer. Dash has failed. All around us, Hobs are working to help who they can. The Lammers too, and among them the pale bats. We head down to one of the oldest warehouses, and I pull my shawl closer about my head and keep my neck bent. There are servants here who might recognize me. Quickly, Jannik and I thread through the maze of buildings till we find a long-abandoned storage facility, a relic of better years.

Under the fading red light of the last sun, the leaping dolphins of my House crest glint feebly from beneath decades of black grime. It's been many years since anyone used this place. The door is old wood, heavy and splintered and tacky. Someone has been here. There are footprints in the dirt.

I don't want to go in.

"Come on," Jannik says, and tugs at my hand. I'm glad of his presence, of the comforting familiarity of my poet mathematician. No. It's the magic that's comforting, the subtle play of his bat-nature through my palm, tingling my arms, and making the hairs on my body prickle.

I shake my head. Truth can wait for another day.

We go farther into the darkness, all the way to the back, where I see a familiar figure shining in the gloom. My heart leaps.

I let go of Jannik's hand and run forward.

Ilven turns to me, looking over her shoulder through a fringe of hair so pale it gleams like surf. I pause in my headlong flight.

"Ilven?"

Her eyes are silvered coins, blank and expressionless. Although she's ghost faint, there is color in her cheeks. She's fed. And I know that Dash is gone. I stand, waiting for the boggert to come closer. She drifts toward me, her feet leaving the sandy floor untroubled. One eyebrow is arched in a question. It is a familiar look, and it's this, more than anything else, that makes me bite at my lip in an effort to stop the tears that are stinging the corners of my eyes.

"It's me," I say. "I know why you did it." Her leap from the cliff has plagued me, left me feeling guilty every night. "I used to think I should never have left without you, that I should have waited." My voice trembles. "And then I'd—I'd have seen you, stopped you."

The boggert is a breath away from me, and she pauses, hovering.

"But that's not true, is it?"

"Felicita." Jannik's voice is soft, warning. "Step away from her."

"Maybe I could have saved you once. Twice, even." I want to reach up and brush back a lock of pale hair that has fallen over her face, but I hold my arms still. "In the end, we make our choices on our own. And no matter how stupid they are, we have to live—or die—with what we've done. Sometimes choosing our moment of death is the only freedom we have left."

The boggert blinks, and for an instant I see Ilven's blue eyes, a flash of summer.

"And I've no right to try to save you from that."

She's barely there, her body misted and irregular. She's dissipating, dissolving into nothingness. "No," she says, and I know that she has remembered. "Goodbye, Felicita," the boggert says in Ilven's cotton-soft voice. She has remembered that she's dead, and I can feel the change that ripples through her and then she's gone and all that is left is the remains of her last victim.

Sitting with his back to the wall and his knees drawn up against his chest is Dash.

Like Rin, like the other two corpses that were found, he is ghostly, barely there. He manages a weak smile at my approach.

We must have interrupted Ilven—no, the boggert—before she finished feeding.

"Hello," he says.

It's so incongruous that I stare at him. "Hello?" I say after a few moments. "Hello?" After everything that happened and what we did to each other, he greets me like he's just stepped out for a few hours and now he's back.

"I wasn't talking to you," he says, and coughs. "Although you can believe I've a choice few words stored up."

"I had to stop you," I say. "I had to make you see."

"And what good did it do?"

I say nothing. Dash opens one clenched hand and drops Ilven's hairpin on the ground between us. The scream is trying to come out. It can't. My fingers shake as I scoop the Gris-damned thing up and hold it tight. I want it to prick me, to mark me, and make this whole thing over. Only I'm too much of a coward.

"It's always easier when someone else makes the hard choices. Right, love?"

"I can't." I choke the words out.

"Well it ain't going to be me. You saw to that, you silly flick."

"Dash," says Jannik from behind me, "I shouldn't be feeling this death."

"Oh, but you are." He grins. A sickly thing, with no real humor to it. "Sit down," he says. The vampire walks past me and obeys. "You can sit on the other side," Dash says to me, and pats the empty space next to him.

Exhausted, too tired to argue with him, I fold my skirt over my legs and sit down. My skin crawls at the strange texture of his body against my arm.

"Why?" asks Jannik. "Why am I feeling you die?"

"You should know, better'n me anyway."

The bat shakes his head. "I fed off you, that's it—it means nothing."

Dash tilts his head back and takes a rough breath. "So why did your dear mother insist that you stop feeding off me? There *are* reasons for your stupid laws."

"Shut up," Jannik says, but there's no strength to it.

"You're not going to die," Dash says. His voice is getting weaker. "I don't think we're that far gone."

"Well I'm so relieved now I could vomit. Thank you for clearing up that little worry." Jannik's voice is thick. I glance past Dash. The vampire's white eyelids are down, and he stares ahead, not moving his face to look at either of us.

"What do you want us to do?" I whisper.

Dash sighs. "There's nothing to be done. I just didn't want to die alone." He takes a sharp breath, almost as if he is in pain.

He reaches out suddenly and takes both our hands in his. The touch of his icy flesh makes me start, makes me try to jerk my hand away, but I still myself and accept that this is my apology. And his. Silently, I squeeze his hand once in reassurance.

"You changed things," I tell him softly.

"Did I now? So it was worth it, was it?"

I think of the dead, of the wounded, of Dash's own death waiting for him. The thing that I still have to do. I am filled with an ache so vast that it strangles me. "No."

"That's where you're wrong." Then he falls into silence.

We sit together, the three of us, and pass vigil in the dusk.

The sun has just set when I hear Dash's breathing change.

I swing my head up from where I've rested it against the wall, and I can just make out the dark gray shadow through Dash: Jannik.

The bat is sitting with his head bowed and his knees drawn up in a mirror of Dash's pose. We are all still holding hands: me on Dash's right, Jannik on his left.

I squeeze again, harder this time, and Dash laughs a soft moth-laugh that flutters against my cheeks and makes me too scared to cry in case I wash it away.

After that, he doesn't breathe again.

Jannik pulls his hand free and folds his arms over his head. After a moment, I realize his shoulders are shaking, and he's making a choked noise.

Do bats cry? Do they feel like we do? I brush the back of one hand across my eyes and stand, careful not to touch the jellied corpse next to me. "We have to go."

Jannik doesn't look up or take his arms from over his head. "Go where?' His words are muffled. "Are you planning on flying us home?"

"We can walk—"

A hysterical laugh escapes him. "I am not fucking walking anywhere," he says.

"Have you suddenly gone lame?" Grief makes me hard and angry, hating myself and him for feeling anything, especially when I still have Dash's sentence hanging over me, his final gift to my House.

Jannik lowers his arms and looks up. There is blood smeared across his face. "No," he says. "But his death has near killed me." He makes a hiccuping sound somewhere between a laugh and a sob.

"What are you talking about?"

The bat leans his head back and stares at the shadowed ceiling. "I'm talking about my own stupidity. I fed too much from one donor, and ended up becoming too . . . attached."

There's something he's not telling me. I wait.

"I'm not going anywhere unless I feed again," he says, still carefully not looking at me.

Anger flares sharply. "You're—no." I cross my arms over my chest. "You're lying," I say. "I'm not fooled."

Jannik twists his head and stares at me with his awful blood-covered face, his eyes white blanks in dark sockets. His cheeks look pinched, thin. "Why would I choose now to lie to you?" he says, and I see the tips of his fangs. "Not everything in this world revolves around you, high-Lammer."

He's right. I sink to my knees. "Feed? Like you did with—" I glance nervously at the corpse. There is nothing of Dash left in it. "What happens if you don't?"

"For all that Dash was so certain that his death wouldn't kill me, it may just do so in the end." He's matter-of-fact, bitter. I reach out and touch his hand.

"I—I can't do it."

"Then go away," he says dully.

I stay where I am, still crouched before him, still touching his wrist with my fingertips. I could go now, leave Jannik here, find Owen, and mark him. Dash couldn't destroy us on his own. And now it's up to me. I can't leave the sea-witch to run through Pelimburg unchecked, not when I know how to stop her. If I could lecture a boggert about choice and death, then I can damn well face up to it myself. I will wear my guilt, and I will make my choices.

Me or Owen. It should be easy. Except that it isn't.

I don't want to do it alone.

"No." My voice is a bell shiver, a high tone. "Do what you have to." Even as I say it, fear and revulsion twine in my stomach: two snakes, twisting and coiling over each other.

"You're certain?"

"No," I say. "Quickly, before I change my mind." It comes out of me in a rushing breath, too fast and frightened. I shove my hand out, my wrist toward his face, and look away.

One breath. Two. My arm is shaking. Is he never going to do it?

Then I feel warmth on my skin as he takes my wrist, pulls it closer. The tingle of magic is almost overwhelmed by the hammer of my heart, the strange bellow wheeze of my lungs. "Shh," he says, and sinks needle-fangs into the raised blue vein. My arm throbs.

We stay like this—a *tableau vivant*—for more breaths than I can count. To keep myself calm I imagine that the air filling my lungs is red, then orange and yellow. I work through the rainbow and each breath is filled with clean vibrant color, and I send that brightness curling through my body, stretching out to the very limits of every limb, and then I breathe it out again, fouled, faded, and grayed, taking away with it all my fear. My thighs begin to ache, the strained muscles cramping, and I breathe through that too.

He lets me go, and I tumble backward, dizzy and emptied. The sand bites into my palms, scraping them raw.

"Here," says Jannik. His voice is back to normal again. He's untying his olive necktie. "Hold out your hand."

I obey, and he carefully binds the wounds on my wrist. I don't really want to look, though I do anyway. There are two neat punctures, and the blood wells up in thick dark rivulets, running in ticklish streams down my arm to drip and puddle in the sand and dust.

The pale skin of his hands is marred with a fine red rash. The tiny blisters spread even as I watch.

"Thank you," he says very softly as he pulls the binding tight.

I swallow and nod.

"What about this?" I raise one hand almost to his cheek, where more of the blisters are spreading fast.

He shakes his head. "Scriv in your blood." He stares down at his fingers, flexing them and watching the raised blisters burst. "It will pass." His voice is tight, controlled, and I wonder if they burn. Jannik helps me to my feet. All I want to do is get out of here. I'm shaky and weak.

"Wait."

He crouches and slips his arms under Dash's body, easily lifting him. The boggert drained her final victim well, and it seems to me that he is nothing, an empty husk that she has left behind.

"What are you doing?"

"Taking him to Whelk Street."

"We'll come back for him," I say. "Jannik, please, there's something I have to do. Something—I can't do it alone. Please."

And he seems to understand. He sets the corpse back on the ground and crouches there for a moment to straighten Dash's collar.

I want to point out that Dash will never care now, but I bite the words down and wait.

He stands, offers me his arm. "Where do we need to go?"

And because I know my brother far better than Dash ever did, I know that we will not find Owen by the docks, looking over the remains of his burning wherries and warehouses. He will be with his wife, with the little unborn Pelim heir.

I DON'T THINK OF OWEN as we walk through the twilight to the Pelim residences in New Town. I think of the dead, I think of the sea-witch walking through Pelimburg and claiming our people. I picture the faces of Hoblings I have never met. Esta's brother, Rin, a gelatinous mess of a body, sacrificed to Dash's cause. I picture the Whelk Streeters. I even manage a little pity for Dash.

Owen opens the door himself, something I did not expect, and the act throws me off course. I stand on his doorstep, one hand in Jannik's, and I can think of nothing to say or do.

"What is it?" he snaps. "I've no time for this. Go find some other House to beg from."

"Wait," I say, before Owen can close the door. "I—"

He frowns, recognition warring with disbelief. I don't give him time to say anything, just thrust out my hand, the little hairpin held tight, and stab it into his cheek.

It clatters onto the stones between us, and all that shows of my ill-timed attack is a meager kitten-scratch below his right eye.

It's enough.

The air booms, and I feel the magic take. It's as if all the winds have changed direction at once, drawing the sea-witch here. My skin crawls and sweat prickles up my spine between my shoulder blades. She's coming.

"What have you done?" Owen whispers. It's a pointless question—any War-Singer worth his scriv can taste what's happened here, and Hob fancy or not, Owen knows as well as I do that there is a sea-witch walking through Pelimburg and that she is no longer aimless.

The drag of her tidal magic claws against us both. Perhaps she senses that I am bound to Owen by blood, perhaps she is too wild and blind and uncontrolled an entity to understand who her true target is.

She could take me instead.

This realization comes to Owen at the same time. I see the knowledge light up in his eyes, and he lunges forward to grab at my collar. "Oh no you don't," he says.

I try to jerk out of his grasp and the fabric tears, but he catches at my arm and pulls me closer to him. The blood on his face is running thicker now, dripping down his chin. I did not think I had struck him so deep.

Jannik grabs at Owen's wrist and tries to pry the two of us apart, but Owen has always been strong, even without scriv, and Jannik is weary from a day of sun and the poison of the scriv in my blood. Neither of us makes a good warrior.

And perhaps it's only fair, after all. What made me think I was more worthy of life? I'm just a runaway girl. Owen has a family, he carries our name forward. Who did I think I was?

"I'm sorry," I tell him, and stop struggling.

He looks at me in disbelief, then releases his hold. I drop to the stone steps, bruising my knees. The hairpin lies at my fingers, glinting like a green eye. Accusing. I'm no better than Dash, it says. I'm no better than Owen, than all the men who have tried to manipulate me into doing their dirty work or my so-called duty. And I am so tired of men always deciding my path.

Fingers shaking, I pull the hairpin toward my knee. It scrapes along the stone. Somehow, I make myself pick it up. It feels heavier than it should, weighed down with all the things that have been laid upon it—such burdens of death it has carried. So what's one more?

I jab the pin down into my thigh and it bites deep. The pain is less than I expected. When I can make my fingers move again, I let the hairpin go and look up at my brother. His face is white, almost as pale as Jannik's. They're both staring at me.

"I'll wait here," I say, and the words seem to drift out of my mouth, puffing up. The world is spinning around me, and I place my hands against the ground and try to keep myself from flying off into the skies. "You should go."

The magic of the sea-witch is drawing closer, smothering the air. It's like a huge wet blanket has dropped over the city. There are no stars above us, no clouds, just the implacable weight of her approach. "She'll take me." I'm sure of it, and it feels good and right. Guilt I barely knew I had lifts from me, and I am released.

Owen doesn't move.

The street goes black.

She's here.

"Run," I say, my voice breaking. I don't understand why he won't leave. I've given him a chance. No matter how small it is, he should take it. After all, I'm already dead.

"No."

"Felicita, this is madness." Jannik kneels down to try to force me to rise. "You marked him first, it's not going to matter what you do now."

I pull my wrist out of his hand, shaking myself free. "You're wrong, and if Owen would just listen to me for once in his life—"

The witch is upon us. The air is thick with the smell of iodine, of rotten fish, of the peculiar stink of seals and seaweed. I turn my head, determined to face her.

She's a swirling black mass, vaguely Lammic in shape, and colors slide under her liquid skin—sea colors: greens and reds and grays. There is a shimmer to her, and her eyes are fish scales. She's wreathed in dark brown and orange kelp, and strands of fine red weed hang from the arm she reaches out to me.

Yes.

I've tricked her. I'm closer to her than Owen, and my blood is enough to make her think I'm the sacrifice.

Then she reaches past me and Owen is consumed.

There is no breath in me to scream. The winds that have been tugging me go still, and the veil drops from the sky, revealing again the stars and the grinning moon.

The weight that was pressing down on Pelimburg—all that wild magic—vanishes. I look to where my brother was standing just seconds ago, and there is nothing there to indicate that he ever existed. They are both gone. She has returned to the sea with her sacrifice.

In a daze, I allow Jannik to help me to my feet. The hairpin is still sticking from my thigh like a tiny dagger, and I pull it out viciously, wanting it to hurt me more.

"She's gone," Jannik says. "There will be no more deaths."

And that, at least, is true.

I sob once, then with Jannik's hand still in mine, I turn and run away from what I have done this day. A strange excitement is burning through me, and it seems all my earlier tiredness is gone, replaced now by this madness. We run through Pelimburg breathlessly. I've saved them, all of them. I pretend that I did not really kill my brother in order to do it.

When we stop, panting, I do not even know where we are.

"We—" Jannik huffs, tries to catch his breath. "What do we do now?"

"Jannik?"

He raises an eyebrow.

"What would you do to change your future?"

"We've discussed it. There's nothing I can do. My mother is free to do with me as she wants."

"Like mine was with me?"

He stays silent.

Owen's death has made me realize one thing. No matter what the results, it is my choices that define me. And I will fight for them, even when it seems that failure is inevitable. Perhaps most especially then. Jannik is staring at me, waiting for me to talk, and so I make my first choice as Felicita, returned. "Then what if I could give you a huntsman's gambit?"

"Explain."

I take a deep breath and plunge into a strange new world, one where I awkwardly knit together the holes I've ripped. I talk fast, hoping to make him see the sense of this partnership I propose, despite how bizarre it must sound. At least he listens, saying nothing, although his face gets more and more serious as I speak.

Afterward he says, "It's not much of an offer."

"It's better than what you have here!"

"Is it really?" he says. "Just what does either of us gain in this scheme of yours?"

"Freedom."

"A strange sort of freedom."

"Better than none at all."

That makes him smile, just a quick flash of fangs.

"Well," he says, "I believe that our bargain is settled."

19

JANNIK'S CARRIAGE RATTLES along the broken seashells that cover the last stretch of the road up to House Pelim. The mansion rises before us, a myriad-eyed giant waking from sleep. I hold my breath, flex my fingers, and remind myself that I am not a child.

"Do you want me to come with you?" Jannik and I have already faced his mother down. She was condescending, laughed in our faces, and told Jannik to do whatever suits him.

So that settled that.

I shake my head. "You stay in here. It'll be enough of a shock when I turn up on the doorstep. Arm in arm with a bat might just kill her."

He looks out the window at the cliff edge, at our famous Leap.

The driver pulls the unis up in the circle and comes to open the carriage door and help me out. I press my damp palms on my borrowed dress—pale rose, something I would never wear normally—and walk toward the front stairs, my head held high.

Firell opens the door and claps one hand over her mouth. She makes a muffled moaning sound, her eyes growing wider and wider.

"Just fetch my mother," I say with a sigh, when her show of histrionics is over. "Please." It is time, after all, to give Firell back her name and reclaim my own.

She runs off, skidding on the polished floor.

While I wait I try to summon up all my reserves of courage. The well is rather empty.

The wind yowls in the forests that edge our land, the sea mews add their plaintive cry, and the unis stamp in their traces.

And then a sound so familiar that my heart freezes. The *click click click* of my mother's shoes on the slate tiles of the entrance. My palms are wet again, but I don't want to wipe them in case I stain this borrowed dress. Suddenly I worry about the most mundane things—the color of my hair, the thinness of my face, the way my hands are rough now and the nails broken.

These same work-torn hands held Ilven's hairpin and marked my own brother for death. I fold them behind my back.

When she sees me, her expression doesn't change. She is thin-lipped, frowning, her hand on the edge of the door, anchoring herself in her house, while I wash up like flotsam on her doorstep.

"Mother. It's me," I say, as if she has somehow forgotten that I exist. Perhaps she thinks that I am just another boggert risen from the deep, dragging Owen up behind me.

Her fingers tremble against the door, and the wind blows fine wisps of her dark gray hair loose, but except for those two things, she might as well be a wooden carving.

"I'm not dead." So obvious, but what else do I say? "I ran away, made you think I took the Leap." I have never felt so childish and selfish as at this moment, hearing aloud my own cruelty. "I'm so sorry."

Finally she speaks. "Why are you here?"

Not at all what I expected. Somehow I thought she'd pull me to her bosom like a lost child, fold me up in her arms, and tell me that everything was going to be all right.

"I wanted you to know," I say. "May I come in?"

She steps a little to the side, giving me just enough room to slip into my childhood home. She looks past me at the black carriage waiting outside. "House Sandwalker?"

"Yes." It is impossible to explain.

She closes the door and *click clicks* her way through to the pristine formal lounge. The one where she receives guests.

Firell brings us tea and little cakes. She has set salt licorice in a small bowl in the center of the cake tray. She has re-membered that it is my favorite.

This makes me feel stronger, and I offer her an uncertain smile as she puts the trays down. In answer I get the barest of nods, and this small acceptance does more for me than I believed possible. Light-headed, I cling to my seat.

Mother and I sit perched on the edges of the uncomfort-able but beautiful chairs and stare at each other across the tea table.

"Please." My mother gestures at the silver tray of tiny cakes. I take a piece of licorice and set it down on my plate.

"Explain," she says, once Firell has poured our tea and withdrawn, leaving us alone in the gauzy-curtained room.

So I do. I leave out the worst, about how I had a hand in the attack on Pelimburg, about the thing I did to condemn Owen. Instead, I make his death my reason for returning.

Through it, she remains expressionless, not even touching her tea.

When I'm done, I take a hasty gulp of my own drink to cover up my nervousness.

"You cannot come back."

So she will side with honor. I expected it, true, but I had hoped . . . Ah well, if anything, it makes easier what I have to say next.

"I know." I set my cup down and stare at the little spill of tea in the saucer, gathering my thoughts. "I have a proposition for you."

"Go on."

"I will leave Pelimburg."

My mother nods in approval.

"I thought to MallenIve." And now the part that gives us both an out. "It might be possible for me to take over the apartments there and oversee our business ventures in MallenIve." It is a solution that allows my mother to save face and to blissfully continue her existence here without my presence spoiling her pleasures or shrinking her social circle. But it also gives her a chance to hold on to what little family she has left. It gives me a chance. "There may be some talk at first." I know this, and I rush to convince her that it will not be all that dreadful. "But people will soon forget, once I am gone."

"So they will." She touches her cup as if she is about to raise it, to finally take a sip, but then she puts her hands flat on the table and shakes her head. "There will still be rumors, and our standing will fall."

"You can tell them anything you want to save face," I say. "Tell them that I was kidnapped, that Hobs made me do it, that I took up with some cult—whatever lie will put the best spin on your story."

My mother grimaces. "Save our House face at the expense of yours?"

I bow my head. It's what I expected.

She speaks again, her voice a steel whip. "All very well," she says, deciding my fate as neatly as she would slice a tea-fork through a cake. "Only you've never shown any aptitude for business. How do you propose to make your way in MallenIve? Indeed, to secure our holdings there."

"I plan to be the face of Pelim," I say. "Making the contacts we need, cultivating the ones we already have." I swallow some more tea and try to keep my voice airy. "My husband will be the one who deals with the financial aspects. He has rather a head for figures."

"You've secured yourself a match in MallenIve already?" She's aware that no House here will spit upon me, let alone tie me to its bosom.

"Yes," I say. It takes all my courage to continue, knowing the rage my mother will unleash. "In a manner of speaking."

It seems that after the city heard that my brother had been devoured by the sea-witch, my resurrection raises almost no questions. All I need for my wedding is two witnesses, and the official accepts the Pelim House lawyer and Jannik's father, hollow cheeked, gray, and tired.

My mother does not attend even though I had half hoped she would find some measure of forgiveness for me.

It comes as a shock that I keep my House name, that Jannik becomes a Pelim. When I question this, the lawyer merely shakes his wizened head.

"You will understand someday," Jannik's father says before he takes his leave. He gives us the ghost of a smile, and it is surprisingly warm in such a pale, cold little man.

There will be no wedding feast. Our House is trying to keep the recent developments—my return from death and subsequent marriage to a bat—as quiet as they possibly can. I look down at the dress I'm wearing, yellow, for weddings, but the shade is not quite the right one, and it's certainly no wedding gown. It's a dress I wore last season, just once. There was no point in buying a dress for such an insignificant moment. Nor time to have one made. My mother wants us gone from the city as soon as possible. She's even brought Owen's widow into the old family home, in waiting for the new Pelim heir.

Understandable, really. As long as I am here, I remain a humiliation. The gossip has started, whispered no doubt by our army of servants. From our House to Malker—who will revel in this chance to sink their own scandal under ours—and so, like a disease, it will spread from one mouth to the next. Mother has sent word to her own family in MallenIve that we will be taking over the Pelim apartments, but I expect little welcome there. I can only guess what she wrote in her letters.

Jannik and I take our few belongings and make our way to the docks. The shambles of broken, burned-out warehouses is being slowly rebuilt. Hobs and Lammers together are hoisting wood and slate, and there are even a few vampires in the crowd, working with them. The dock is busy, the people industrious. Through the noise and bustle I see small moments of quiet community, people sharing tea or 'grits. Sometimes it is enough even that they greet each other, when before they would have not made the effort.

While my mother has made no move to see us off and Jannik's family has withdrawn as carefully and quietly as wyrms, a company of familiar faces is waiting at the docks to wave goodbye: Nala and Lils, standing hand in hand holding their red kerchiefs high, Esta, still scowling, and Verrel, looming over them with Kirren yapping from his arms.

When Jannik and I brought Dash's body back to Whelk Street, I felt the final door to their companionship shutting in my face. They took him back, and with that our partnership ended.

They no longer needed me, and I was a high-born Lammer, not one of them.

The separation seemed inevitable, so it lifts my spirits to see them now. Perhaps, after all, Dash did manage to change something.

THE JOURNEY BY BARGE is slow and tedious. Even with the extravagant berth paid for by Jannik's family, we are hemmed in on all sides by large wooden crates of produce. The wherrymen hoist the sails, and the fresh wind coming off the ocean gives us a chance to coast upriver. We are the only passengers, and every Hob here knows our story it seems. No one says a word to us.

Jannik and I stand together on the *Gray Moth*'s deck and watch Pelimburg fall away as the Casabi curves through the vineyards that lie beyond the city. Then the vineyards of Samar slowly give way to other pastures. Little towns flick past, toy bright and small. The sun is dipping below the fields when Jannik puts his hand on my shoulder. His touch sends a shiver through me. Not disgust and not just the headiness of magic.

"Come to the cabin. You've still some packed food."

I agree even though my stomach is too knotted up for me to eat. I don't ask Jannik what he plans to do, although I've heard that there are butchers in MallenIve who specialize in the clean blooding of animals for bat purposes. In the dank little cabin, I try to sleep, try to remember what little I've learned of MallenIve, that city of scriv and palaces. I've left behind everyone I know, my family and my motley collection of friends, for something bigger. MallenIve is a monster, a city known for her vices and pleasures. And yet—and yet she is endlessly faceted and fascinating, a city full of magic, and when people speak of her there is a fire in their eyes and their voices are hooked with desire.

There is scriv in abundance, the tented irthe orchards are thick with windle grubs spinning the most expensive silk, the theaters and music halls host the richest of talent. As the seat of the ruling House Mata, she is the fount of all our fashions and art, our science and magic. The Bone University houses keen minds, men and women of power. I could hire the best tutor for myself and there would be no word to stop me.

MallenIve is my chance at a clean slate. All my misdeeds will be washed away by her vast indifference. And the urge to leave behind all that I have done is greater than any obligation I might feel to stay and face my guilt.

Lils and Nala at least understood. Standing on the dock and watching us leave, they had the look of people who would run too if they were given the chance.

I'm lucky.

The night is spent rocking fitfully in this flat-bellied monster. All through the long darkness I lie awake, expecting that any moment we will sink under the weight of the cargo or be attacked by one of the nixes that still make their home in the muddy water, or that the summer's torrential inland storms will spring unannounced from a cloudless sky and we will all be swept to our deaths.

Across from me, on his own narrow bunk, I can see the shadow of Jannik as he sleeps, the regular rise and fall of his chest. I shake free from my covers and pad softly over to his bed. He shifts as I lie down next to him, stretched out body length to body length, but his dreams do not release him. The bunk is not meant for two, and he is warm, almost feverish. Breath held, I put my cold hands to his cheeks, and he murmurs.

The language is soft and lilting, and while I don't know what he's saying, something in its cadence comforts me.

I close my eyes and sleep.

Dawn comes cold and clean and I leave before Jannik wakes. I sit at the head of the barge, next to a Hob wherryman, and we pass the rising of the sun in a quiet salutation. The Casabi stretches around us, wide and pinkish in the early sunlight. The summer rains will soon be here, and the river will be swelling, flooding her banks, and for a while all river trade will slow to nothing. The *Gray Moth* is the last barge to leave Pelimburg this season, and she is heavy laden with more than just House cargo.

She carries the promise of something greater.

Acknowledgments

No book grows in a vacuum, and many people have given me their help, insight, and encouragement. Without them, this book would be a shriveled thing, and they deserve all my thanks.

My fantastic agent, Suzie Townsend, for everything she's done for me. Her enthusiasm for the project kept me going, and her incredible feedback helped shape the book it became.

The team at FSG, most especially Beth Potter, who performed works of magic, guiding me and helping me knit together a stronger, better book. My thanks also to Jay Colvin, who designed a fantastic cover, and to the copy editors and proofreaders, Alicia R. Hudnett, Chandra Wohleber, and Judy Kiviat, who did their best to make me look literate.

My army of beta readers: Bee Retief, Amy Ross, April Castillo, Sophie Wereley, Brianna Privett, Andrew Carmichael, Elissa Hoole, Gary Couzens, Nerine Dorman, and Glynnis Rambaud. You suffered more for my art than I did, and you should all get medals.

The Musers: a circle of friends better than any I could have ever asked for.

And there's one last person who I can't thank enough, but I shall have to try. Brian, this one's for you.